Renate Dorrestein is one of Holland's best-loved novelists. Her books regularly win prizes and appear at the top of the Dutch bestseller lists. *A Heart of Stone*, her first novel to be published in English, is also published by Black Swan.

Hester Velmans's translation of *A Heart of Stone* won the Vondel Prize for Translation in 2001.

Also by Renate Dorrestein
A HEART OF STONE
and published by Black Swan

WITHOUT MERCY

Renate Dorrestein

Translated from the Dutch by Hester Velmans

BLACK SWAN

WITHOUT MERCY
A BLACK SWAN BOOK : 0 552 99989 X

First published 2001 by Uitgeverji Contact, Amsterdam, as
Zonder genade.
English translation published 2002 by Doubleday,
a division of Transworld Publishers

PRINTING HISTORY
Doubleday edition published 2002
Black Swan edition published 2003

1 3 5 7 9 10 8 6 4 2

Copyright © Renate Dorrestein 2001
English translation © Hester Velmans 2002

The right of Renate Dorrestein to be identified as the author
of this work has been asserted in accordance with sections 77
and 78 of the Copyright Designs and Patents Act 1988.

Set in 11/13pt Melior by
Falcon Oast Graphic Art Ltd.

Black Swan Books are published by Transworld Publishers,
61–63 Uxbridge Road, London W5 5SA,
a division of The Random House Group Ltd,
in Australia by Random House Australia (Pty) Ltd,
20 Alfred Street, Milsons Point, Sydney, NSW 2061, Australia,
in New Zealand by Random House New Zealand Ltd,
18 Poland Road, Glenfield, Auckland 10, New Zealand
and in South Africa by Random House (Pty) Ltd,
Endulini, 5a Jubilee Road, Parktown 2193, South Africa.

Printed and bound in Great Britain by
Clays Ltd, St Ives plc.

For Frans, for now,
and for Elisabeth and Barbara, for later

Contents

PART I

Do Not Pass Go

What Jem used to say

'Dad!' said Jem. 'Come on, be serious now. How many fingers am I holding up?'

'Eleven?' he said. 'Really, son, I can't see a thing.'

Jem walked round behind him and gave the knot in the blindfold another firm tug, for good measure. His bare feet slapped over the kitchen floor. There was the fizz of a soft drink being opened. The clatter of something being poured into a glass.

It was Sunday morning, 7 a.m. Even with a blindfold on, you could tell that outside the garden was in full bloom and that the sunlight was already winking off the rims of the child's bike that had been flung down on the ground next to an overturned bucket and a tennis ball. It was the height of summer. There was that singular silence that exists only when most adults are still asleep. Soon the talking, the analysing and the arranging would start up again, decisions would be arrived at, matters that couldn't wait would be tackled, plans made, tasks assigned. But not just yet.

Two glasses were slammed down on the table with a

11

thud, and Phinus turned his face to where he guessed Jem was standing. He asked, 'Do you remember which you put in which glass?'

'Yep, the Coke's in Bert and the Pepsi's in Ernie.'

'OK, I'm ready.' He stretched out his right hand.

But quick as a flash, Jem's fingers closed round his wrist. 'Wait. What are we betting? The swimming pool, this afternoon?'

'*Again?*'

'Yeah, and not just a quick dip. You've got to do ten laps, all the way up and all the way back. Or you'll never learn, and then one day you'll drown.'

'Jemmie, in our family we're not in the habit of falling into ditches. Besides, your mother passed her life-saving test.'

'Mum could never get you to the side safely.'

'She certainly could.'

Jem let the subject go. 'Go on then, taste!'

He reached for the glasses and for a short, disorienting moment, his hands hovered in the void. Then they found the edge of the table and clung to it as if to the side of the pool. Sunday morning, ten past seven – and suddenly he'd been struck by a disconcerting insight into the natural order of things: Jem would lose him some day, Jem would, it went without saying, outlive him, as well as Franka. Where, and from whom, could you request enough time to raise a child safely until adulthood? But when did children become adults? When they'd no longer fashion a set of false teeth out of a piece of orange peel, or when they—

'You don't dare!' cried Jem.

'I'm concentrating.'

Jem shrieked with laughter. 'I'm going to count to three-ee . . .'

Sunday morning, twelve minutes past seven. He picked up a glass. The carbonation fizzed against his nose. He put down the glass, picked up the other one. This one had a lot more bubbles. Insipid bubbles. Listless bubbles. Rather flabby, too.

Next to him Jem was puffing with excitement.

Warming to the exercise, he took alternating sips from the two glasses. Sweeter? Less sweet? The difference in taste was marginal. The difference lay largely in the fizz. 'Ha!' he said. 'You want to know something?' He sat up straighter. 'This bubble is the pithiest. Explosive yet also compact, a bubble with personality, distinguished and well-defined, someone's put a little thought into this. Whereas this one' – he found the other glass – 'is much duller, a washed-out fuddy-duddy bubble without any sex appeal. Jem, my boy, I'll stake my all on it, the first is Coke and the second is Pepsi.'

'Ooh! You peeked!' Jem threw himself on him, fists pummelling.

Phinus, good-naturedly, let himself be punched as he pulled the blindfold down. 'It's Bert! I won!'

From behind him came Franka's sleepy voice. 'Well, well, guys. What have you been up to?'

'Just a game,' Phinus said, turning round.

She was standing in the kitchen doorway, blinking, in an old shirt of his that reached halfway down her thighs. Their eyes met, and she smiled briefly. 'So, did Phinus make mincemeat out of you?' she asked Jem.

'Your turn, Mum! You have to guess which one has the fuddy-duddy bubble, Pepsi or Coke. Shut your eyes.'

'Piece of cake.' Phinus stood up and planted a kiss on her tousled hair. Then he walked to the fridge and took out eggs, bacon and butter. He put a frying pan on the burner and began cutting oranges in half, whistling under his breath.

'What's a fuddy-duddy bubble?' asked Franka.

'One that isn't sexy!' yelled Jem.

'Very good,' said Phinus with satisfaction. The ability to make distinctions, that was what life was all about. He swiftly squeezed the oranges. He turned the last piece of orange rind inside out, then picked up a knife, grinning to himself.

'Not sexy?' said Franka. She had sat down at the table across from Jem. They were bathed in wide bands of dusty sunlight pouring in through the seldom-washed windows. 'And what then, according to you, O expert of mine, is sexy? A naked bottom?'

Solemnly, Jem said, 'Nah, when their hair goes like this.' His hand made a sinuous motion.

'Yes, that *is* nice.'

Phinus hovered behind them wearing his orange-pith teeth, ready to send them into gales of laughter.

Franka asked, 'And what do you suppose they'd think was sexy about *you*?' Then she glanced over her shoulder. 'Have you got the hiccups, Phinus? Do you want a sip of Coke?'

It must have been the red Coca-Cola truck that just went by. The slightest provocation is enough, the most innocent sight, the most everyday subject. The world has turned into a minefield: memories are waiting in ambush everywhere, ready to jump out. His hands are clenched round the steering wheel.

'What a sigh,' says Franka, next to him. She touches his knee. 'Do you want me to take over?'

'No, not at all.' He glances in his rearview mirror. There isn't much traffic.

'Let's make a quick stop at the café on the Afsluitdijk.'

He puts his hand on top of hers and gives it a squeeze.

They drive past the sluices. Miles and miles of dyke separating the North Sea from the IJsselmeer stretch out before them, right across the sea, the sea which gives and takes, as various ballads remind us. It is Friday afternoon. It's nearly Easter.

It's so windy in the car park that they each have to struggle to get their door open. Phinus takes Franka by the arm on the slippery steps up to the café. Her flimsy raincoat whips around her legs, his hair is standing on end; in the glass door's reflection they look like any other windblown couple.

Inside, every wall – even the wall above the glass case displaying almond cakes, sausage rolls and bottled chocolate milk – is hung with framed black-and-white photos showing whiskered men in oilskins heroically subduing the elements. 'A nation that's alive builds its own future.' They have made a habit of stopping here, on every weekend trip to the islands of Terschelling or Vlieland, both on the way out and on the way home, here at this tacky coffee shop that's hardly any bigger than a shoebox, to look at these pictures, at the steadfast dredgers and stern builders, men who were able to tell their children, 'I have taught the seas to behave, I have connected two distant shores, I have opened up remote provinces and made possible the reclamation of new land. I have created order out of chaos.'

Franka has sat down at a little table by the window, beyond which the IJsselmeer sparkles in the spring-time sun.

Carrying a tray, he hurries past the potato and fish salads, the wrapped sandwiches and the sign, *Warm sliced ham on a roll, with sauce.* He orders a cappuccino and an espresso.

'What kind of sauce do you think they serve with the ham?' he asks as he puts the coffee down in front of Franka.

'Mustard, don't you think?' She sounds tired.

'In that case it would say *mustard.*'

'Why, are you hungry?'

'No, are you? Perhaps they mean—'

She leans forward. Mildly amused, she suggests, affably, 'Why don't you ask?' She has let her chin sink into her hands.

He looks at the bright red welts at her fingertips. What if one day she ends up devouring every nail? Will she just go on nibbling indefatigably, night after sleepless night, first her fingers, then on to the little bones in her hands? Will she keep on gnawing, from her wrists up to her elbows, then her shoulders, until she can no longer feel her empty arms, simply because she no longer has any arms at all?

She gets up. 'Just going to the loo.' Her eyes are trapped by his, and she raises her eyebrows. 'Why are you looking at me like that?'

'I was just suddenly thinking how much I love you.'

She laughs. 'So big, yet such a softie.'

As she turns round, she tugs the skirt of her yellow suit straight. She has clearly tried her best for this outing: no tracksuit, no baggy sweater. Somewhere in the far reaches of her consciousness or her wardrobe, she came upon this outfit and thought: Phinus likes to see me in this.

The skirt stretches round her bottom. She's gained

16

some weight, a good sign. Now all she has to do is find a way to get to sleep.

He himself has always been a healthy sleeper. He is out like a light as soon as he sees his pillow. For him, no hours of wavering over the choice of lorazepam, Dalmadorm (15mg or 30mg?) or a double whisky ('What was it I took yesterday, Phinus?'). Insomniacs claim there's a world of difference between lying awake at one o'clock and at five o'clock, between not being able to fall asleep and not being able to stay asleep, between the effects of hot milk and of herbal tea. They turn on the TV in the middle of the night or they peer listlessly at the moon, the stars and the planets. They'll read a report that needs to be read anyway. They poke at the cold ashes in the fireplace. They wait for deliverance, sometimes with resignation, sometimes in despair. They are acquainted with an aspect of life of which sleepers know nothing. They know the night, those eight hours out of the twenty-four-hour day that are so lonely, terrifying and maddening, hours during which all the little teeth of blame and shame ratchet together so finely that human beings have been specially designed to evade it: after sixteen hours of activity, the heart rate slows, your body temperature drops, you have to clench your teeth to bite back a yawn, your thinking begins to get a little foggy. Not long now before your consciousness gives you the slip and you find yourself shuffling safely off to the land of Nod in your slippers, as it were.

But not Franka, not any more. She hasn't been able to sleep a wink for six months. She is utterly worn out. She says she sometimes sees stars before her eyes. She is hardly Franka Vermeer any more, she is mainly an exhausted mass of cells, sinew and protein hankering for unconsciousness. And yet she doesn't dare close her eyes, because as soon as she surrenders to sleep, she is right back in the morgue, in that terrible night without end.

At the Harlingen exit, he is suddenly beset by doubt. Maybe he should have rented a cottage on Terschelling, after all. Then they could have ridden their bikes over to Oosterend, as usual, and scavenged for mussels on the mudflats. But he'd wanted a place without memories this time, that was the point. Something quite different, for once, from what they always used to do.

'Weren't we supposed to turn off here?' Franka asks, twisting round to peer at the sign for the ferry.

'Nope.'

She leans back again.

'You'll never guess where we're heading. It begins with an A.'

She sends him an indulgent look over the top of her sunglasses. 'Or else we could play I Spy With My Little Eye. Or recite the names of the seven dwarfs. Except that you're the only one who knows them. Remember how you always used to—'

'Mmmm,' he agrees quickly. His collar is suddenly sticking to his neck. 'Take out the map for me, will you? I have to pick up the N355 at some point.'

She unfolds the map and studies it. 'Oh, it's not for a while yet. Is that where we're going?'

'No, I'm not telling you another thing. It's a surprise.' Surreptitiously he pats the little *Alliance Gastronomique* guidebook in his breast pocket. An inn in a rural hamlet of Groningen province, it sounds modest enough. But what about that seven-course dinner laid on for them the night of arrival, which is part of the deal? Franka will feel all the world's have-nots reproachfully staring at her with every bite. It may not be too late to work something out with the kitchen. *Three courses maximum. My wife isn't such a big eater, you see.*

'Hey! Watch out! Phinus! Stay in your lane!'

He slams on the brakes. The car swerves, the tyres squeal. A whirlwind of colour and noise tears past, narrowly missing them.

For a brief moment it's quiet. Then she says, in a voice that's shrill with shock, 'If it had been me at the wheel, we'd have had it.'

The adrenaline rush makes him exultant. 'Fortunately your husband possesses excellent re-flexes. It was nothing, Franka.'

'He was driving on the wrong side of the road! Isn't that what they call a ghost driver?'

Tsohg, he thinks automatically, it was a revird tsohg. It sounds to him like the name of a wind instrument of some long-extinct race, an ancient instrument that touched human lips when humans still had tails and evil had not yet come into the world. The tsohg was renowned for its pure tone. Anyone who'd ever heard the tsohg expertly played, would know the difference between tears of joy, tears of regret, and tears of grief.

'It was just an idiot,' he says. 'Another hour, and we'll be there. Close your eyes, love. A little nap will do you good.'

Over the comfortable bed in which Phinus Vermeer wakes up every morning, the bed in which he reads the weeklies and the Sunday papers on Sunday mornings and in which, in happier times, he and Franka made love countless times, hangs a reproduction of a neoclassical painting by Sir Lawrence Alma-Tadema. Young virgins in pleated gowns dance gracefully across a marble floor, their long hair flowing. Some play the flute or shake a tambourine.

It's a picture that, every day as he opens his eyes, reconfirms his view of man's most fundamental impulses. Recreation and play are a basic need of all ages and all generations, for all ranks and stations in life, as long, that is, as the bare necessities of survival are met. At Jumbo Toys, in his toast to the New Year, he always likes to make reference to *homo ludens*. Deep down, all man really wants, Phinus will declare, is to play.

('My father,' Jem used to say, 'spends his whole day at work playing Snakes and Ladders or dominoes, and he gets paid for it, too.')

The fact that at the present time, at the beginning of the twenty-first century, *homo ludens* is pursuing increasingly passive forms of recreation hasn't made any impression on Phinus. He believes absolutely in man's sporting, playful and irrepressibly curious nature. Not long ago he introduced, with considerable success, a new line of board games for adults called 'After Dinner Games'. By explicitly incorporating the time designated for play into the name, you plant the idea in people's heads that, rather than sprawling in front of the TV for some quiz show, they could stay convivially seated at the table with a board game.

Franka found it all just hopelessly old-fashioned and patronizing. After a long, difficult day, her idea of relaxation is to lie on the couch watching a B-movie, a generous bowl of popcorn within reach, and not some game that urges you to guess why a woodpecker never gets a headache, or how come sea water is salty. Franka has reached the age of thirty-eight without knowing the answers to such questions, and she finds that, even now, she has no desire whatsoever to read stuff off a plastic card about the woodpecker or sea water, thereby gaining the right to move her counter on one square, thanks very much.

It has always amused him to be married to someone who couldn't care less about having to 'miss a turn' or a 'triple word score', someone who will never in her life spit on the dice in order to coax a six out of it, someone who couldn't tell you the difference between a bishop and a castle and who has never sprained her thumb trying to solve the Rubik's Cube, that miracle of puzzle perfection – millions of possibilities, just a single correct solution . . . Doesn't it simply make you drool? The genius of the design alone, with its cheerful Mondrian colours, and then the brilliant execution – *Christ!* – the nearly inaudible clicking of the ball bearings inside the twenty-seven little cubes which together make up this god's gift to the puzzle enthusiast! But it's the one-dimensional jigsaw puzzle only for Franka, after that she draws the line. Of his entire, prodigious assortment of games, this is the only one that appeals to her: the classic jigsaw. It calms her, she says. It's so deliciously mindless.

Mindless.

That's Franka all over. Where out of politeness others may occasionally laugh – uproariously, in his case – at jokes they don't find particularly funny, she will remain deadpan, frowning. When she does laugh, it is sincere; otherwise, she simply refuses to crack a smile. He doesn't know anyone else who is so imperturbably herself. He has a wife of spirit and substance. And she likes to do jigsaw puzzles.

As soon as the new puzzle catalogue comes out, she'll underline her preferences and give him her list, with a self-explanatory gesture. More often than not, he'll drive out to the plant in North Holland the very next day. He fetches the boxes out of the warehouse in person, and signs for them. It gives him a thrill that at that very moment, his laconic, independent Franka is thinking of him while at work: will he have them with him this evening, or will it be tomorrow? He gets a kick out of suggesting when he gets home, 'Why don't I start dinner early tonight?' keeping a straight face, and seeing her biting her lip to refrain from asking about it.

She comes and sits with him in the kitchen. She pours two drinks and enquires casually, 'Do we have anything special planned for tonight?'

'Wait, I've got to keep an eye on the sauce.'

She waits, even though she knows that he can whip up a superb sauce with his eyes closed or bake a superlative cake with just a snap of his fingers. She waits, and plays the game.

He sprinkles some snippets of fresh lovage over the sauce. He brandishes the peppermill, a pinch of this and a dash of that, and a dollop of butter to finish it off. *Homo curans*, as it were. 'How does it smell?'

'Wonderful. Of course, for me, your casseroles and your pies are really what it's all about,' she says, poker-faced.

'What, nothing else?'

But Franka doesn't give anything away. She refills the glasses. She is certain of it now. She can read him like an open book, or, better yet, like the instructions for Stratego or Touché, concealed inside the cardboard lid, in the tiniest letters imaginable, printed in the greyest grey.

The kitchen where Phinus prepares his casseroles and sausages daily is located in an old house in Amsterdam. They bought it when Jem had just turned seven and they had come to consider themselves, after an extended probation period, a tightknit family. The house is neither charmingly nor distinctively old, it's old largely in the sense of leaks and lack of amenities.

They began by ripping out the prehistoric bathroom. They had a new boiler put in, they called in plasterers, plumbers, tilers, countertop installers and electricians. They worked their way from one floor to the next. They argued and collapsed in fits of laughter. They were a good team. Not every marriage is able to withstand a renovation, the endless decisions required, the mess, the inconvenience and the constant torment of radios blaring at full blast. Phinus was chief foamer-at-the-mouth, Franka was chief what-can-you-do shrugger. Thus did they tackle the job, hand in hand, shoulder to shoulder.

The only thing was that Jem started being troubled by nightmares at around this time. He'd regularly wake up screaming. Franka said it was because his bed kept being moved around, first here, then there; he'd settle down of his own accord as soon as the house was done. 'Children get upset by change, they're such little conservatives.'

Getting up in the middle of the night from sheets crunchy with grit, Phinus thought of the crocodiles that used to lie in wait under his bed when he was a child. A crocodile was a serious problem. In the hall, where not a single light switch worked, he remembered how in those days he had tried to transform the monster into a camel, that silly, near-mythological beast that had to buckle all its joints in order to let a person climb on its back. As an added bonus, a camel would not fit under your bed.

Jem was seated on top of the covers, his knees pulled up to his chest. He had bags of exhaustion under his eyes.

'Let's see here,' said Phinus. He bent down. His long arms thrashed around under the bed. 'Not a crocodile anywhere! All clear!'

Jem looked at him blankly. Finally he said, with some pity, 'Of course there's no crocodile. But it's still spooky in here.'

'Ghosts, you mean?' His feet were freezing, he should have put his slippers on. 'In here? Where, then?'

'Everywhere. Wherever you look.'

'Even if you look at it this way?' He lifted Jem up off the bed and hoisted him up on his shoulder.

'Yes,' came the dejected answer from on high.

'Well I never. And what about this way?' Seizing Jem by his pyjama top, he let him topple down forwards over his chest, and grabbed him by the ankles. The boy gave a shout of surprise. 'Now, what do you see from this angle?'

'I see everything upside down!'

Phinus flung him onto the bed. 'Precisely!' he said, out of breath. 'That's what's known as looking at the situation from the other side, in other words, turning things around. And if you turn a ghost around, what do you get? Think about it. G-h-o-s-t, only back to front?'

Jem sat up. 'Tsohg,' he declared, frowning with the effort.

'Tsohg?' said Phinus. 'Never even heard of it. If you ask me, there's no such thing as a tsohg.'

Jem began to laugh, uncertainly. 'But Dad—'

'Problem solved,' said Phinus. 'Let's go back to sleep, shall we? And if you really can't get to sleep, well,' he lowered his voice, 'just think about the friendly lemac, who pads on gleaming little hooves through the desert to see if anyone anywhere needs his help.'

'Lemac?' said Jem. He crawled under the covers.

'Yes,' whispered Phinus. 'If you're scared, there's always a lemac watching out for you.'

'What does it look like?' asked Jem, his eyelids drooping shut.

'They have the softest lips. Animals are our friends. Don't ever forget that, all right?' He tucked the covers in. But he was already too late for a kiss: Jem was asleep, he was well on his way to a dream no one would ever know about.

The final result of the rebuilding – when all the money was used up – wasn't an unqualified success. Yet Franka – it's so typical of her! – loves the house in spite of its shortcomings, perhaps precisely because of everything that isn't perfect about it. He himself has to work a little harder to see it that way. It's difficult for him to ignore the broken tiles in the hall or to restrain himself from having a couple of ugly pipes boxed in. On occasion he'll still sketch out an idea on the back of an envelope. But the thought of everything turned upside down all over again, the prospect of grit and plaster dust, holds him back.

('My father,' Jem used to say, 'whenever he spots a mess anywhere, rants and raves just like John Cleese in *Fawlty Towers*.' His adolescent's voice would break. 'Cracks me up, man!')

Luckily, thanks to some colourful touches and a deft arrangement of the cheerfully eclectic furnishings, it is possible to distract a visitor's attention from the - deficiencies. The guests aren't going to go looking at what's behind the façade, especially if there is home-made sushi on the menu.

Oh, the guests! Their chatter and laughter still reverberates in the high-ceilinged rooms. What a lot there used to be to celebrate! Good report cards, anniversaries, the arrival of the new herring – Franka and Phinus liked to turn anything into a party. Over a table littered with bottles and dishes they'd exchange satisfied looks, united in their collaborative success.

There are no parties or dinners any more nowadays. That era is over. Yet the house is still teeming with people much of the time, thanks to the constant comings and goings of Franka's protégés. Drug addicts and school dropouts, illiterates, sullen girls without any future and swaggering hoodlums with too much of a past: the kids who fill the records of the social work agencies. Sometimes he'll find them seated at his own dining table when he comes home. Poor bastards, to whom he can never say, 'I live here, so would you please just sod off.' At the strangest hours of the day you'll find glassy-eyed weirdos wandering around the place, the kind you can't have a normal conversation with. In his own house he can't leave a ring or a watch lying around without some juvenile delinquent getting itchy fingers. There are full ashtrays everywhere, stinking the place out. And at night the phone will ring, or there'll be a policeman at the door again because one of the problem children has managed to get him or herself into trouble.

Yet he used to be so proud of Franka's professional commitment, her total devotion, her uncompromising principles. He doesn't understand why, of late, her admirable abilities, as well as her pathetic clientele, should inspire in him a certain repugnance. But then, he understands so very little any more, about anything at all.

Without realizing, he'd begun picking up speed, and he lets up on the accelerator. The next exit must be the one for Aduard, a hamlet in the Groningen countryside, land of cardboard and potato flour – he has, of course, thoroughly done his homework, and uncovered all sorts of obscure names – of *borgen* or manor farms; of sea-clay bricks called *kloostermoppen*; *wierden*, which are primeval manmade hills; distinctive village squares called *hamrikken*; agricultural lands of the *opstrekkende heerden* type, and huge farms built in the vernacular head-neck-trunk style.

The landscape lies before him sullen and inhospitable, dissected by poker-straight canals. Fields with rigidly ploughed furrows as far as the eye can see, nothing but perfect 90 degree angles, and, on top of the dykes, the poplars maintaining a fastidious distance from each other. Crows peck furiously at the clay. Their vicious eyes follow him as he drives past grim parishes strung along the road like beads on a string. To be honest, he had been expecting something rather more picturesque, more richly embellished, more rustic.

Next to him Franka is dozing, her hands folded in her lap, her head lolling sideways, this wife of his who these days tends to take little catnaps everywhere, except at home in bed, where all her demons lie in wait for her between the sheets.

He's thinking: if we can first just simply be together again, if we can first just, if we can just have a good time again together, yes, that's it, then the rest will come by itself. Cautiously, he signals, gets into the left-hand lane and then makes the turn. The road dips under a viaduct. The pillars are covered in graffiti. They seem etched into the concrete. As if they are the outlines of creatures which have, by brute force, secured a hiding place for themselves inside the hard cement; creatures which have hurled themselves against the thick walls, gnashing their teeth. And which, as soon as it's dark out, will burst out of there again, as they do every night, to prowl along the quiet streets and stretch out their claws towards anything that breathes. They are the embodiment of an earlier stage of man, when man had yet to rise up out of the primeval slime.

He can't help a quick glance sideways, at Franka.

How can you tell, if the conjugal bastion begins to show signs of internal, invisible cracks? Well – cracks? He mustn't exaggerate. It's just that they're not hitting it off at the moment. The spark is missing, for now. It happens to the best of us. And no interest in sex, that isn't a capital crime in itself, either. As long as she isn't going to expect anything of him later tonight, at that romantic inn. He slips a finger behind the knot of his tie and pulls it a little looser. *God in heaven.* If only she could be coaxed into doing a jigsaw puzzle. But since she's stopped sleeping, she just doesn't have the energy for the two foot six by four foot Mont Blanc, in five thousand pieces. It makes her see double, she says.

He had always assumed that in their marriage the passage of time would be marked by a gradual, mutual scaling back, back to the Austrian Alps at a thousand pieces, or a Vincent van Gogh at a mere five hundred. Both of them wearing reading spectacles, a magnifying glass at hand. A special table just for puzzles, by the window. Even at seventy pieces, you could still get a pretty good Snow White, a sweet little pony and foal, or four puppies in a laundry basket. Garfield they'd be able to handle well into their nineties: just twenty pieces.

The charm of this shared pleasure may very well lie in its quasi-clandestine nature. It's definitely not the kind of thing you brag about to your friends. It's so innocuous it's all but indecent. Let's not tell anyone, it's just the two of us against the rest of the world. It's bad enough we're expected to be grown-up all day. Other couples buy each other teddy bears, that's a lot dafter.

Suddenly it isn't clear to him any more how they are supposed to grow old together now, without that comforting ritual to cling to: first you work on the border and the corners, and then you fill in the picture by assembling, with painstaking devotion, the different elements, conjuring them into a coherent whole, like a promise that everything will turn out all right in the end if you can just sit down and calmly work it out together. So he keeps trying to tempt her: with a cartoonish map of the United States in five thousand pieces, a still life with roses in three thousand. The boxes end up in the cupboard, unopened. Sometimes when he opens the door in search of a pair of scissors or a pen, a few will slide off the pile. An avalanche of boxes: ominous symbol, perhaps, of everything in his life that's foundering? But of course it is possible that, at times when he isn't there, Franka will take out a puzzle the way she used to, and spend a contented evening with it, her stockinged feet hooked round the chair legs. He has tried to remember the order in which the boxes are stacked, but when, after an evening of working late, or a drawn-out business dinner, he sneaks a peek behind the cupboard door, he'll suddenly find himself doubting his memory. And then he'll think to himself, it's only some jigsaw puzzles. It isn't the writing on the wall, just some ordinary boxes with little pieces of cardboard inside.

And yet last week she had reacted enthusiastically to the Lago Maggiore, from the new collection. 'Impossible, all that blue!'

When she immediately emptied the contents of the box onto the table, his heart began hammering like a pile-driver. 'You do the sky, I'll do the water?' she suggested as she started pushing the pieces around with her chewed-up fingertips, sorting them by colour.

'I'll get us something to drink,' he said. In the kitchen he blew his nose.

'Champagne?' she said when he returned with the bottle and glasses.

'It's almost past the use-by date. It's got to be drunk.' She cracked a smile.

While he poured, she studied the picture of the puzzle on the box lid with a look of concentration. Perhaps she was seeing Phinus's image materializing right through Lago Maggiore, and marvelling: this is the work of my husband. 'Just look at this section here,' she said. 'That's going to be complicated.'

He took the lid from her. 'Yes, tricky.' But then the smile died on his lips. 'Oh no! Look at this! The logo's reversed!'

'So, what does it matter?'

'Someone in production should have caught it!'

'Oh, Phinus,' she said, almost pityingly: you spoilt baby with your frivolous problems. You and your insignificant worries about pawns or bits of cardboard.

He swallowed his indignation. Let's not spoil the atmosphere, not after waiting so long for an evening like this. He lifted his glass invitingly.

She casually took a sip from her own, not looking at him. The glass had a crack in it.

'What I'd like,' he remarked abruptly, as he picked up a puzzle piece, 'is a new dinner service.' Elegant glasses that matched, teacups with handles, a footed gravy boat, plates that weren't chipped round the edges. Neatly stacked in a locked cupboard, out of reach of junkies, klepto-whiniacs and crackpots.

'Keep your hands off my water,' she said.

'It belongs to my mountain.'

She snatched the piece out of his fingers, glanced at it and then gave it back. 'What were you saying about a dinner service? Don't we have everything we need?'

'Sure, from Woolworth's!' Suddenly, unaccountably, he was so incensed that his hands were shaking.

'What's wrong with that? Perfectly good stuff, and not too pricey.'

'I just want something nicer to drink out of than those clunky mugs of yours.'

She looked up at him for a moment and then bent over Lago Maggiore again. 'We are not going to buy stuff we don't need. I think that's showing off.'

The nervous twitch in his left cheek started acting

31

up. He only just managed to suppress the urge to smash the champagne bottle on the edge of the table, the table with the dented top, onto the colourful Third World tablecloth, onto the bleached pine floor with the dusty skirting boards and the piles of newspapers and the bank statements left lying around and one bright red sock, for crying out loud – *How often do I have to tell you: take a pair of socks, place them back to back, a little tug on both ends, roll them up into a ball, fold the cuffs over once and back again* – and next to the sock a withered houseplant sitting on a saucer from Woolworth's, crusty with calcium deposits. Chaos and disorder surrounded him day in, day out, junk thoughtlessly accumulated engulfed the house with its leaky gutters, its defective pipes, its cracked tiles, because we don't get all uptight about a little mess, do we, we have loftier goals than the poor sods who get all worked up about whether a logo is printed on a product correctly, we despise anxiety and fuss about material things, and that's why we live here like pigs – *How many times do I have to tell you: take the rubbish bag out of the bin before it's completely full, shake it a little, press out the air – I said FIRST LET THE AIR OUT – and only then do you wrap the tie round it, twist the ends three times and fold it back and now three times more . . .*

'What's the matter?' she asked. 'You look so agitated. Here, this corner is yours.' She slid a piece over to him. 'You aren't looking for a fight, are you, now that we're sitting here together so nicely?'

'A fight? I'm the most peace-loving man on earth! How long haven't I been walking on tenterhooks, to spare you?'

She said calmly, 'You know perfectly well how

long. But I never asked to be spared anything, did I!'

'Well, that's rich! You won't even let me tidy away Jem's things!' Instantly he could have kicked himself. But his helplessness only made him angrier. Tripping over his words, he blurted out, 'Tell me, how long are you intending to go on breaking your neck on his skateboard? And how long are we going to keep his bike as some kind of relic in the . . .' His voice faltered, because out of the blue, he remembered how he had taught Jem to ride a bike, and an even earlier memory came tumbling out: the little boy in the child seat on the front of his own bicycle, tiny fists clamped round the handlebars between his – *You're steering, Jem, aren't you!* – and his entire body remembered the rapid, deft sequence of manoeuvres required to wrestle an excited, thrashing child into the seat, to place the little feet onto the flipped-down footrests, tug the jacket down, and at the thought his right leg almost gave in to a familiar impulse, irresistible and involuntary, to swing itself over the crossbar, and he had to press his foot into the floor with all his strength.

Franka cried, 'I'll save his things as long as I want!'

The muscles in his calf trembled with the exertion. If he didn't watch out, his leg would do its own thing, with the most dire consequences, because the minute this leg managed to wrest control of the paternal motor function in Central Command, every molecule in his body was bound to fall in step with that leg, and his nose would remember the fresh smell of a child's sweat, and his fingers would remember how to pry pebbles out of a grazed knee, and on parent-teacher evenings smelling of chalk he would feel his heart wavering again between pride and defensiveness and everything, everything, would come back to him again: the first, halting words, followed with disconcerting speed by the first swimming lesson, the first skating lesson, and, before you know it, the first shaving lesson: *You begin at the cheek, look, this way, come on, pay attention, how many times do I have to tell you, there are rules for everything, and they're not there for nothing, don't be so stubborn, begin at your cheek!*

'You're not even listening,' Franka shouted. She was on her feet. 'You only ever think of yourself.'

Quivering with self-restraint, he stared at her. *Jem's mother.* 'And you don't?' he said.

And what do you do after that kind of fight? Sulk? Snivel? Ignore each other, if not overtly? Go on stubbornly insisting you were right? Do you dig in your heels, that's the question, or do you bury the hatchet, mend your fences, kiss and make up, laugh it off and drag precious goodwill back into the house?

Come, wounded heart, simmer down, and see if you can't make some gesture that will make it up between you, so that peace and harmony may be restored. That is a wiser course to take than to insist on thrashing it out. Because he who remains silent cannot say the wrong thing, or hear himself utter words he will shortly regret. And after a marital row, isn't a little outing together a capital remedy for any remaining negative emotions? To have enough time and attention for each other again, in a fresh new environment?

And what do you know, she said yes, his elusive, indecipherable wife – *it's true, she said yes!* – when Phinus, oozing with hope and goodwill, came up with the idea for a weekend out of town.

* * *

34

And so it is that the two of them now drive into Aduard at nightfall, in search of the celebrated Onder de Linden Inn, which is recommended in the *Alliance Gastronomique* guide with these words: 'Enjoy the tranquillity, the beauty and the culinary pampering.'

The deserted village high street rolls by, dull, straight and narrow. The few shops are already closed and the streetlights are about to come on. Just before the bridge over the canal, it becomes apparent that they have already reached the end of the village proper. Phinus stops on the shoulder. He takes the guide out of his inside pocket, looks up the number of the inn and dials it on his car phone. Drumming his fingers on the steering wheel, he waits for the connection. Nothing happens. He takes the receiver out of its holster to give it another try. No dial tone. 'Not again!' he mutters. Is the worthless piece of junk broken again, just for a change? Oh, the pointless busyness of modern existence, getting things fixed just so they can break down again!

'What did you say?' asks Franka, waking up with a start. She shakes her head and looks around, still half asleep.

He clicks the phone back into its holder. 'Just going to ask for directions.'

He gets out, his back stiff from sitting so long. It's chilly out. He buttons his jacket and thrusts his hands deep into his trouser pockets. On the left side of the road stands De Lantaren, some kind of teen hangout, by the looks of it. As he turns towards the ramshackle building, he suddenly notices, a little further on, two people on the bridge.

'Good evening,' he calls.

The figures turn round. Two young girls. They are

both wearing puffy bomber jackets, one of them has her hair shorn halfway up her skull, the other one has a pierced nose. They chew their gum languidly as he approaches.

These are no hearty farmers' daughters exchanging by the fading light at the water's edge some last comment about the milking of the cows or the cutting of the peat, these two are graffiti made flesh, they are the type of youngster that belongs in echoing car parks and badly lit underpasses. He clears his throat elaborately. 'Good evening. I'm looking for—'

The taller of the two, the one with the pierced nose, interrupts him with a sour look on her face, just discernible in the dusky light. 'Over there.' She points.

'The Onder de Linden Inn,' he specifies.

'That's what I said. There.'

He throws a doubtful look over his shoulder at the high street. Then his eye is caught by the row of linden trees in front of a magnificent old building. Naturally, when someone asks for directions around here, it's got to be Onder de Linden they're looking for. Why else would anyone come to this backwater?

'Thanks,' he says.

'What for?' drawls the tall one.

'For your help.'

The short one with the buzz cut fixes him with a clear gaze. She remarks, 'Maybe you'll die tonight, sir.'

'And a pleasant evening to you,' he says, flustered. He hurries back to the car, pressing his hand against his cheek where that cursed nerve is dancing the hornpipe. He can't have understood her right. He mustn't get spooked by seeing tsohgs everywhere.

'Well?' asks Franka as he gets in again.

'We're here.' He turns the car round and sets course for the inn, less than six hundred metres back.

'Great. You must be stiff from all that sitting, after that long drive. First thing we do, we'll order you a drink.'

What Franka lost

He parks the car next to the inn, on the gravel. The silence is unreal. In Amsterdam, even in the dead of night, you can always hear a laugh ringing loudly off the tram tracks somewhere. And if you should find yourself in the great outdoors, you'll hear the equally reassuring rushing of the surf, or the rustling of the treetops. Here, on the other hand, there is no noise at all.

Furtively he feels his armpits. He's got the feeling that he has started to smell, but his shirt is dry.

When he has locked up the car, he notices Franka taking in the surroundings. Onder de Linden is located in a beautifully restored historic building. On the sheltered terrace stand little box trees in large pots. There is a courtyard with clipped hedges and, behind it, a kitchen garden.

'How lovely!' she exclaims. 'How did you find out about it?'

'Really? Do you like it?'

She puts her arm through his. 'Sausage,' she says

affectionately. 'Who wouldn't be enchanted by this?'

In the hall, candles burn in glass bowls. The flagstone floor gleams dully. In the hallway, a gigantic flower arrangement lifts its raffia bows to them: welcome to the world of starched table linen, of smoked salmon with horseradish and a twist of deep-fried aubergine on the side, the world of ranks of silverware and glittering crystal. Phinus can already picture the discreet ministrations of waiters in long white aprons, as well as tomorrow morning's breakfast, with its assortment of six kinds of bread, fresh fruit, eggs to order, and a pat of fresh creamery butter under a small earthenware dome, with the sunlight of Aduard shining generously in through the window.

Why shouldn't Franka and he be entitled to enjoy themselves again for a change?

The hostess meets them in the hall. She enquires politely about their trip, perhaps they would first like to recover a little, with an aperitif, and then have a look at the room?

In the bar with the beamed ceiling, a fire burns in the hearth. They install themselves by the fireplace and order some white wine.

'Do you find, as I do,' he says, 'that certain situations call for specific words to come into your head? I mean, one doesn't just sit down in a place like this, no, one nestles by the hearth. Nestle. Such an absurd word. But totally apt. Or crunch. Snow crunches. What else crunches? Nothing, right? It's extraordinary.'

'Twigs sometimes crunch.'

'No, those crackle.'

'Perhaps the mystery of the ham and the sauce can be solved here as well,' she says, picking up her glass. 'God, am I bushed.'

'You'll get a good night's sleep later. It's dead quiet out here.'

She shakes her head as if chasing away an insect.

He observes her tensely. 'Shall I order us a little nibble?'

'If I feel like having something, I'll tell you.'

'OK. OK. Do you want a newspaper?' He waves at the reading material lying on the bar.

She smiles. 'Yes, certainly.'

'What are you laughing at now?'

'Nothing, Phinus.' She gets up to fetch the *Gazette of the North*. 'Want part of it?'

He accepts the business section from her. 'You do like it here, don't you?'

She opens the newspaper. 'This is totally my idea of getting away. It's a treat, having a drink with you someplace, and reading the newspaper together.'

Half reassured, he concentrates on the stock market news. From time to time he glances at Franka's cropped blonde head. She is absorbed in an article. The fire crackles. He stretches his legs and takes a sip of wine, slowly surrendering to a wonderful feeling of relaxation. His gaze drifts outside, where, on the other side of the box trees, cabbages and herbs are marshalled in neat formation. He thinks, it's just the way it used to be when I was little, here. And for the first time in six months, his heart feels a little lighter, because the land of long ago is free of the guilt that has lately been tearing him apart; free of regret, free of shame.

In the vegetable garden with the aunts, wellies under their summer frocks. Aunt Irmgard as always rather peeved about the plantings' progress, Aunt Leonoor

40

thrilled at the sight of each new lettuce leaf, Phinus looking on in his little boots. This is how we plant the carrots, see, and the potatoes this way, and remember, you never eat the seed potatoes, always keep a box of them stored away in the shed, because if you should run out— Oh, shush please, you'll give the child a fright . . .

One day, Aunt Leonoor, on her knees amongst the rows of vegetables, her fingernails black with dirt, waved him over. 'Look, that's where you came from.'

In the heart of the cabbage she was pointing at, he beheld a caterpillar.

So first you were a caterpillar, then you turned into a baby, he'd seen one or two of those, and then you turned into an orphan.

But orphans, said Aunt Irmgard, were simply children, just like any other children! OK, except that they didn't have any parents of course. No need to get all worked up over the petty details.

Now, don't frighten the poor child, Irmgard!

It was so reassuring to hear them happily bickering. As reassuring as the smell of their ample bodies, or the self-assured sound of their tread. The way the aunts smelt, the way they walked, all of it, erased every doubt: they were confident of their place in the sun, the sun which would grow pale if Aunt Irmgard didn't bitch any more, which would be extinguished if Aunt Leonoor didn't cheer any more, which would tumble right out of the sky if they no longer slept together in the big bed that creaked and groaned under their weight.

They read the books of Rudolf Steiner and Mellie Uyldert. They knew that an apple boosts energy, that lemon balm relieves stomach problems, and that you must never burn the wood of the elder (rather, you could make excellent divining rods from it). But they were also clued in on worldly affairs. They sat in front of the television in the dead of night to see Cassius Clay box. They each owned a moped and a helmet. They drank Campari out of a tall glass (Leonoor) and Dutch gin out of a small snifter (Irmgard), and they concocted bright pink and brilliant yellow dips, from a packet. For Phinus, there was Ribena.

The three of them manned the sub-post office in the village square. They postmarked envelopes, counted out money and weighed packages that would then fly from their set of scales to the other side of the world, where the children walked around on their heads and Ribena was poured into glasses in a stream running up instead of down. There were ostriches down there, and tarantulas as big as ostrich eggs, and kangaroos too, of course. They kept their baby in a pocket in their tummy so they wouldn't lose it.

Phinus had one in his room, made of felt, called Kanga, just like the one in Winnie the Pooh. Whenever he found a caterpillar, he stuffed it inside Kanga's pouch. It was probably just a matter of persistence.

In the morning, after breakfast, he helped the aunts sort the letters and packages. The aunts would stick thimbles of ribbed rubber onto their thumbs and index fingers and briskly leaf through the piles he pulled out of the post bags, you couldn't keep up with them, they turned it into a race, snorting with delight. At the same time they'd talk about the contents of the letters: another tax demand for so-and-so, at long last a letter for poor Marie Jansen from her son who'd emigrated, and, look here, a dentist's bill for her round the corner, for her new set of dentures. They would laugh to see him pressing a piece of mail up against his eyes, longing to divine its mysteries just as easily as they. 'Once you've learned how to read,' they promised. But he didn't believe them, because they didn't ever read the letters, they didn't even open them, they only glanced at the envelope.

They told him plenty of other fairy tales. About his name, for instance. They maintained that everyone's name was written in a book into which, just before you emerged from your cabbage, an angel would stick a golden pin. A second angel would write down that name in vermilion ink on a little card, and a third one would immediately fly it down to the vegetable patch, and tie it with a piece of string round your big toe, so that people would know your name. It's true, Phinus, cross my heart, *we* can't tell you why you were named Phinus. Oh dear, so many why's, well, that's the age. We really can't tell you any more than you already know. Do we ever beat about the bush? Don't we always tell the truth? That you draw so well, for instance, that's right too, isn't it?

His drawings were all pinned up on the wall. In those, the aunts were as tall as giraffes. They towered over the little boy in the yellow galoshes. He'd be holding a little bunch of cornflowers up to them. Or he'd be running after them, his little fork hands stretched out.

In the evenings, the aunts sat on the edge of his bed and played I Have a Little House on the Moon with him, or they'd philosophize about life. 'As an orphan, you may be more inclined in your life to follow authority,' said Aunt Irmgard pensively. 'Be grateful! Be obedient! But we certainly hope we'll never catch you at it. You don't need to earn our love.'

'An orphan,' Aunt Leonoor observed, 'sometimes has the urge to skip his youth, only to have it catch up with him much later in life. An orphan lives in the future, because he longs for a life like that of other people. Don't you make that mistake, darling. Now's your time to be young and carefree.'

He had taken that piece of advice to heart. And he had, all things considered, managed to pull it off pretty well.

There's a drone of voices all around them. The bar has filled up with guests. A slightly older couple, a group of friends, two women who clearly have something to celebrate. The dress is casual, yet smart. From the sound of it, they're all from the city. That is to be expected, in a place like this. One thing worries him: what if they run into people they know? With the Easter weekend coming up, anyone could have had the same idea. He shifts in his chair, uneasily. He wants to have Franka all to himself. All will be well again once he finally has her all to himself.

'Waiter,' he says, to get her attention.

She drops the newspaper and looks at her watch. 'Oughtn't we to go and eat instead? I'm getting quite peckish.'

'But wouldn't you rather get the bags out of the car first and go upstairs – we haven't even seen our room yet – and perhaps freshen up a bit?'

She folds up the newspaper with swift movements. 'Oh, I don't need to change, I haven't brought anything dressier than this.'

He tugs at his tie to make sure it's straight. 'Then let's go in and sit down.'

She walks ahead of him into the dining room in her

yellow suit, a little unsteady in her high heels. An attentive maître d' settles them at an impeccably laid table (pale yellow damask on top of a green cloth) and a waiter rushes forward with delicious-smelling bread and a little halibut appetizer. She says, in a relaxed tone of voice, picking up her napkin, 'We should have done this ages ago.'

'And there I was thinking you might not . . .'

She sends him a probing look. 'That I might not be ready for it yet, is that it?'

'Can't we talk about something else, just this once?' He has to cough to hide the anger in his voice. 'I was just worried you would think it's too fancy here. You're sometimes such a Spartan.'

The sommelier interrupts them to enquire if they wish to see the wine list.

'What would you suggest?' says Phinus with some relief, and then he's perturbed again, for had he not wanted to be alone with his wife, undisturbed? How can he – how, while all the time – what will become of their weekend away, if this – or, even worse, if that, or if not?

A fine rosé to start, to be sure. And then a white Bordeaux perhaps. That will take them through the third course. To follow, with the main course, a—

'Dear heaven,' says Franka, 'what are you planning to do to us?'

'A light red,' snaps Phinus brusquely. 'What kind of Beaujolais have you got?' The stress is making him grimace.

'Your tic,' she mouths at him, softly and discreetly. Then she turns to the sommelier. 'Let's have a quick look at that list after all.'

Franka Vermeer, woman of the world.

'What's the matter?' she asks as soon as they're alone again.

'I was thinking of all the cholesterol that's in store for us.'

'Phinus.' She takes a piece of bread and drizzles some olive oil on it. 'What a hypochondriac you are these days! It just isn't like you. You're looking appalled at the mere thought of—'

'No, no, I—'

'You are, it's making you sweat!'

He sets his hands flat on the table. 'Just say it: you think I smell.'

'What gives you that idea!'

Wildly, he rips open his jacket and leans his body towards her.

'Which one of you . . . ?' asks the sommelier, offering the wine list.

Phinus promptly controls himself again. 'Shall I take a look?'

'And could we have a large bottle of blue Spa to start?' asks Franka.

'Will San Pellegrino do?'

'In that case, we'd prefer a Ramlösa,' he says. Just as he's about to consult the wine list, something moves into the periphery of his vision. A blur comes closer, a voice calls out enthusiastically, 'Phinus! You here too!'

'Hello, Katja,' he says, spent.

'What a lovely surprise!'

He gets to his feet. Katja is a buyer for Intertoys, Katja is a major player (and Katja and he, some years ago, at the annual toy fair in Nuremburg, did once end up in bed together, but it didn't come to anything because Phinus, literally on the edge of the hotel bed, had been overcome with remorse. That bed had a royal blue bedspread on it, Franka's favourite colour. Katja's red-lacquered toenails had been no match for it, and he'd stroked her hair apologetically – astonishingly stiff hair, actually, a sort of helmet of straw – and had felt, all things considered, pretty shitty about the whole thing.)

'And this is my husband, Mark,' she says. 'You remember, Mark, Phinus works at Jumbo.'

'Franka,' Phinus introduces his wife.

Now they are on their feet, the four of them standing rather woodenly around the table. Mark is studying his toes, Franka the wainscoting.

'Your Yali is quite a hit,' Katja gushes. 'And I wouldn't go near it! What a hoot, eh?'

He tries with all his might to picture Yali in his mind and thus to return to his old self. Yali! Yali walked away with the Toy of the Year Prize. An ingenious game in the form of a scale, with marbles at either end. The object of the game: to get to the other side as quickly as possible without upsetting the balance. EVERY TURN IS A GAMBLE WITH GRAVITY. For the technical nuts and bolts they'd consulted the National Research Institute; it hadn't been a doddle by any means. He'd enjoyed it hugely. In his line of work it wasn't every day that you got to sit down with those super-smart engineers.

'Care to join us?' he asks.

Katja looks at her husband.

Enthused, Phinus goes on, 'That kid who thought up Yali is coming in next week with a new idea. He's definitely one to watch. It's to him we owe the whole revival of unplugged games.' He pulls out the chair next to his, for Katja.

A waiter instantly materializes to make the necessary

adjustments to the table configuration. The bottle of rosé arrives too.

When everyone is seated, Franka asks, 'So, Phinus and you are colleagues, more or less?'

'Something like that!' says Katja elatedly. She presses her knee against his under the table.

Franka is smiling. Is she pleased with the extended company, thankful to be relieved of the prospect of an entire evening spent alone with him? His mood plummets.

The conversation ranges over the unique spot in which they find themselves, over other gastronomic jewels hidden here and there deep in the countryside, over summer holiday plans, over Mark's activities in the computer sector.

'Our children take after him that way,' says Katja. 'The computer gene, I mean. By the way, have you two got—'

'The menu?' says Phinus. 'Yes of course. That appetizer, the celeriac, endive and sweetbread tart, is a most unusual combination.'

'But tell us, Franka, what do you do?' asks Mark.

'Oh, social work.' A flush has crept over her cheeks. She accepts a cigarette from the pack Mark offers her. 'I work with young people.' She leans over towards the candle on the table and sucks at the flame.

'Sweetheart,' says Phinus. 'You don't smoke.'

'That, I'd never have imagined for Phinus,' says Katja. 'Please don't take this the wrong way but,' she turns towards him, 'you always struck me as the more light-hearted type. The kind who'd be married to an ABBA girl, say.'

'That's what's known as a Spice Girl these days,' says Mark.

'Whatever.' Katja looks cheerfully from one to the other. 'What's the difference? Behind every man there's a disappointed woman, I always say. Don't you agree, Franka?'

Franka blows out smoke like a pro. 'So, you think of Phinus as light-hearted, do you?'

'Absolutely!' shrieks Katja.

'But we were talking about your work,' says Mark to Franka. 'Do I understand that you spend your entire day surrounded by those scowling wastrels in hoods?'

'Oh, someone has to try to keep them on the straight and narrow. If we all chose to turn our backs . . .'

'They're spoilt, lazy and selfish, that's what's wrong with them,' Mark sums up.

'Except ours, of course,' says Katja complacently. 'And yours too, probably. Surely it's simply a matter of upbringing? Not that Mark is ever home to contribute in that department. Anyway, first let's drink to this happy coincidence.' She raises her glass. 'Cheers, guys. Are you spending the night here too? If so, the four of us could visit the museum in Groningen tomorrow. Or did you have other plans?' Under the table she again presses her knee intimately up against Phinus's leg.

He is, when it comes down to it, not a man to have affairs. Life, with all its pitfalls and snares, is nerve-racking enough for him without cheating and clandestine assignations; making one woman happy requires quite enough effort on his part. Even if it's no more than the constant attention she deserves as a matter of course, simply for being his Frankie. The daily concern for her comfort. Don't forget your umbrella, love. Isn't it too draughty for you over there?

I can take it back for you, if you like. Shall I give you another helping?

But with him it goes deeper. When, fourteen years ago, he gave her his word 'I do', that well-considered vow encompassed the best of himself, namely, his faithful devotion. A promise so grave — because it's such a sweeping commitment — isn't one you can just go back on. It takes more than ten scarlet toenails, a few glasses of alcohol and messy happenstance.

Just what kind of circumstances *do* lead to infidelity, that is something he has known only a few weeks. He's known it since the afternoon that . . . *No, forget that.*

On their wedding day, he'd promised Franka that from this day forward he would be one of the pillars of her existence. And, years later, he could still nip everyday irritations in the bud by thinking back on the moment when he told her I do; how determined and serious he'd been then, and how happy it had made him. He didn't just belong to himself any more, he was now someone's husband as well, a notion so exotic and exciting that he just couldn't get over it. All during their honeymoon in Paris, he'd hoped that just once she would say it out loud. To a waiter: 'No, no, that's for my husband.' To a taxi driver: 'My husband's just coming.'

What an extraordinary, phenomenal institution it was, marriage! Suddenly he had a shiny label stuck to his forehead: I belong to Franka. I am her husband. *You are the one with whom I cast my lot, through thick and thin. Together we can face anything.*

You could tell from the wedding pictures. Here was a man with a mission. Next to him Franka, with a touch of irony in her eyes: cool it a little, Phinus. Or perhaps the mockery was aimed at herself, and she was thinking: well, now you've really gone and done it, the widow who swore she didn't need this, ever again. Clinging to her hand was little Jem, happy and without a care in the world, looking straight ahead, hugging a teddy bear to his tummy. A whole family, in one fell swoop. The three of them together, until death do them part.

Which, just three years later, very nearly did come to pass. It was the height of summer, that supremely happy-go-lucky season. They were just packing their bags to go on holiday, when they got the results of a routine medical check-up.

They unpacked their suitcases again. They stuffed a few T-shirts, a dressing gown and some underwear in a bag, and called a cab. There are rides you don't forget all your living days. Your own neighbourhood, your own city, the parks you have passed a thousand times, everything, including the daisies on the verge, everything suddenly looks unfamiliar, that's how shaky the ground feels under your feet.

After the operation, Franka was brought to intensive care. Phinus anxiously had to scan the rows of beds before he recognized her among the identical motionless bodies with tubes up their noses, hemmed in by intimidating beeping machines. Her face pale, her lips cracked.

'Darling,' he said, distraught.

'It's OK,' she whispered.

'I'm here now.'

She moved her head back and forth on the pillow.

'It went well, they say. Everything's clean. You'll be home in ten days. Let's be glad it was discovered in time. You'll be as good as new in no time.'

She shut her eyes. She mumbled, 'How can you say that?'

'Frankie,' he began, *I've buried you a hundred times over in the past twenty-four hours, I've thought of myself as your widower, I've already bought black clothes for Jem, in a manner of speaking, I've seen the smile die on his little face and have known that we'll never, ever be carefree or happy again, I've hoisted him up on my shoulders and held him firmly by his little feet as we walked behind your coffin through the cemetery, surrounded by our friends, their faces drawn and nearly unrecognizable, Franka, Franka, what are you doing to us, how do I explain this to someone who isn't even five years old, what shall I, what will I do, if you're no longer here, if at night you don't snuggle your bottom against my stomach any more, where are you, where will you be then?*

With her eyes shut she whispered, 'It was so quick, everything, so . . . it feels as if I've gone and lost my uterus in the shopping centre, or on the train, or that it's like money that's blown out of my wallet, so suddenly, one moment I was still whole, and then after that stupid smear test . . .'

Phinus held her hand and tried to picture her in a shopping centre, shopping, among women with pushchairs, dragging whining toddlers by the hand, and as it dawned on him that Franka would now never walk there pushing a buggy with their baby in it, he suddenly felt so robbed of his own future that he had to get up off the bed in order to hide his distress.

In his fear of losing her, this aspect of the situation hadn't even crossed his mind for one second. They used to think they had all the time in the world, and they hadn't wanted to saddle Jem with too many changes at once. What was he to do now? Comb all the shopping centres of the Netherlands on all fours? Crawl, panting, through the discarded cigarette butts and cash register slips, Muzak droning in his ears, his trouser legs collecting wads of old chewing gum, the sickly smell of croissants and chips rising from all sides? This kind of thing could only happen to a damn slob of a scatterbrain – *How many times must I tell you?* – like Franka.

He couldn't come up with a single comforting gesture.

The next day he found her bed empty. According to the nurse he bumped into in the corridor, she had been in the shower for hours. 'That's not unusual, don't let it worry you, Mr Vermeer.' He pictured her in a cloud of steam, the hot water clattering down, huddled on the tile floor, the plastic identity bracelet still fastened round her wrist, hair plastered to her skull, mourning all by herself. He took the elevator down, bought a bunch of roses from the florist in the foyer and left them on top of the folded-back sheets, thankful that he didn't have to face her.

He picked Jem up from the childminder's and drove back to Scheveningen with him.

Instead of visiting Aléria and its Roman temple and the Gorges de Spelunca in the Aitone ravine, they'd ended up in a little hotel in Scheveningen, enough at least to give Jem a bit of a change of scene, yet not too far away from the hospital either.

'When will Mummy be better?' asked the boy from the back seat.

'Know what?' said Phinus. 'You can call her tonight. Then she can tell you all about it herself. OK?'

In the rearview mirror he looked at Jem's full-moon

face. Better not bring him with you, Franka had said. It would only frighten him, to see her looking so sick.

Jem was sucking his thumb, holding on to his ear with the other hand. Suddenly he let both hands fall. He started singing in a loud, clear voice, 'There's a cow walking over the earth, there's a cow-ow on earth, there's a cow, a cow, a cowow on eaaaaarth!' He gave a deep sigh. 'That's what I just saw out of the window, Daddy.'

'What else do you see?'

'The road.'

'And on the road?'

'Cars.'

'What else?' Phinus felt around behind him, found a little ankle, squeezed it.

'I see the sun!'

'Where?'

'There! Right by that cloud.'

'Which one?' It was raining.

It rained the entire week, nonstop, so that the wooden walkways of Scheveningen's beach establishments were covered in large puddles. On the terraces, the beach umbrellas were furled and tied with heavy rope, to secure them from the gusting wind. At Zeezicht, with its all-you-can-eat menu of mussels and spareribs, the electric heaters glowed red under the striped awnings. On the deserted promenade, geraniums drowned in their cement planters, the trampolines were abandoned, the merry-go-round was mostly at a standstill, and on the wet beach the deck chairs and sunbeds were stowed under canvas.

But since they were, after all, on holiday, Phinus and Jem made forays out every day. They erected bulwarks in the sand, which the sea promptly

54

swallowed up. They poked at jellyfish with sticks, while the wind made their eyes water and the whirling sand nestled in their nostrils. With their hands behind their backs, leaning forward like long-distance skaters, they plodded past beach tents with names like La Playa, Summertime, Blue Lagoon or El Dorado. Credit cards & Smart cards accepted here, Pancakes with genuine butter, Toilets 50 cents, Wilkommen, Kees' Bar is open, Dogs not allowed, Yes we have mussels, alive, alive-oh.

Inside Sea Life, the big aquarium with its slanted glass front, they made the acquaintance of the sea anemone, the spiny lobster and the angelfish. They learned that a flounder can live to be thirty years old, that a grain of sand is composed of over 250 million parts, and that twenty-one per cent of the Netherlands is reclaimed from the sea. In a shallow open tank that they could look into from above, they tickled lazy sting-rays on their stomachs. 'Kindly pet only the stingrays and the starfish,' warned a sign on the wall. 'All other creatures, including the sharks, may be damaged by touching.' The sharks were small and not very scary. But it was troubling to think you could damage them by accident, just by touching them. If even sharks couldn't stand up to a little knock, then what *could* you be sure of?

At the end of every afternoon, before going off to eat pancakes, with an orange juice for Jem and a beer for Phinus, they'd buy a postcard for Franka with 'Greetings from Scheveningen' printed on it, in the gift shop at the entrance to the pier. There were also dried crabs for sale, keyrings shaped like lighthouses, bottles with tiny galleons inside, and little baskets of coloured seashells. Jem couldn't get enough of it. He had five sandy guilders to spend, but he just couldn't decide what to spend them on. Every time they were in the little shop, his fist would disappear into the pocket of his windbreaker to take out his holiday money, only to put it away again. 'It's so hard to choose,' he said, defeated.

'Yes, it is,' said Phinus. 'Because once you've made your choice, you're stuck with it.' He was tired. Tired of the rain, tired of the nonstop entertainment he had to provide, tired of driving back and forth to the hospital, including the obligatory detour to Jem's childminder. These past few days, he'd even felt too drained to shave, and every evening, after tucking Jem in and reading him half a page out of *Pluk van de Petteflet*, he would collapse in bed, unwashed. He slept and slept, as much as twelve hours of the day. The books he had brought remained unread, the crossword puzzle from the newspaper unsolved.

In the mornings Jem had to wake him by pinching his nose shut or tickling the soles of his feet. Every time it felt as if he were being dragged up by the hair, out of murky, stagnant water. Once he'd surfaced, he just didn't have it in him to stick his head under the tap or put on a clean shirt.

No wonder that the woman standing behind the counter in the gift shop was beginning to eye him with increasing suspicion. With pursed lips she rang up his daily postcard, all the while staring with distaste at Jem, his tow-coloured hair stiff with salt and a crust of dried snot on his upper lip.

'Come on, Jem, let's go,' he called.

'I want this one!' Blowing out little spit bubbles of excitement, Jem rushed out from behind a shelf. In his outstretched hand he held a red plastic tiara with yellow starfish. 'It's a *crown*, Daddy.'

Phinus examined the piece of rubbish. 'Are you sure?'

'Yes,' said Jem, nodding vehemently.

'Then hurry up and pay for it.'

And Prince Jem, the princeling from the dark and dangerous forest, mounted his white steed and galloped to the till, glowing from head to foot.

'That's for girls,' said the sales lady condescendingly. 'That's a *tiaaara*.'

Shocked, Jem looked round at Phinus.

'So what?' said Phinus.

'Surely you're not going to let the little boy go around wearing that!'

'And why not?'

The woman rolled her eyes heavenward. 'It's a tiara. For girls.'

'Who says?'

'Everyone knows that.'

Jem had already stopped counting out his money. His little hands, blasted red by the sand and wind, squirmed around the rim of the counter, timidly, as if he was afraid he might hurt the wood.

Phinus's knees started knocking with frustration. 'Bitch,' he stuttered. He snatched the hairband out of the woman's hand, grabbed Jem by the hood and pushed him outside ahead of him.

On the promenade, heavy raindrops hit them in the face. From the pier came the ringing and rattling of slot machines. On the beach a seagull skimmed past the marker posts with their colourful recognition symbols for toddlers: a strawberry, a mushroom, a butterfly, a seahorse. *Don't forget, will you: we're sitting next to the banana.*

'Here,' he said to Jem, who was standing beside

him, his head bowed. 'Put your crown on, quick.'

Jem shrugged.

'Come on! You wanted to have it, didn't you?' He squatted and stuck the tiara impatiently into the blond hair. 'Wow, it looks great!'

Jem's eyes filled with tears.

'My poppet. It's a super-duper crown. Really truly. You made an excellent choice.'

'Not true!'

'Come now, don't whine,' he snapped. 'Just because that old witch—'

'Was that a witch?' Jem fingered the tiara uncertainly.

'Couldn't you tell she was? Off you go to the merry-go-round. Go choose yourself a handsome, valiant steed.'

Shoulders drooping, the boy trudged towards the carousel with its curlicue-painted wooden horses that rose and fell on their gilded poles. He turned round and cupped his hands like a megaphone. Anxiously, he shouted, 'Was it exactly five guilders?'

'I have your change,' Phinus lied, in a loud voice. 'You still have two fifty left.'

A cautious smile appeared on Jem's round toddler's face. Then, huffing and puffing, he climbed up on a horse with a blue halter and threw his arms round its neck. The carousel reeled into motion. The little boy waved at Phinus on every jingling turn. 'Here I am! Over here!'

'I see you!' he shouted back encouragingly as the rain dripped inside his collar. He waved both hands high in the air.

'You'll wait for me, won't you, Daddy?'

Suddenly he was struck by the thought that, the

moment Jem swept out of sight again, he could simply walk away. The thing that would now be an irreversible fact for Franka for the rest of her life didn't have to be so for him. He still had a choice. He could still make the dream come true, the dream that stemmed from the time when he used to stuff caterpillars into Kanga's pouch. Had he ever doubted that he would have children of his own? A whole retaining wall of children is what he'd intended to build up around himself, children of his own flesh and blood.

'Dad?' yelled Jem. He was hanging sideways off his horse's flank so as not to lose sight of Phinus, waiting for some sort of reaction from him. Jem, who had never known his own father because Franka had only just become pregnant when her first husband had been killed in a traffic accident. Jem who'd known from the time he was very young that he was *such* a special little boy ('Really, it's incredibly special!'), so special that he had *two* daddies. One dead and one alive: one to just think about, the other on whose lap to sit. Jem who, just like Phinus himself, had learned even before he knew how to tie his shoelaces to take life as it comes and not be stingy with his trust.

'Well, of course,' shouted Phinus, not sure if it was sheer gratitude that prompted him, or the onset of resignation, 'of course I'm waiting for you, Jem, right here. I'm here, really I am.'

'What is it exactly,' asks Mark during the first course, 'that makes a game a good game? Do you have a theory, Phinus?'

Phinus puts down his fork, somewhat taken aback. It's hard to believe, sometimes, that other people actually take you seriously when playing is what you do for a living. 'A good game ought to surprise you,' he says, 'but it mustn't rely too much on pure luck and chance. The players want to see their own skill or ingenuity rewarded as well.' He smiles shyly, but he's beginning to get fired up. 'What's more, an ideal game is a game that isn't won in only one way. But you do have to be able to explain the rules in just a few words. Take chess, for example. Now there's a game you couldn't possibly market nowadays, something that complicated, every piece saddled with its own rules and regulations. Even Monopoly survives today only because one generation that's been initiated into its mysteries can teach it to the next.'

Katja's face assumes a patronizing expression. She presses her napkin to her lips, glances at the cloth and then declares, 'That's because of the TV ads, mate. You have to be able to get across how something works in thirty seconds or less these days.'

'I know that,' says Phinus, 'but look at that Aztec board game, which was invented around—'

'Wait a minute, wait a minute,' urges Mark, with a sly grin. 'You just mentioned marketing. So that's your definition, then, a game is good if it's saleable?' He raises his eyebrows provocatively. 'And to be saleable, it has to be kept as simple as possible?'

The muscles in his neck begin to tense up. But Franka puts her hand on his before he can answer. 'And what, may I ask, is so bad about simplicity, Mark? It's the limitations that reveal the master.'

'It's about time you heard it from someone else!' Katja crows.

'That's an impressive endorsement, coming from someone who's in charge of Barbie dolls and Skippy balls,' says Mark. Unruffled, he slices off a piece of his rosemary and honey marinated lamb.

Katja hoots. 'You wouldn't think it, to see him sitting there with gravy dripping down his chin, but he has, I assure you, just been named department head. As I always say, Franka, behind every successful man stands a flabbergasted woman!'

Franka stares at her salad. Her embarrassment is tangible.

'More wine, anybody?' asks Mark. 'What were we talking about? Oh, right, the ideal game.'

'A good game has to teach the player something,' stutters Phinus. 'It isn't just—'

'Sure, but that's true about all of life.'

'Aha, the insight moment,' says Katja. 'Pay attention, people, here comes the insightful moment. Tell me, what have you learned lately? Speaking for myself, I won't even begin to go there any more. The moment of insight gives me a headache. You know, the way a disaster can nevertheless give rise to something good. Do we really need that kind of thing, at our age?' She rests her hand on Phinus's sleeve.

He suddenly has to fight the urge to panic. He blurts out, 'One point to you, Katja,' pretending his napkin has fallen to the floor and thereby shaking off her hand.

'They say that misery unites people,' Katja continues stubbornly. 'And that setbacks create intimacy. But in our house I've never noticed any such thing.'

'Katja is rather more the type for a fair-weather marriage,' Mark explains.

The feeling of claustrophobia has just about reached its limit. Phinus jumps up, nearly upsetting his chair. 'Excuse me, I'm just . . .' He narrowly manages to dodge the waiter who is approaching with the main course.

In the loo he splashes handfuls of cold water on his face, gasping, quite undone by his own undoing. What has become of the plot of his life, a storyline which might hold the occasional surprise but which, with just a little ingenuity and sleight of hand, he could always get back on track again? And above all, why does everyone have to *talk* all the time? About anything and everything, you name it, the most outrageous thing you can come up with, and next thing you know, it's the subject of conversation. How many more conversations is he expected to endure? Maddening, exasperating, nonstop crap and nonsense, consummate hot air, *exchanges of ideas*.

When he looks in the mirror, he sees a wild man, and it makes him jump.

What Phinus won't tell

Thanks to the Calvados with the coffee, it is almost midnight before they get up from the table. Katja kisses them both good night three times, while Mark looks on with an expression that says he's never seen anything so ludicrous.

Phinus goes outside into the fresh night air with Franka to fetch the luggage from the car. As they walk through the parking lot under the starless spring sky, every little pebble underfoot makes itself heard.

'Don't you hear it now?' she teases after a moment. 'Gravel crunches too.' She laughs. 'I say, what a creepy-drawers, that Mark, don't you think?'

The sense of unanimity warms his heart, and he suggests, 'Shall we walk along the canal for a bit? Fresh air brings on a good night's sleep, they say.'

'Fine. But no wonder Katja has her eye on you, with a husband like that at home.'

'The canal is to our left, sweetheart. Try not to lurch like that.'

'Well, we had all that wine. She kept fiddling with you.'

'Did she really? By the way, shall I try that endive tart at home some time? The secret, I think, is a squeeze of lemon in the filling.' He steers her out of the car park and gives her a push in the right direction. In the high street only a single window is still lit.

'What a goody-goody you are, really.' She giggles, then claps a hand to her mouth.

'A goody-goody?' He stands still. He sees the wedding ring glinting on her finger. *Mrs Vermeer.*

'How little you know yourself, Phinus. But come on, keep walking, because I'm getting cold. We should have brought our coats.'

They walk past De Lantaren, from which spills the muffled sound of thumping music, and cross the bridge. On the other side it is dark, there are no street-lights. A sandy towpath gleams pale along the embankment, which runs as straight as a rail.

'Not that I don't get a kick out of noticing that my husband may be to some other woman's taste,' she says after several minutes. She leans against him affectionately, against this big softy of hers, this faith-ful dog who wouldn't know how to cheat on her even if he wanted to. How certain she is of herself. Her trust in him is just about the last thing left between the two of them. He'd be crazy to smash it to pieces.

'Are you sulking now?' she enquires ingenuously. 'Am I not allowed to call you a good boy, then? That's just what's so adorable about you! So attractive and yet so responsible.' She giggles again.

'Will you stop it,' he says in a stifled voice.

'But I consider being a goody-goody a virtue, I swear!'

To put an end to it, he blurts out, 'So what it boils down to is, you're just hopelessly bored with me!'

'Come on, who said that? Don't be so childish.'

'So now I'm childish as well.' He hunches his shoulders and stomps off ahead of her along the dark path.

'Phinus, don't be so touchy!'

The sand is soft and heavy underfoot. Next to him the inky black water laps at the embankment. Be careful, it lisps, careful, you've come all this way with Mrs Vermeer, to this godforsaken backwater, in order to get close again, closer, closer, closer to each other, so just try your best and let her keep her illusions, let her, let her keep them intact. Why, why suddenly give in to the urge to make a clean breast of it, why now, why this minute, after all these weeks? Just because she's provoking you a little? Remember, sometimes intimacy is possible only by grace of deceit. If you love her, then keep your mouth shut, beat around the bush, lie through your teeth if you have to. Because it wasn't just a little roll in the hay, Phinus. A roll in the hay doesn't begin to describe a roll on top of a newly set gravestone. Even Franka will realize that. She won't have a moment's rest until she's dragged the whole lurid story out of you. And then you'll have to tell her everything, then you'll have to begin at the beginning. With Jem.

It's as if in one split second all the alcohol in his body has suddenly evaporated. The full weight of his conscience makes him gasp. What, compared to his real guilt, does that one moment of infidelity even matter? That was only a . . . a . . . a *by-product*. Stymied, he stands still.

She catches up with him. Her ebullience is all gone. 'What's *up* with you all of a sudden?'

Evasively he says, 'I've been feeling so panicky lately.' As soon as the words are out of his mouth, he regrets them.

She studies him with a frown. In the distance, a duck quacks drowsily. 'You're doing it to yourself,' she says finally, in an even voice. 'Because you insist on carrying on as if nothing's happened.'

'I see it differently. What's happened, happened. We have to go on.'

'We have lost our child, Phinus!'

In sackcloth and ashes, he raises his hands. 'All right, let me say it one more time. You can't expect, you simply *cannot*, in all reasonableness, expect it to be the same for me as it is for you.'

'But that's just an excuse!' She hits him, hard, in the chest. And again. 'And what's worse, it's a lie! Do you know that you grind your teeth every night in your sleep? Why don't you just say that you miss him! I miss him too! And it gets worse every day!' She bangs one fist jerkily on top of the other, as if she's doing the hand jive. 'I miss him more every day! Every day!'

'Then don't be so fixated on it all the time.'

'But that's just what I want! I don't want to forget him! Why do you want to forget him so badly? You'd prefer to act as if he never existed. Just now again, at dinner! Not that I feel a great need to discuss Jem with perfect strangers myself, but still—'

'That's why you're such a wreck now, Franka, a zombie! Let it go.'

'I'm asking you! Why—'

'You never sleep a wink and you—'

Fists clenched, she faces him on the canal bank.

'How can I sleep when I dream about him all the time? That he's walking into the kitchen, or dropping his bag in the hall, all those ordinary things, that I'm telling him to hurry up with his homework, or we're making popcorn together, in the saucepan with the little clouds, and I hear music coming from his room, and he's laughing himself silly over Mr Bean, or—'

'Stop it, you're working yourself up into a state!'

'And then when I wake up . . .' Finally she is silent. She clutches at her collar to close it.

A gust of wind suddenly makes him cringe. Oh, why is fate always snapping at her heels? Not yet forty, and she has already suffered the kind of losses one would normally need a war for. Was it written in the palm of her hand, then, that she would lose Jem before his time, even without Phinus's help? Yet is that enough to exonerate him?

'To talk about your loss with your husband, is that really too much to ask?' she says bitterly.

'If it were up to you, we'd never talk about anything else.'

'I just wish I got it. That I understood why this happened.'

In a pinched voice he manages, 'You know perfectly well why! Because he was stupid enough to be in the wrong place at the wrong time!'

She takes a step back, onto the grass. 'Because he was *stupid* enough?'

'Yes. Who just lets himself get shot? The others, all three hundred of them, left that disco unscathed.'

Her contorted face softens. 'So, you're angry with him! Which only proves how much you loved him.' She looks at him hopefully.

This is the way she used to stand with Jem at the

garden gate every evening when he returned home on his bicycle. Jem excitedly shouting, '*Da—!* There's my daddy!' Jem stretching his little arms out towards him, babbling about this and that, pulling at his tie, squealing. Jem who, upon seeing Phinus standing at the foot of the stairs a little later, would pitch himself headlong into his arms without warning. Jem who was once awarded an A at school for his presentation on Games Throughout the Centuries ('Look, Jem, we'll start with the Aztecs'), a presentation in which those centuries all led up to the one proud fact that Jem Vermeer, eyesight minus seven, weight 35 kilos; offspring of one mum and two dads; indefatigable Petitioner Against Bullfights and other matters pertaining to animal rights such as the Annual Royal Swine Hunt – *Please, your most esteemed Majesty*; that this Jem Vermeer, besides all his other accomplishments, was Juvenile In-House Consultant to Jumbo Toys, which put out Halma, 'and Stratego, and Mastermind, and Mikado, and Frog Soccer, you know, and Backgammon and Script-O-Gram'. He'd shown them the games, one by one.

Afterwards, in the playground, one of those pests in his class had taunted him, 'Halma your mama, loser. You haven't even got a Game Boy!'

'Jem doesn't have a Game Boy! Jem doesn't have a Game Boy!'

They had yanked the large carrier bag out of his hands and kicked the boxes around the playground, until all of them were ripped and the paving stones littered with wrecked game pieces and torn cardboard.

'I expect they were jealous of you, little monkey,' said Phinus as calmly as he could, while preparing a cup of hot chocolate for the weeping boy. 'You showed them up, the lot of them. You walk away with an A-minus for a terrific presentation, no problem. And that's not all. You happen to sit on the test panel for Jumbo. You are one of the people who get to decide which new games will make it into the shops.'

'I don't want to do that any more,' said Jem. Hunched over at the kitchen table, he hiccupped a few last times.

'But what would we do without you, for our trials?'

'All the kids on the panel are nerds.'

'Nine-year-old nerds don't exist.'

'They do. I want a Game Boy, Dad.'

'But a Game Boy will turn you into an autistic goon, you saw that for yourself today. Bleep, bleep, bleep! Jesus, Jem! Is that what you want? And square eye-balls, and those goofy thumbs? Just because of a bunch of rotten bullies . . .' Should he go and have a word with the school? Inform them that they had nine-year-old scum going around destroying other kids' innocence? And kicking a bag full of brand-new games to pieces in the process! Or would he only be making things worse for Jem? Well, look who we have here, it's Mr Vermeer, he works on Mastermind, doesn't he? Oh yes, and on Frog Soccer, of course.

'Let's go,' he said. 'Come, fetch your coat.'

Twenty minutes later found them standing in the checkout queue at Bart Smit's, the toy store. Jem would get kinks in his thumbs and a dazed look in his eyes, but he wouldn't be the biggest geek in the playground any more. Standing among bright toys and whining children, Phinus suddenly realized with a shock: we've let ourselves be beaten. We let the loud-mouths win. In his day, the aunts would simply never have allowed it. They would have jumped on their mopeds, they would have taken those brats down a peg or two. Boys will be boys, of course, but there were limits, and this really was going too far.

To suppress his gloom, he tried making light of it. He tugged at Jem's sleeve. 'Hey, kiddo, if you'd prefer me to go and work somewhere else, just say the word, OK?'

Jem opened his eyes wide. 'But you like it there, Dad.' He lowered his voice. 'From now on I just won't tell anyone about it any more.' He pushed his warm little hand into Phinus's and pulled him one step closer to their destination, the till where his dream was about to come true, thanks to Daddy, Daddy who had at least a hundred guilders in his wallet, and a cash card too, and, if all else failed, a credit card.

'Why don't you just come out with it!' Franka's voice, high-pitched with stress, carries quite a way across the canal at Aduard. The sky above her is a solid black. She grabs him by the lapels. Even though she is a head shorter, she gives him a thorough shaking.

Stiffly he puts up with her assault.

She lets go. 'You loved him enormously!' Her lips are trembling.

The wind makes the water ripple. The canal reeks of mud, an earthy smell redolent of a rained-out camping trip, of clothes that refuse to dry, of a waterlogged package of muesli spilling its contents on the groundsheet. Jem was a toddler, they had tied plastic sandwich bags over his little feet. They had . . . 'Stop it!' he roars. 'Cut it out, for heaven's sake!'

'Don't be such a baby,' she snaps. 'You're just pissed off because you can't accept that you can't always have control over everything. You're still labouring under

70

the delusion that it's possible to hold all the cards! That there are set game rules for everything, and as long as you stick to those . . .'

Natter, natter, it just goes on and on, until you're ready to drop. Wouldn't day still follow night if everyone just shut up from now on? Would the horizon tilt to a vertical position? Would the seas dry up? The birds develop gills? Human beings begin and end their lives without language, without words or explanations. Why, then, is there need for so much drivel in between, what's the point, for crying out loud? 'I've had enough, do you hear me?' he screams. 'I can't be held responsible for my actions if you keep this up, this – this prattling.'

She fixes him with eyes narrow with fury. 'How can I share my life with someone who belittles my feelings this way? How long do you think I'll put up with it?' Then she turns and walks away.

For a moment he holds his breath as Mrs Vermeer stalks away from him with resolute step. Away from the wretch who is, unbeknownst to her, the one responsible for all her grief. Alone beside the icy water he digs his hands into his pockets. Shivering, he hunches his shoulders. He kicks at a clump of grass with the tip of his shoe.

The moon displays itself briefly, only to disappear promptly behind the clouds again. Just a single star blinks in the sky, like a lone observation post through which the Creator keeps an eye on his creatures below. But he who wants help from Him ought to know better. The Creator dazzles us, above all, by his phenomenal aloofness; we look up to heaven in vain.

What's he supposed to do? Dig a hole in the ground, like King Midas's barber, and whisper his secret to the patient earth, before hastily burying it again? But the rushes would whisper it to the wind and the wind would blow it from east to west, from north to south, first a light breeze, but swelling, little by little, into a storm, a whistling hurricane, a desperate, howling confession, audible in all corners of the world: 'It is my fault. It's all my fault!'

Franka's silhouette on the dark path is now almost impossible to make out. Within a few minutes she'll be back in the village. Instinctively, he glances over at the other side of the canal, where all of Aduard should be asleep by now. But no. In the distance two figures come sauntering up the bridge, clearly visible under the streetlights. As soon as they install themselves at the railing, he recognizes them. *Maybe you'll die tonight, sir.*

They must have come out of De Lantaren, those two, one of those dives where everyone is soaked to the last nerve cell in Ecstasy, where everyone gets plastered on brain-pounding house music. One of those dumps where it's considered an excellent distraction if someone starts waving a weapon around on the dance floor. Livens things up a little, anyhow.

Jem might have stood a chance if he had realized that there were creeps you'd better steer clear of. But how was he supposed to have figured that out? As a little boy, his babysitters had been underage whores ('Give them trust, and you give them a future') and later on his mum had looked on, smiling, as her son was taught to play Hangman at the kitchen table by bicycle thieves bristling with methadone ('What if everyone washed their hands of them?'). Would Jem have been alive today if he had been taught the art of making distinctions, instead of a naïve trust in even the most criminal scum? *Goddammit, Franka!*

He peers into the darkness. She has almost reached the end of the towpath.

The couple on the bridge nudge each other: they have noticed her too.

'Franka!' he calls, suddenly alarmed. He starts jogging after her.

The girls turn their heads in his direction.

'Franka! Watch out! Wait for me!'

Looking back over her shoulder, she almost trips. Now she's scrambling up the bank, to the bridge. The tight skirt and high heels don't make it easy for her.

The girls have posted themselves in the middle of the bridge; Franka won't be able to get past them. The tall one has linked arms with the little one. Their black jackets gleam in the streetlights, and the shorter one's half-shorn head lurks spookily.

Can't Franka see the danger? Does she see just a couple of ordinary girls, the kind she comes across every day on the job? Or is she merely gripped by a single thought: to get away from him?

Not that that would be anything new. He often likes to bring up the subject himself, with a certain amount of pride, at parties and anniversaries. 'Oh, she did everything she could to give me the brush-off, believe you me,' he will tell anyone who'll listen; let it be known that this relationship, this marriage, came about through his efforts. It was his project. Make no mistake, it was he who in the end managed to bring Franka to her knees, Franka who is known to all as a woman of mettle. Franka, beautiful, unconventional Franka, who could have had any lover she wanted.

The first time he saw her was in the park, at lunchtime. It was nearly Easter then too, the feast of the resurrection, but because Easter fell late that year, it was almost warm enough to be summer. The fresh green chestnut trees and hedges were already in full leaf, and the city was gripped by a mood of feverish anticipation. At all hours of the day and night, the terrace cafés were packed. People talked in shrill voices, they spilt their drinks and laughed at nothing. They were all looking for someone, their eyes roaming like searchlights.

The only one who seemed unaffected by the intense atmosphere was the young blonde woman with a small child in tow whom he spotted one day from the bench where he always ate his sandwiches. She was seated at the edge of the pond, sorting twigs and stones in the grass with quiet concentration, objects which the little boy, engrossed, proceeded to drop into a series of colourful plastic cups. He was just a little mite. When the game was over and they headed home, he had to hold on to the bars of his buggy as he toddled along.

The next day they were there again. This time the cups were filled with sand, carefully levelled off, and turned upside down. *Mud pies, I see.* They were down on their knees, the little boy and his mother, both equally absorbed in the game. It was a rare thing to see, an adult who could play like that. Phinus watched, fascinated.

Now a handful of pebbles was carried to the water's edge — careful, hold on tight to Mummy's hand now — and dumped into the pond. They sank. The twigs followed — they float, see that? — and Phinus got up, newspaper and all, walked over to them and

74

suggested, squatting down, 'A paper boat is a good one too.'

The mother looked at him in surprise. The dappled light streaming through the leaves of the willow at the water's edge dotted her cheeks like confetti.

'Look, here's how you do it,' he said quickly, tearing a page out of the newspaper, folding it over and pressing the crease securely. 'Always be sure to run your fingernail along it,' he explained to the little boy, 'otherwise it'll fall apart again before you can say boo.'

The child was too young yet to talk. Mutely, but with great interest, he looked on.

'It's a hat,' said the woman gaily. 'Look, Jem, a hat for your little head.'

'Going strictly by the rules, it's a boat,' said Phinus. 'But of course everyone is free to make of it what they will.'

'Oh, good.' There wasn't a trace of sarcasm in her voice.

Together they launched the boat into the water and pushed it away from the shore with a stick. It was buoyant enough to stay afloat for a few minutes.

When it had sunk, she commented, 'Still, a hat's fun too, and it'll last longer.'

'Nothing lasts for ever.'

A bitter expression flitted across her face. 'It's time for Jem's nap.'

The next day, when she took her place by the pond with the little boy, there was nothing to indicate that she noticed Phinus's presence on the bench. The ritual of hunting for twigs and stones began all over again. Sand was scraped together and shovelled into the cups. Phinus's hands were itching. Cautiously he rose to his feet. 'For mud pies, you might consider using something shallower, that way they'll come out sturdier,' he said.

'Dear me, you seem to be an expert on everything.'

'Listen, I don't want to intrude, of course, but . . .'

'Well now, that's very sensible of you,' she said calmly. 'Because I lost my husband just a year and a half ago, and I'm nowhere near ready for something new, not even for a one-night stand. So don't waste your time on me.'

Taken aback by this overture, words briefly failed him. She was too quick for him, in more ways than one.

'But thanks for the advice,' she ended in a conciliatory tone which made him suspect it wasn't the first time she'd had to give strangers the brush-off. 'If we do decide to bake mud pies, I'll definitely bring some little bowls next time. Only, these aren't supposed to be pies. They're mountains, with knights and dragons on them. See? Those pebbles are the knights.'

That afternoon he looked it up in Elisabeth Kübler-Ross. One year was sufficient to get over a bereavement. There were five well-defined stages. He suddenly felt elated. The thought that this woman, Jem's mother, might have seen in him someone who wanted to court her was both astonishing and thrilling. He had done nothing except simply be himself.

He returned to the park and waited for his chance.

After an intensive siege lasting half a year, they rented a house together, with a garden and a sandbox for Jem.

It was about time, said Franka, to tell her parents, and her parents-in-law. That way her grandfathers and

76

grandmothers, her uncles and aunts, her cousins, nieces and nephews were guaranteed to get to hear about it. Her brothers, on the other hand, she would call herself, and her brother-in-law, her two sisters-in-law and their partners too.

She was – how to describe it – she belonged to a whole galaxy. An entire Milky Way. Everything was connected, orbiting along fixed trajectories, with blood ties drawing complicated dotted lines through the universe in which Franka existed with her Jem. In this enormous constellation, the two of them were as insignificant as two pinpricks.

In his own universe, he had never been one of many. It was one of the first startling insights she gave him.

The aunts, who were enchanted with her, agreed. 'One characteristic of an orphan, of course, is that he's the quintessential egoist. And a clinger at that,' they remarked fondly while serving mint tea, known for its restorative properties, in the garden. Drink up, my girl, you'll be needing it. Oh Phinus, why don't you show her your old room? Your fold-up bed is still up there, with Kanga on it. Crazy, he was, about his stuffed animals! And his drawings, Franka, oh my, we've saved them all, at the bottom of the dresser he used to crawl into sometimes, when he was little. It was his hideaway. He'd sit in his hut for hours, with the door open just a crack.

Upstairs Franka lost no time pulling down the narrow bed. The worn straps that lashed the blankets to the mattress still smelt exactly the same. 'Were you lonely?' she asked, lying down on top of him.

At the bottom of the stairs Aunt Irmgard called out in a booming voice, 'Young people! You are not to take advantage of the situation!'

77

'Frankaaa!' he yells. He breaks into a run as he covers the last few yards of the towpath, then swerves up to the bridge. 'Franka, wait!'

She doesn't slow her pace. Her heels click angrily on the asphalt. There's no other sound to be heard. A little way on, on the far bank, the village is plunged into silence. There's no music coming out of De Lantaren any more. What time is it? One o'clock? Half past one? Later? When does a joint like that close, out here in the sticks? What time does a place like that kick out the last overheated guest, into the long, tedious night?

He cranes his neck to see what the girls are up to. But Franka's shape is in the way, blocking his sight. And right at that moment the streetlights flicker out.

Adrenaline thumps in his ears. It swallows up the sound of Franka's footsteps, just as the darkness has engulfed her slender form. For a few drawn-out seconds he feels himself to be the only human in the whole wide world. A world which turns slowly but inexorably, without any reason, without any purpose, simply because, according to the laws of the universe, it must turn – as long, that is, as there are still town councillors like those of Aduard, tree-hugging know-it-alls pushing a politically correct green energy policy, who would never do anything to burden the environment needlessly. Blindly he stomps over the uneven tarmac of the bridge.

Next to him a dark shape looms up, and he is startled. But it's only the bridge operator's hut. Gradually Franka comes into sight again, a pale blot walking ahead of him. He is so close on her heels now that he could have smelt her perfume trailing after her like a fragrant streamer, if she used scent, that is. He is so close that he could have hooked his fingers into her hair, if she'd had long hair. If she had been someone else, one of those girls in a women's magazine, he'd have caught up with her by now.

Suddenly, right ahead of him, there's a stifled cry. The blot that is his Franka crumples: she falls. Two figures bend over her.

With a loud yell he covers the last few yards. He lunges, he grabs at the nylon jackets, he seizes one of them by the collar. Panting, he hauls the short one to her feet, picks her up bodily and slams her to the ground with all his might. Her body has hardly hit the ground with a heavy thud before he's nabbed the tall one. He gets a good grip on the front of her jacket and punches her in the face with his other hand. The girl's head rolls from side to side like a rag doll's. As she begins to scream, he rams a fist into her mouth. *No whining, no complaining, no reproaches, no more questions. SHUT UP!*

'Stop it! Stop it!' screams Franka.

Dazed, he lowers his hand and looks at her. She's trying to scramble to her feet. Her skirt is hiked all the way up to her bottom, tears are rolling down her face, and he thinks to himself, hush now, your old man's here. A moment later he's doubled up in pain, kneed in the groin. For an instant everything goes black. Then he sees a long shiny implement pointing at him.

His attacker backs off, her arm outstretched. It's the tall one. Blood is gushing from her mouth and one of her eyes is mangled.

With an effort that makes all his bones creak, he drags the short one up from the ground and holds her limp body in front of him like a shield. The tall one shows no inclination to put down her weapon. She yells something, and the next moment he can't see a thing any more, while his face feels as if it's exploding. He hurls his human shield away from him in order to grab his head with both hands.

Franka is screaming bloody murder.

Why hasn't anyone come to their aid? Do the good citizens of Aduard roll over in their beds when they hear a brawl on the bridge, afraid of risking their own necks? It's only then that he realizes his face doesn't hurt. With stinging eyes, he peers at his hands. They glisten. But not with blood. It's green hair dye.

The short one is lying lifeless on the ground at his feet, stretched out neatly on the dotted line dividing the road into two lanes. He steps over her stiffly. Out of the corner of his eye he notes the taller one's presence, but she has retreated a safe distance to the bridge railing, shifting her weight nervously from one foot to the other.

Franka is sitting dead still on the tarmac, huddled up.

He bends over her, the hair paint dripping down his cheeks. 'Are you hurt? Are you in pain? Can you get up?'

She struggles against him as he pulls her up. As soon as she's on her feet, she cries out.

'What is it? Your leg?'

'The right one,' she mumbles. She tries to wriggle out of his clutches. 'I thought you . . .' She shudders. She must be suffering from shock. This time he, too, was very nearly shot dead, and right before her eyes at that.

'Yeah, so did I. I thought she had a gun.' He tries to catch his breath. 'But it's nothing. Everything's fine.

Don't worry. I'll get the car.' Carefully, he helps her to sit down again, the hurt leg stretched in front of her. The bridge smells of fresh tar. Below them the water makes a babbling sound.

'Easy for you, innit, taking on a couple of girls!' the tall one screams suddenly. She has edged a little closer. She has one hand pressed against her bloody eye, but aside from that she doesn't give the impression of being much impaired by her wounds. The realization that more than a good hiding may be necessary to teach this sort of creature a lesson makes him shudder.

'You were asking for it.'

'We weren't doing nothing! You were the one yelling at her to wait up, arsehole!' she shrieks.

'Well, thanks for your help, in that case,' he says. His voice sounds feeble to his own ears, his tone markedly less sarcastic than he meant it to sound. He looks at Franka for support. She doesn't seem to have heard him. She's massaging her temples, pale as a sheet, without taking her eyes off the girl lying face down on the road.

'How am I supposed to get Mel home now? On my back, I suppose?' the tall one growls.

Now all three look at the lifeless heap. To conceal his uneasiness, Phinus plunges his hands into his trouser pockets.

'And what if she's dead?' It's almost as if she gets a kick out of saying it. 'Then you'll get banged up, serve you right.' She sidles closer to her motionless friend. She pokes her in the ribs with a foot.

'Stop it,' he says, sick with revulsion.

She makes a snorting noise. 'You got a problem, moron.'

He makes a huge effort to concentrate, but panic has poked a gash right through his head, causing all his thoughts to come tumbling out in one big muddle. If only Franka would do something. This is her territory, for Pete's sake. All she has to do is snap her fingers and brats like these spring to attention for her. Brusquely he says, 'I'm going to get my car.'

'And then?'

He has no idea. He motions with his head. 'You're coming with me.'

'Hell, no.' The girl takes a few paces backwards and steps on the can of hair colour, sending it tinkling over the edge of the bridge. There is a soft splash.

'I'm not leaving you here with my wife.'

A grin splits the scab on her lips: apparently it's the kind of admission that pleases her. Her nose ring dangles from her torn nostril.

He turns to Franka. 'I'll be back in two minutes.'

'And then what?' she too demands, suddenly alert.

How is *he* supposed to know? Why must he be responsible for solving all the world's problems? He has to fight the temptation to throw himself down and pummel the ground with his fists and feet. Instead, he takes out his handkerchief, wipes the paint off his face, then takes off his jacket and drapes it round her shoulders. 'Back in a sec.' His own words, so ordinary and humdrum, briefly serve to make him feel in control of the situation again. He beckons imperiously to the tall one. 'You, walk ahead of me. So I can keep an eye on you.'

She starts to move without a word, slowly, as if she has all the time in the world. Her thighs are massive beneath the jacket.

They march into the village single file. There is no

sign of life anywhere. At Onder de Linden, too, all the lights are turned off. All the orderly hustle and bustle of the inn is done for now, the stoves have long been turned off, the staff have gone home and the guests are sleeping off their seven-course menu and the petits fours with the coffee, enjoying the deep slumber of the thoroughly sated. It will be hours yet before the inn bestirs itself again: the comforting rituals of rising and shaving and showering in the guest rooms, the logistics of cooking eggs, cutting bread, squeezing juice in the sparkling kitchen. Each undertaking equally methodical and predictable. It feels as if he's been expelled from the paradise of orderly routine and cast into the wilderness, where there's nothing to hold on to, and his hands are shaking when he opens the car door.

He sinks down behind the wheel. All that hurling and slinging has wrenched his back and it isn't easy for him to find a comfortable position. He sticks the key in the ignition. The dashboard lights up. According to the clock it's 2:15 a.m. The CD player clicks on, and the first sober bars of the *Matthäus-Passion* ring out. '*Kommt, ihr Töchter, helft mir klagen*,' beseeches the choir of King's College, Cambridge.

'Don't you have anything better?' the girl complains. She makes herself comfortable next to him, her feet up on the glove compartment.

'It's Good Friday,' he finds himself saying.

'What's good about it!' She heaves herself up a little, reaches for the sun visor and flicks it down. Cursing under her breath, she examines herself in the little mirror. Then she slumps down again. 'Well, what are we waiting for?'

'*Erbarm' Dich unser, o Jesu,*' sing the angel voices.

Strenuously, he puts the car into reverse. With leaden arms he turns the wheel and manoeuvres the vehicle over the gravel of the car park.

'OK, step on it,' says his passenger.

What Phinus thinks money can do

He has a vision of Franka on the bridge: teeth piercing her lip, a gash in her head, a bicycle chain round her neck. And blood everywhere. Only a few minutes have gone by, but it feels like years, years fraught with dangers against which he has been unable to defend her. It's just like one of those harrowing dreams where time keeps racing on while you find yourself battling shadowy obstacles, dazed and out of breath, growing increasingly desperate as the realization begins to sink in that you'll get there too late, definitely too late, no matter what you do.

Only when the raised bridge barriers loom into sight does he realize he has been driving the car in first gear the whole way – several hundred metres.

Ignoring the girl sitting next to him, that chunk of graffiti made flesh, he jams on the handbrake, flings the door open and jumps out of the car. Behind him the engine keeps purring calmly, and the Cambridge voices soar and fall: signs of civilization, in sharp contrast to the countryside around him. The pitiless black abyss of the night sky. The over-abundance of oxygen, which makes the head spin. The silence, so complete that you can hear the rustling of insects as well as the swishing of countless tail fins down in the mud of the canal. At this moment every-thing around him is, without question, busy devouring everything else, skin, bones and all. Hedgehogs and martens come crawling greedily out of their holes, their eyes glinting with hunger. Owls silently spread their wings and then, quick as a flash, their claws. It is night: nature showing her true colours.

It seems to Phinus as if he is being drawn against his will into a secret: so *that's* why sleep knocks us out at night, so that we won't have to be aware of what's going on outside our bedroom window. We sleep because otherwise the night would remind us that we, too, are nature's sons and daughters: just as callous, just as cruel and just as heartless as she is.

Franka is still sitting in the middle of the bridge, in the same position. In the beam of the headlights he can see the runs in her tights and tracks of mascara on her ashen cheeks.

'Are you OK?' He puts his hand on her bowed neck and slides his fingers inside the collar of the suit that she put on specially for him. The fragility of her vertebrae. It wouldn't take much to snap them, like toothpicks. 'Just put your arm round my shoulder. I'll help you to the car.'

'And those girls?' Her voice is flat.

He follows her gaze. A little further on, the tall one is bending over her companion. She is talking in an urgent whisper to the skinny girl, who is now sitting up.

86

There she sits, the wench, unbroken. Weeds never die. They're going to get off lightly, just a little shaken up. 'Come on, get in,' he tells Franka.

Limping, she reaches the car, grabs the passenger door and then says, 'What were you thinking, Phinus? What in heaven's name have you done?'

'What do you mean? They attacked us!'

'Sure, with a can of paint!'

He can't believe his ears, she's got it all backwards. 'Come on, we're going to bed.'

'You beat up two children and now you just turn your back on them? In the middle of the night, too! Please go and ask them if they need any help. Please.' She lowers herself into the car.

Nervously he crouches down beside her by the open door and turns off the *Matthäus*. The gluttonous sounds of the night immediately make themselves heard again. He picks up her handbag from the floor of the car. 'Here, you'd better take a sleeping pill. That way at least you'll be able to sleep later. Or else you'll be a wreck tomorrow.'

She finally looks at him. Her eyes are sunk deep in their sockets, the grooves along her nose appear sharper than usual.

'Frankie, come on. You look like a ghost.'

Still she says nothing, but accepts her bag from him and takes out the little box with the sleeping pills. Blankly she sits there weighing it in her hand, as if she can't make up her mind: what time is it now, will I get to sleep even if I don't take a pill? He has seen it happen so many times lately, in the middle of a conversation, as she's reading the newspaper, sometimes even while on the telephone. Only insomniacs can sleep standing up. He may not even be able to wake her when they get back to Onder de Linden. He'll have to carry her up to bed. And tomorrow morning she'll open her eyes, refreshed, and say with a little laugh, 'Goodness, the things I was working myself up about last night!' Under the starched bedclothes, she'll stretch her arms towards him. She'll get that look in her eyes, languid and determined at the same time. She'll sling her leg over his hips, press her breasts ardently up against him.

He shuts the car door and turns round.

The girls are sitting side by side on the asphalt, the big one sprawled full length, propped up on her elbows, the little one cross-legged. Two disconcertingly young faces are tilted up at him. The little one with the shaved head jeers, 'According to Astrid, you thought I was dead. That must have given you a scare.'

Astrid, the big one, honks with laughter.

'I could report you, keep that in mind, you two, for assault.'

'And *we* can report *you*, loser,' says Astrid. 'We're beaten to a bloody pulp.'

'You attacked my wife.'

'She nearly knocked us over!' says the little one vehemently.

He hooks his thumbs, deliberately, into his waistband. 'Funny. I just heard quite a different story. Your girlfriend here told me only a minute ago that you were kind enough to detain my wife because you heard me shouting at her to wait for me.'

'Do you beat *her* up too, then? Is that why she had to get away from you so badly that she didn't even notice us standing here?'

The other one puffs out her fat cheeks. 'Or does she have to fuck you nonstop?'

Her tone leaves him speechless for a few seconds. Such insolence, even after a thorough hiding! No, these two aren't afraid of anything, not even the devil himself.

With a sudden lurch, the short one gets up. She takes one step in the direction of the railing, doesn't make it, and starts throwing up right where she is. The vomit splashes all over his trouser legs.

'Gross, Melanie!' shouts Astrid, jumping backwards.

The small one gags one last time, wipes her mouth with the back of her hand, and collapses back on the ground.

He hunts for his handkerchief, gingerly lifting first one and then the other foot out of the vomit. Could that Melanie have concussion? What will Franka say? Should they call an ambulance? But won't that automatically mean a police report? And how can he plead self-defence, justifiable use of force, with the girl sitting there looking so frail and puny? No match, surely, for a six-foot-two fellow with the bearing of a well-fed businessman. And that Astrid, with her ugly battered mug, she's a hefty girl, to be sure, but how old can she be? Sixteen? Not even?

'Mel's looking pretty fucked-up too,' Astrid says in an ominous tone.

'That's what you get when you have too much to drink.'

She wipes her nose with her sleeve. 'Booze is for stiffs and old farts. Us, we don't drink.'

He thinks of the quantity of bottles he drained tonight, not to mention the two glasses of Calvados with the coffee. The word of a drunk against that of two molested children. Abstractedly, he smears green paint all over his trouser legs and shoe with his soiled handkerchief. He walks over to the bridge railing and chucks the foul rag into the water. *Don't panic!* Yet even in Aduard there must be insomniacs who, out of desperation, go out for a midnight stroll. And even here, somebody might very well come driving by unexpectedly, on his way home from a birthday party, a celebration. Any moment now someone could come along and misconstrue the situation in a single glance.

They have to get off the bridge.

'Help her get in,' he says.

'What for? We're not idiots.'

Melanie lifts her head up. 'What's he want, Ast?'

'I'm offering you a lift.'

'You don't say!' Astrid folds her arms. 'A lift? Sure, why not, from a bloke who beats up women and children.'

'I think it's starting to rain.' At his wits' end, he sticks his hand out, palm up, for appearance's sake.

'Oh, fuck.' She looks up at the black sky and then at her friend, who gets up with a sigh and opens the back door.

As soon as they're in, Astrid announces, 'It's over the bridge, to the right.'

'Pipe down! My wife's asleep.' He glances over at her. Franka's breathing is deep and regular.

Lowering her voice, Melanie says, 'Actually, why don't you just head straight, after the bridge.'

'But Mel—'

'No, really . . .' Her voice sinks even lower.

'So, where to, then?' he asks, his foot hovering over the accelerator. At that moment, a set of headlights looms up in his rearview mirror, and he immediately rams the car into gear and roars off.

The road on the other side of the canal is dead

straight. Here you don't easily shake off someone who's on your tail. He pushes the pedal to the floor. Dark farmhouses flash past. A stand of birches. A tractor parked at the side of the road. A ploughed field. A sign in clumsy white lettering: Potatoes and Firewood for Sale. A bicycle pump dangling from a post.

Mile after mile, and still the car following him stays right on his tail. The girls whisper in the back seat. In the distance, the road comes to a T-junction. Peering into his rearview mirror, he waits until the last possible moment. Then he turns the wheel hard to the left. The car swerves. He has to slam on the brakes in order not to skid off the twisting side road.

'What are you doing?' complains Melanie. 'I feel sick.'

'Oh shit, she has to puke again.'

'Help her, then,' he says. He stops the car. 'Here, in the ditch.'

He is far enough from the village to dump those two tsohgs right here. It will take them at least an hour to walk back. And while they're doing that, he'll be driving home with Franka. She has to see a doctor; who knows, her leg may be broken.

Behind him he hears shuffling over the upholstery, the opening of a door.

Once he's legged it out of here, they can't do a thing to him any more. Sure, they can enquire at Onder de Linden. Vermeer, the most common name in the Netherlands, that's all they have on him at the inn. And once they realize the bird has flown after a night of extravagant wining and dining, they'll assume he must have given them a false name. Their bags are still in the boot, they haven't even been up to the room. *They've left no tracks!*

91

Half hanging out of the car, Melanie throws up on the verge. Then she pulls herself upright again and says indifferently, 'We can go on now.'

'Shouldn't you two get out for a breath of fresh air? Because otherwise . . .'

'Otherwise what?' asks Astrid.

'He's afraid I'll barf all over the upholstery,' says Melanie. 'Of his lovely Mercedes. Licence plate SF-HS-57.'

He lets go of the steering wheel. His voice cracks as he asks, 'What's that supposed to mean?'

She gives him a little tug on the ear, as if she's chiding a naughty child.

At that moment Franka suddenly sits bolt upright. 'Where are we?'

'Hello there, madam,' says Melanie promptly in her politest voice.

'Oh,' says Franka, dazed, turning round. 'Sorry, but I just couldn't keep my eyes open. I'm knackered.'

'Just go back to sleep, don't worry,' says Melanie. 'We'll show your husband the way.'

Franka says groggily, 'Can I leave it up to you, Phinus?' She leans back. Instantly she's surrendered to sleep again. It's clear she must have taken that pill after all.

Astrid snickers, 'Phinus? What kind of a name is that!'

'Could you turn up the heat, Mr Phinus? We're just about freezing our little bums off,' says Melanie.

Automatically, he slides the tab over into the red. The action reminds him that his car is no longer his passport to safe anonymity. He's trapped. Those two have him by the short hairs.

The urge to smash their bravado nearly chokes him.

Scum, that's what they are. Utter scum with nothing at stake, there's no risk, seeing that they're minors. No one can touch them, they can rough up your wife, they can murder your child ... And at that thought, he breaks into a cold sweat: Jem in those faded jeans, that scruffy T-shirt, Jem the way he set out that evening, with his whole future rolled up in his pocket like a shiny new ribbon, Jem of the earnest brown eyes behind the foggy glasses, the eternal baseball cap worn backwards, Jem of the unshakable ideals, Jem who'd go so far as to compare an ant trap to the gas chambers, *Jem, come back to us!*

Here he is, sitting in a car with a delegation from the underworld that swallowed up Jem, the person-ification of that evil in duplicate, *in the back seat of his own car*. Has the evil now found him as well, or did he allow himself to be found? Has he perhaps been looking for it, without realizing it? Doesn't he have a score to settle, after all? What's to stop him from skewering these two harpies on a pole by the side of the ditch? These two snot-noses, who have nothing to fear but a scolding, at most, from the juvenile court judge, and who'll then end up under the wing of the social workers, those gullible Frankas who can't wait to rehabilitate them into society, and who invite them home for a nice cup of tea at their own kitchen tables. How about a nice bickie to go with that? A cigarette, then? Must have had a miserable childhood, right?

He is startled by Astrid banging on the back of his seat. 'Hey, Phinus, are we gonna stay here till we start sprouting roots?'

'How quiet he is, all of a sudden,' remarks Melanie. 'Must be thinking of his sins.' Her voice is dripping with smugness. She knows there is nothing he can do

93

to them. No, worse, they could easily claim that he forced them into the car against their will. They'll say, 'We did try to defend ourselves with a can of spray paint, but he beat us to a pulp and then he was going to take us to some deserted place outside the village and rape us.'

'OK,' he says quietly, trembling with fury and impotence, 'out with it. What is it? Is it money you're after?' His tic is acting up, he can feel his entire face twitch.

It's quiet for a moment in the back seat. 'Money? But what do you want to pay us for?' asks Melanie, all innocence.

'Blood money.' Astrid starts to laugh, in that honking way of hers.

'We don't accept credit cards,' says Melanie.

'But we will accept a debit card, with a pin number,' screeches Astrid.

He relaxes slightly. They're only kids, after all, eager to profit from the situation. He pats his breast pocket. 'Will cash do?' he asks curtly. 'How much?'

King Midas is an ass. An ass!

'How much?' he had asked Jem, taking out his wallet in the doorway to the bathroom. 'What do you need to get in? And do you know how much the drinks cost in that joint?'

Jem shrugged his bony shoulders. His hair was still damp from the shower. He was standing in front of the mirror with a towel round his hips. There were flecks of toothpaste on his skinny chest. 'No idea. But we could go to the Eko-café instead. I've got enough money for that, from my paper round.'

'But she wants to go clubbing. The — what did you tell me? — the Escape. Wasn't that it?'

Jem stuck his toothbrush back in his mouth. 'Dad, just bugger off for a minute, will you? I'm running late already.'

'Do you want to make a good impression on her or not?' He was beset by a mild case of despair, the despair arising from the compelling, almost dictatorial need to see your teenager happy; the despair, too, of realizing there was little you could do to contribute to it. Realizing you would always fall short, no matter how much you gave him. 'Here,' he said, starting to peel off the notes. 'Eko-café, no way. You're clubbing. Escape-ing. And if it gets very late, take a taxi home.'

'We're going by bike.'

'I don't think cycling's safe.'

'It is, after four a.m.' Jem took a sip from the tap, then spat into the sink. 'It's between the hours of two and four a.m. that you shouldn't be out on the streets.'

'How did you get to know so much, all of a sudden?'

'Everyone knows that, man.'

'But do her parents know it too? And is she allowed to get home at such an ungodly hour?'

Jem gave him a scornful glance. Then he began studying the label on a jar of hair gel. Franka was calling from downstairs. 'Boys! Coffee's ready!'

Phinus stuffed the notes into the towel round Jem's loins. Fifteen years old, and already half a head taller than himself. But a little more bulk wouldn't do him any harm. Phinus had to bite his lip to stop some comment about meatballs from slipping out. Just this week, at the Home Show, Jem and his scraggy band of like-minded cronies had posted themselves squarely in front of a hot dog stand to distribute crackers with

Marmite, wearing T-shirts that read, *There are hamburgers, and there are world-burghers.*

'What time are you meeting her?'

'Ten o'clock.'

'Then you'd better get a move on. Where does she live?'

'She's coming here.' Jem twisted the lid off the hair gel and sniffed at it, frowning. 'Shouldn't it say on the package if it's guaranteed not animal tested?'

'We used to pick up our girlfriends at their homes.'

'We're closer to the town centre here.'

'That's not the point.' He was trying to remain calm.

'Your coffee's getting cold!' shouted Franka.

Annoyed with himself, he went back downstairs, where Franka was sprawled in front of the TV. The sound was turned off.

'I've turned into a prehistoric git,' he told her.

'Don't worry, you've always been one,' she said consolingly, without taking her eyes off the screen. 'Isn't Jem going to come down as well?'

He sat down next to her on the sofa, and drank his coffee. 'I'm getting that dread feeling that everything was better in the old days.'

She laid a hand on his knee. 'Be quiet, I'm watching.'

'Then turn up the sound.'

She asked affably, 'Is it all right with you if I do it my own way?'

He locked his hands behind his neck, stretched his legs and *relaxed* with all his might. Who wouldn't trade places with him? Jem was a kid in a million, after all, if you didn't count his adolescent mood swings. OK, he never cleaned up his room. That was, apparently, par for the course. The same went for piss this, fuck that, awesome man, let's chill, Dad. Half the time you didn't know what they were on about. But Jem didn't smoke pot, or hardly, he didn't have the wrong kind of friends, he didn't swear at his mother, and he didn't play truant, except when he had to go to the Home Show. But Franka had agreed to that. 'As long as he's passionate about *something*,' she used to say, 'I'm not worried. They only go wrong if they don't have anything they care about, if there's nothing that touches or inspires them.' And that was something you certainly couldn't say about Jem. Jem was a kid who came home from school all out of sorts after hearing about the hole in the ozone layer or the world's water crisis. From the time he was little, you'd find Jem seated at the kitchen table, working enthusiastically on some project or other, his felt tips drawn up in neat formation, informing his mother's grubby clients, who'd be wandering in and out, in a worried voice, 'Four and a half billion years from now the sun'll be all burned up, you know. And then there'll be no more life on earth.'

One of the junkies had asked him suspiciously one day, 'Are you a leprechaun or something?'

Phinus felt his heart soften. There were kids who did nothing but hang out all day at McDonald's or in computer chatrooms. Perhaps one ought to count one's blessings if a kid like that didn't have the manners of a gentleman on top of everything, and if he seemed to find it completely normal that his very first date was riding her bike over to his house while he wasn't even dressed yet. After all, a person could be *too* perfect. 'And that isn't cool, of course,' he said out loud.

'Shh!' went Franka.

At that very instant, the doorbell rang.

He got up and wanted to button his jacket, but found he was wearing a sweater. He did manage to appear to give the gesture some meaning by scratching his stomach. 'Shall I open the door?' he asked needlessly.

'Jem!' Franka called.

There was no answer from upstairs. In his mind's eye Phinus pictured a heap of T-shirts, trousers, shoes, all rejected in a fever of despair. He hurried to the door, thinking up a number of jovial greetings and promptly rejecting them again. He switched on the hall light. He pasted a smile on his face. 'Hello,' he said, as he opened the door.

'Hi,' said the girl on the front step.

What he saw first was a shocking quantity of red hair. Then a teeny dress in a leopard print, with creamy white arms and legs protruding. One hand was clutching a small bag, the other pushed the hair back from her face. Her full lips glistened. Really, nothing could possibly be further removed from the Animal Liberation Front. This one certainly wouldn't turn down a nice slice of liver sausage if you offered her one. 'Won't you come in?' said Phinus, dazed. 'Jem is still busy – Jem isn't quite ready, I mean, Jem is coming.'

Nonchalantly she stepped across the threshold.

As he showed her into the living room, he had to restrain himself from gesticulating triumphantly behind her back at Franka. *Look at this! That Jem!*

'Hi,' said the girl again, as impassively as before.

'I was just in the middle of *ER*, but I'll turn it off,' said Franka.

'Oh, don't, my mother always watches it too.' She plumped herself down on the couch, all legs. 'Dr Benton is her idol.'

'Then your mother has excellent taste. Just look at that poor darling, working his fingers to the bone again.' Franka pointed at the set with the remote control. 'That man is so serious and so dedicated.'

'But not very relaxed.'

'No, those two things don't usually go together, do they?'

The girl leaned forward. She said, shaking her head, 'Poor sucker!'

'Nice scent you're wearing,' said Franka.

Phinus wondered why he was still standing in the centre of the living room. In a loud voice he asked, 'Drink, anyone?'

'Oh, let's,' said Franka congenially. 'Will you pour us one?'

He got busy with bottles and glasses. Apparently you didn't introduce yourself any more these days. And as soon as you stepped over the threshold somewhere, you just went and flopped down in front of the box, as if you were in your own home. He felt uncommonly let down.

'Oi,' said Jem, entering the room in shapeless trousers and a worn T-shirt.

'Hey, Jem.' The girl flashed him a smile, baring a dead straight set of milky-white teeth.

Quickly Phinus pressed two glasses of Coke into Jem's hands before he could start stuttering or turn red as a beetroot. He gave him an encouraging jab in the upper arm.

'Let's be social, shall we?' said Franka. She turned off the television.

'Cheers, young people,' said Phinus. He was all prepared to start breaking the ice. Then he happened to glance at Jem's shoes, enormous canvas contraptions

99

with the laces untied. He crossed his left foot over his right knee, shot Jem a meaningful look and tapped discreetly on his own shoe.

'They're *supposed* to be untied, Dad,' said Jem.

'That doesn't make any sense,' he said. 'In that case, they wouldn't have laces.'

'Your email just cracked me up,' the girl said to Jem.

'Yeah, how phat was that,' said Jem modestly. He took a sip of his Coke.

Reluctantly Phinus gave up on the shoelaces. 'Well now, tell us. How do you two know each other? From school?'

'Oh stop it, Phinus,' said Franka. 'Next you'll be asking her what her father does for a living.'

'He's a vet,' said the girl, tickled. 'And my mum too.' There was a challenging glint in her eyes. *No match for our Jem. Everything God has forbidden, she's already done at least three times.*

'Aha,' said Phinus. 'That explains a lot. So then animals did have something to do with your finding each other.'

'They did?' asked Jem.

'Oh, never mind, a man's entitled to have a theory.'

Jem rolled his eyes ostentatiously: sorry, that's the way my dad always acts, just ignore him. He put his glass down on the table and stood up. 'Shall we go?'

With a seductive roll of the hips, his girlfriend got up and made some adjustments to the jungle of hair.

'You do have lights on your bikes, don't you?' Phinus asked helplessly. 'And remember, Jem is taking you home tonight. No cycling alone in the dark.'

'Or else you can sleep here,' said Franka.

'We'll see,' said Jem. He walked to the door, his shoelaces trailing.

'His hair looks good like that, doesn't it?' said Franka to the girl. Franka, too, had stood up and was now giving herself a good stretch. *Everyone in this house was acting pretty damn laid back.* 'Come on,' she said, 'I'll walk you out. That way I can make sure Jem doesn't put his baseball cap on at the last minute.'

'Sanne won't let me,' said Jem. He gave the girl a hearty jab in her side, as if she wasn't a sex bomb.

'In that case we are eternally beholden to you, Sanne,' said Franka.

'You're welcome.' Sanne giggled, and followed Jem out of the room.

'Well, have fun then,' said Phinus to the empty air. He leaned back, deflated. The laughter and chatter coming from the hall was salt rubbed in the wound. His eyes watered with frustration. What were they going to be consuming, come to think of it, on his tab, in that kind of club? Cocktails? Coolers? And slow-dancing, did kids still do that?

Franka came back inside five minutes later, still chuckling to herself. 'Well, that Sanne's quite the little number,' she said. 'But oh, how sad you look!'

'I'm so unhappy. Suddenly I'm so terribly unhappy.'

'He's growing up,' she said drily. Standing behind him, she threw her arms round his neck and pressed her cheek against his.

'I'd been so looking forward to being with him when he had his first beer.'

'Oh Phinus, I'm afraid you've already missed a few rounds.'

'Yes. And now it's too late.'

She had to laugh. 'What a lugubrious voice! If it were up to you, he'd still be that little boy waiting upstairs in bed for his goodnight kiss every night.'

He thought of Jem's room, the way it used to look before the posters of pop musicians went up and all the other alarming signs indicating, of late, that Jem was in a hurry to grow up and make his way in the world. Jem used to surround himself up there with stuffed animals. The time of koala-bear pyjamas, bedtime stories, intimate confidences. 'Remember, Daddy, the doll you got me for my birthday? Sometimes I take him up to the attic, and I wish for him to come alive.'

'Well, in that case I'm glad I didn't give you a tiger.'

'Be serious, Daddy! It nearly worked, one time.'

'And then what happened?'

'And then it didn't work. Dad? Why don't I have any brothers or sisters?'

'Phinus?' said Franka, right in his ear. 'What are you thinking?'

He pulled her onto his lap and buried his face in her hair. All the clichés always turned out to be so astonishingly true: the time had indeed flown. Jem could, in theory, even make his girlfriend pregnant. Jem would have a very different life from Phinus's. A life with children and grandchildren of his own, an unending procession of objects of affection on whom to shower all his anxieties and nurturing urges. He would never know Phinus's deepest fear: that of floating through time and space as a loose, redundant link. No ancestors, no offspring. Never a bequeather of genes. Alone in the vast universe, like a rocket gone astray. One of those people on the street who call the weather hotline on their mobiles to give the impression that they belong somewhere.

He clasped his arms round Franka. 'Will you stay with me for ever?'

'Of course I'll stay with you for ever!' she said.

'Whatever gives you the idea I might not, suddenly?'

Reassured, he drank half a bottle of wine, watched a late movie on the box and finally went to bed with nothing but rosy thoughts in his head: of Franka who loved him, of Jem full of ideals, everyone healthy and sound of body and limb, and nothing lacking in the material department, either. This last thought gave him, as he switched off his bedside light, an extra sense of satisfaction. Franka wouldn't have approved, of course, if she had known how much money he had given Jem, but was it right for the poor boy to have to sit and sip an organic apple juice at the Eko-café on his first night on the town?

A crisp banknote was the grown-up equivalent of the goodnight kiss of yore.

Contentedly he turned onto his side; he had seen to it that Jem would have the night of his life.

What fate can accomplish

The girls are conferring in the back seat in whispers. The rain drums monotonously on the roof of the car. Phinus has no idea how far they are from the civilized world. In the distance a small point of light flickers, distorted by the water trickling down the windscreen: a lamp illuminating some garden path or driveway perhaps, or a farm's attic window. There isn't even a moon to cast some light on the narrow unmade road.

He wonders if he has enough cash on him. How much will they have the nerve to ask for? Next thing he knows, he'll have to drive to a cash machine too, God only knows where. He is startled when Melanie raises her voice: 'We don't want your money, Mr Phinus.'

'We don't need no hush money,' Astrid chimes in for good measure.

He turns and looks at them over his shoulder. They avert their faces, as if they've decided he isn't worth another glance. Discomfited, he shifts into gear and starts driving slowly, as if he might shake them off that way.

'It isn't fair,' Melanie continues, a moment later. 'Just because you can pay someone off with a few guilders once it's over, you think you can get away with beating their brains out. That's what I call the rich lording it over the poor.'

'But whatever, we're fucked up good anyway. And we were going to go out tomorrow, too. We can kiss that idea goodbye. I'm not going into town with my face all smashed up.' Unexpectedly, there are tears in Astrid's voice.

'And Ast had bought a new outfit too, specially.'

'At H&M! The top alone cost me nineteen ninety-five! And then the trousers as well.' She leans forward. 'And it just so happens they were the trousers I'd been waiting for all my life, cocksucker.'

'Don't forget your new lipstick,' says Melanie.

'From the Body Shop.'

He pictures them relentlessly shopping, in their girlish incarnation, arm in arm, two girls of fifteen, sixteen, cheeks rosy from cycling, eyes peeled for bargains. And afterwards, at home in a little room with a dormer window, absorbed in their purchases. Side by side before the mirror. Heads together, in grave consultation. What if you wore your hair another way? You could shave it a little higher. Is that the way it goes, nowadays? 'I'm sorry,' he says, suddenly all too aware that he hasn't got a clue, not a clue, about their lives. He doesn't know any girls their age. *Except for Sanne, of course.*

There's a brief silence. Then, 'Sorry!' sneers Astrid. 'Is that it?'

'It's a start,' says Melanie.

105

He glances sideways and observes that her hand is resting casually on Franka's shoulder. Her nails are coated in flaking black varnish. 'Pretty face, by the way.'

'Yeah,' Astrid says bitterly. 'Not a scratch on her. Unlike us.'

He gives himself no time to think it over. The car swerves as he hastily removes his watch and passes it back over his shoulder. 'Here. OK? Take it. My wife gave it to me, on our tenth wedding anniversary.'

'It isn't a Swatch,' says Astrid after a few seconds. 'But even so, I wouldn't spit on it.'

'Some – gizmo?' aks Melanie, astonished. 'Does he consider some old gizmo his most valuable possession?'

'It isn't just any old thing, it's a symbol, it represents all the time we've been together.' He hates it when he stutters like this; why is he stuttering anyway, isn't he telling the truth?

'Tsss. How romantic. And what kind of present did you give her? Some fancy lingerie, I bet.'

'Oh, gross,' growls Astrid. 'Garters, on such an old bag.'

'Is she wearing it now?' Melanie's hand descends a fraction, as if she's about to unbutton Franka's shirt.

'It won't be your size anyway,' says Astrid. 'She's a C cup at least. Or did you want to take it for Mother's Day?'

He just barely misses the red and white barrier that has suddenly loomed up in a bend in the road. The tyres skid on the wet grass of the verge. With considerable effort he manages to steer the car back into the middle of the road.

'Phinus, will you watch where you're going?' mumbles Franka, half awake.

He's thinking to himself, I'm trying to protect you, goddammit! The blood is pounding inside his head. In slow motion, he pictures her tumbling sideways, out of the car, her head grazing the pavement, her arms waving desperately, her heel getting caught in the open door, *and he can't find the brake, he can't stop*, the door slams shut on her leg, blood gushes from her flesh, and, in his panic, he steps on the accelerator, dragging Franka along until her skull cracks open on the road and all her reproaches spill out like strawberry jam from a broken jar and are washed away by the rain: 'How can I go on sharing my life with you, Phinus, when you belittle my feelings this way!'

'*That* was close,' complains Melanie.

'It must have been a pretty exhausting evening for you, though, stuffing your face for hours and hours . . .' Astrid clicks her tongue. 'Goose liver, caviar, steak—'

'Stop it, Ast, I'm going to puke again.' Melanie leans forward. 'Did you have a posh night out like that when you'd been married ten years and you got given that watch?'

'No,' he says.

Franka's expectant face when she gave him the little box, in the morning, in bed. The bedroom curtains had billowed softly in a friendly breeze, as if to affirm that curtains do indeed know how to exemplify happiness. Happiness so ordinary and normal, that your name had to be Phinus Vermeer ('So big and yet such a softy') for it to bring tears to your eyes: to know you were connected to someone. To wake up together, beneath Lawrence Alma-Tadema, each of you with a crease in your cheek and a trail of calcified drool in the corner of your mouth, and then *to behold pleasure*, *delighted pleasure in the face next to yours: 'Well, good morning, are you here too?'* That overwhelming certainty: she is glad I exist.

'Now you'll never have an excuse to keep me waiting any more,' she had said, pulling out the gift from beneath her pillow. She had slept on it, like a child sleeping on a wish. Her eyes grew wide with excitement as she handed it to him. *For my husband, the one I can always count on.*

He had sworn to her: no, we won't make a big fuss. Jem and I will just rustle up a few bites, and you are going to your mother's for a coffee, so you don't get in our way.

Jem kept a straight face, but kicked Phinus conspiratorially under the table. When you're eleven, a shared secret is more exciting than the circus. They'd been planning it for weeks. The tasks were divvied up between them: Phinus was chief dogsbody, Jem was kitchen head honcho. Together they would get the job done splendidly, hand in hand, shoulder to shoulder.

At half past ten – Franka was having a decaf at her mother's – the kitchen was in a state of pandemonium. There was butter on Jem's cheeks, he had a tea towel tied round his sweaty forehead and a flowery apron tied round his middle that reached down to his ankles. Standing on tiptoe, he was stirring something in a bowl sitting on the counter. Nervously he asked, 'Is the oven hot enough for the cream puffs?'

'Just try doing one thing at a time,' advised Phinus, only half paying attention: through the kitchen window men in sweaty T-shirts could be seen putting up a blue and white canopy. Others were walking back and forth with metal tables and chairs.

'But we'll never get it all done!'

'Wait. I hear the doorbell.'

It was the florist, with ten pots of hydrangeas, in every imaginable shade of pink and blue. Phinus carried the pots to the garden, where he was waylaid by the sound technician, who wanted to know where to plug in his equipment. Then it was necessary to have a consultation with the tableware rentals man, just as the wine merchant arrived with crates of champagne and orange juice. Franka's women friends would giggle, 'Well, yes, what can we say, Phinus does have big hands and big feet.' And her uncles and aunts, her brothers- and sisters-in-law, the entire family network, the whole kit and caboodle, would be able to assess with their own eyes how very fortunate Franka was to have such a husband, always generous, loving to a fault, nothing was too much for him, no, not everyone could say the same about their spouse.

When he walked into the kitchen again, Jem had garnished the chocolate cake with wobbly gobs of whipped cream, cut the fruitcake into uneven slices and arranged the finger sandwiches higgledy-piggledy on platters. 'The cream puffs are done,' he panted. 'All that's left to do is to fill them.'

'I'm *frightfully* proud of you,' said Phinus, looking around in shock. He bent down to plant a kiss on the tea towel. 'I'd never have managed it on my own. Hey, shall we stuff a little watercress into those sandwiches?'

Jem's brown eyes grew large. 'Didn't I do it right?'

'Are you kidding?'

Hurriedly Jem started pulling the pieces of bread apart. Just a few days earlier, Franka had remarked with a thoughtful frown, out of the blue, 'Shouldn't he be going to judo? Or to hockey? Instead of always messing around in the kitchen with you?'

'Some day, his girlfriend will be delighted to have a man who knows his way around the kitchen.'

'OK, sure, but other fathers and sons do their male bonding by going to football games.'

'Yes, and yours bake scones together.'

'As long as he isn't doing it mostly to please you.'

'Of course not. He thinks it's cool. When he's in secondary school he'll join a sports club, don't worry. He has the rest of his life to play the tough guy. Just let him have a jolly time hanging on to my apron strings a little longer.' Jem going to hockey or karate was both difficult to imagine and rather alarming. He was too skinny and frail, *just like myself; believe me, I know what I'm talking about, I used to be that kind of kid myself.*

He had pestered the aunts to tears. Everybody was playing football! With a sigh they had finally given in to his demand. Expensive boots, an expensive shirt, expensive long socks. Resigned, they'd muttered something about 'healthy boys', and their faces had assumed a respectful expression.

The ball was hard, the pitch impossibly huge, and the coach a bully. 'Vermeer!' he yelled. 'Get your arse up out of the mud, get up on your feet!' The other healthy boys hung around impatiently, stamping their feet. They wore their sleeves rolled up, even when it was freezing. They were faster than the speed of light, meaner than the devil. They didn't let a chance go by to tackle you or hide your clothes when you were in the shower. If the aunts hadn't prepaid for the entire season, he'd have quit on the spot. He didn't have the guts to tell them about the terrors and humiliations of the football pitch. Every Wednesday afternoon, he'd go with his stomach all tied up in knots, returning home with his shins kicked to pieces. 'What a wild beast,' said Leonoor admiringly as she dabbed arnica on his wounds. 'A real tiger,' said Irmgard. 'I bet you wouldn't mind an extra chunk of sausage in your soup.'

They swelled like peacocks when he described for them at dinner the passes and penalties of his wildest dreams. He traced every move for them in detail, scooting his finger over the worn oilcloth with the ladybird design, with two straw coasters for the goals. '*That's* where it has to go, and *this* is the side we have to defend.' They assumed, unquestioningly, that he had scored the winning goal. They could imagine the spectators cheering, they pictured his teammates hoisting him up on their shoulders for a victory lap. They would stand behind him all the way, with their soup and their arnica, until the day he signed for the first team at Ajax. Every Sunday evening, they filled the gaps in their knowledge with the help of *The World of Sports*. Pelé was their hero. Phinus was Pelé the Second, the boy with the heart of a lion and the unstoppable shot.

It wasn't his intention to lie to them, or even to exaggerate. It was simply another version of I Have a Little House on the Moon, which they used to play with him at bedtime, when he was little.

'I have a little house on the moon . . .'

'And it's all made of gold!'

'With chimneys made of diamonds!'

'And gilded sunflowers in the garden!'

'A red linen tablecloth on the table!' ('Like the one I saw the other day, in town,' Leonoor added longingly.)

111

'And in my little house on the moon I eat . . .'

'Porridge with a silver spoon!'

'No, bee-pollen fritters!'

'And fried chair legs and . . .'

'Chocolates.'

'And sticking plasters and scouring powder, oh my!'

Sitting on the edge of the bed, they would smile at each other. His toes curled up with pleasure at what was coming next.

'I have a little house on the moon and in it lives . . .'

'A man-in-the-moon?'

'No way! Men-in-the-moon make smelly farts.'

'What about a lady-in-the-moon then?'

'Oh please! Those dumb blondes? No way. Well? Who's the only one who's allowed to live in my little house on the moon? My little house made of gold and diamonds, with the red tablecloth?'

Shrieking with excitement, he'd dive under his pillow.

'Where *has* that child got to?' boomed Irmgard with a great show of exasperation. 'The fried chair legs are going to get cold.'

What was the difference, really, between I Have a Little House on the Moon and his triumphant feats on the football pitch? But why, then, was it getting harder and harder to dish up his fabrications about corner shots and headers? The flawless penalty kicks were fast becoming a millstone round his neck, but he couldn't backtrack out of the first division now: the aunts believed in him. How sorry they were that they had to work on Wednesday afternoons! Sitting behind the counter, their minds only half occupied with stamping the post, they just couldn't wait for their champion to return home. His cup of Drinka-pintamilka-day stood waiting for him in the kitchen. 'Now there's a boy with marrow in his bones!' they said.

His stories kept getting more far-fetched, his deeds more glorious. Had he told them that he'd had to take on an entire team of Pelés all by himself, blindfolded and with a square ball, they would have believed him. Where was their common sense? 'Stupid women!' he said to himself out loud.

He got a book about the Dutch national team for his birthday, with pictures of self-confident he-men with enormous hairy thighs. He dreamed he had to take showers with them.

He tried to catch cold by cycling to school with his jacket open. But the aunts secretly added vitamins to his food, or maybe they were doping him up with drugs. Wednesday in, Wednesday out, they craftily kept him on his feet. They didn't give him a chance to escape. Like two fat spiders they kept him caught in his own web of deceit and, without even batting an eyelid, sent him week after week into that purgatory of mud and kicks in the shin and persecution.

Until the day the coach called – it was a Saturday in December – to tell them Vermeer was the most hopeless pupil he'd ever come across and, believe him, he'd had his share of stone-blind, bungling gormless misfits in his day. His own life would be personally much improved if he were to be relieved of having to coach this exceptional basket case.

'How is it possible, darling?' asked Leonoor, hurt.

'Is it just sour grapes? Should we phone the Football Association?' asked Irmgard without a flicker of her usual combativeness; she was just offering him an honourable way out.

Head bowed, he stood before them on the coir

runner in the hall, feeling equal measures of shame and relief. 'I'll pay back the money, honestly I will,' he stammered.

For the rest of the winter, he washed cars and made deliveries on his bike for the chemist. He walked dogs and collected old newspapers. Sometimes he'd earn as much as two-fifty in a weekend. Leonoor carefully stowed the money in a tin that had once held butterscotch. Irmgard carefully kept track in a little cashbook. The column of spidery figures got lengthier as the weather turned warmer and brighter, both indoors and out. The windows were opened. A cheerful spring breeze wafted through the house. And on the first day of the Easter holidays, the aunts fetched the cashbook, put on their reading glasses and added up the columns.

'It's all there, down to the last cent.' Irmgard looked at him approvingly over the top of her spectacles. 'Now you can be proud of yourself again.'

'Here,' said Leonoor. She pushed the tin over to him and had to laugh at his astounded face. 'Go on, you earned it, didn't you?'

'There you go, spoiling the child as usual,' said Irmgard, delighted to have something to bicker about.

'Come on, it's not as if the money hadn't already been spent.'

'He'll buy himself a new pair of shoes with it, that's what he can do with it.'

'And whatever's left over, he can keep for himself,' said Leonoor. She hugged him to her broad bosom.

His face pressed into her flowered blouse, he'd stopped listening to their squabbling. A bottle of Dutch gin for Aunt Irmgard, a red tablecloth for Aunt Leonoor. In his mind he was already pedalling home with his offerings, light as a feather, happy as a clam.

'Make a right here,' says Melanie, businesslike. 'That's it, over here. And remember to signal. Accidents are always waiting to happen.'

'You can say *that* again, Mel.' Astrid yawns noisily.

He leans forward to wipe the condensation from the windshield. Even though it does improve the visibility somewhat, there isn't much to see. The road stretches emptily between the fields, there's yet another flooded ditch shimmering alongside. It's stuffy inside the car, and he opens his window a crack. The night air streaming in feels like a sobering hand on his neck. He wonders, why am I driving here? Next to him Franka stirs in her sleep, as though his thoughts had poked her in her side. She smacks her lips, *What are we doing here, for God's sake?* she sighs, and then resumes breathing deeply and peacefully again.

'That one sure can sleep,' Astrid declares. 'Must be a dead bore for our driver at home.'

'OK, I've had enough now,' he says. 'Where shall I drop you?'

'But Phinus, where's your cap? Doesn't any driver worth his salt wear a cap? And how do you communicate with the dispatcher? How do they know where you are? I don't see a mobile.'

Only then does he notice the holster for his mobile is empty. The phone is gone! That fat bitch must have nicked it when he got out, on the bridge. 'It's broken,' he says, with great self-restraint. 'It won't do you any good.'

'Yeah, sure.' In his mirror he sees her take out the phone and start pushing the buttons. Her battered face assumes an indignant expression. 'Hey, shit, man! The thing's dead as a doornail!'

'I wouldn't look a gift horse in the mouth if I was you,' snaps Melanie. 'Watches, phones, it never ends. I'm sitting here empty-handed with a bleeding headache, and you're just raking it in! Maybe he's got some sexy underwear for you as well.' She lowers her voice. 'Well, here we are then, with a sex maniac . . . and we can't even make a phone call!'

'It makes me sick,' says Astrid. 'Is it that old story again?'

It's at that moment that the red petrol warning light starts to blink. The dashboard clock announces that it's 4.02. Hours to go before daylight. At the thought of being stranded here with these two, his mind simply shuts down.

'Bastard,' cries Astrid, 'don't you dare think I'm doing it with you.' She begins to snivel. 'Always, always, always the same thing.'

'Come on, Ast.'

'Isn't it true?'

'Well, yeah, it sucks, you're right.'

Astrid sniffs. 'That's what he thinks, the dirty old coot.'

To his horror he hears the sound of a zipper, articles of clothing being tugged at. Suddenly he can't see a thing any more because a piece of fabric has been pulled over his head. The car swerves across the road, and Melanie hisses, 'Not over his eyes, moron!'

'That's as close as you'll get to it, pervert. Get that through your head.' Huffing and puffing, Astrid pulls her jeans back on.

He quickly puts his hand up to his head.

'Don't touch, Phinus!' She slaps his arm down. 'See, at least you now have a chauffeur's cap.'

Melanie hoots with laughter.

116

The unmistakable odour of a girl's crotch works its way into his nose, a smell that has the immediate effect of reminding him what a shock it was, that other time, to realize: She certainly *hasn't* yet done three times all that God has forbidden; and what a pervert he felt afterwards. It felt as if his soul had shrivelled up, like flesh under a branding iron. If only there existed some cosmic authority with as much power as his aunts': the power to impose a penance leading to absolution. To be seen, weighed and judged, that was every guilty creature's most fervent desire. To be acknowledged and recognized as the scoundrel you really were, so that a final reckoning could take place, to set you free.

He grips the steering wheel until his knuckles are polished white. He thinks, if only everything could be revealed. About Jem too, even about Jem. Especially about Jem. But it can't, it can't possibly. It would cause too much pain.

'Phinus!' says Franka sharply, wide awake. 'What's the meaning of this?' She sits up and points at his head covering.

'It was just a little game, madam,' Melanie tells her. 'Your husband suggested we—'

'A little game?' She turns round.

'Yeah, look, Astrid's already won this watch.' Dangling it from her finger, she holds it out for inspection.

Franka shifts her position. 'Phinus, take that thing off your head at once.' Her voice is icy calm.

Sick with helplessness, he yanks the panties off his head and throws them over his shoulder.

'OK, and now you can pass that watch back up here.'

'I'm really sorry,' mutters Astrid as she hands it over.

Franka sticks it in her pocket. 'And I also think it's about time you two got to bed.'

'We're nearly there, madam. It's right over there, round the corner.'

'Fine,' says Franka evenly, in the voice of someone who is accustomed to taking control of the situation in a matter of seconds.

It stays quiet in the back seat. A glance in the rearview mirror shows him that they're sitting there docilely, those two, eyes cast down, chastened.

'Left, here,' mumbles Melanie.

The road he turns into is unpaved, it's no more than a farm track. The rain has turned the surface into a sea of mud. A few moments later he notices the open water to his right. It's the canal again. And then in the car's headlights, behind a few scraggy trees, a small, tumbledown cottage comes into view. The mossy shingles lie higgledy-piggledy on the roof, which reaches almost to the ground. Two minuscule square windows peek out underneath. A sign hangs from the gable: 'Condemned dwelling'.

'What's this then?' asks Franka.

'It's an old day-labourer's cottage. Ast and I always come here when we've stayed out too late, and then we tell them at home we slept over at each other's house.'

'That isn't very clever. You're old enough and sensible enough to know that sooner or later the truth is bound to come out. And how do you get in, anyway?'

'It isn't locked. There's just a bolt, on the outside.'

'Well, go on then.'

'Thanks for the lift, eh, Phinus?' says Astrid familiarly. They both snort, smothering giggles. Then they get out.

118

He watches in a daze as they walk towards the cottage. Just another beat, and they'll be out of his life for good, those two emissaries from hell. His breath starts coming a little faster. Wait! The reckoning! There hasn't been any reckoning yet, and now they're getting away.

Franka jerks her head round to face him. 'How could you, how *could* you, in my presence, and with mere children too!' There are tears in her eyes. There isn't a shred of her composure left. 'You can't talk your way out of this one, not in a hundred years! So save yourself the trouble, Phinus, OK?' She digs around in her handbag for a handkerchief. She's furious, so furious she's sharp as a tack, the sleeping pill notwithstanding.

He would like to calm her down, but the girls are about to enter the house. They're fiddling with the door, heads tucked between their shoulders because of the rain.

He flings open the car door. 'Wait!' he bellows. He leaps out of the car, but before he's even standing upright, he senses that this move is about to end in total disaster. He clutches the door for support. The familiar sensation that always precedes a spasm runs up his spine. Next, with an audible crack, his lowest vertebra seizes up. It feels like a chainsaw being drawn over his bones. Gasping for air, he remains frozen in position, half bent over. Sweat is pouring down his forehead. Carefully he places his hands on his hips. He twists his upper body, setting off a fusillade of hellish, shooting pain. It's utterly stuck. He curses. *Not now!*

'What?' shouts Astrid from the house.

He has to wet his lips. 'I can't . . .'

Franka heaves herself up out of the other side of the car, on one foot. 'Is it your back? Not again!'

He can't see her face, his torso is at right angles to his legs. 'That's what happens,' he hears her say. 'You don't do your exercises nearly often enough. Well, can you move, or won't it budge at all?'

'What's wrong with that bloke now?' Astrid calls out nosily.

'My husband's put his back out. Can he come and lie down inside for a bit? He has to stretch. What I mean is, we're going to have to stretch his back for him.'

You take Daddy's other leg, Jem. That's it. Now, pull, easy does it. With all his might, he tries to straighten up. His pinched nerves scream with pain. His head is spinning as the girls hurry forward to help. The rain glistens in their hair and on their jackets. Piranhas.

'You, help him.' Franka nods at Astrid, as she slings her own arm over Melanie's shoulder.

'Well, well, Phinus,' sighs Astrid, 'you *are* jinxed tonight, aren't you! Do I have to push you? What's the story?'

From his bizarre stance he can see only her midriff. Her jacket is hanging open. Underneath she's wearing a poison-green sweater that leaves her navel exposed. This, too, is pierced. Her stomach is the colour of semolina pudding. 'You just have to lead me in the right direction,' he stutters. It sounds like a religious prayer.

'Sort of like a seeing-eye dog?' She honks with laughter.

All the saints in all the heavens have turned a deaf ear to him, all the gods from here to Ouagadougou are pretending they're not in, in every alcove in every church, every statue under every stained-glass window stares straight ahead, unmoved; in all the universe, not a single atom has even considered giving him some small, encouraging push, to help him find absolution from his guilt. The only thing the assembled powers on high did manage to do was to dump Astrid and Melanie in his path. Or is it the other way round: are they the avengers, not he? The pain is so bad that he can't think clearly any more.

His shirt is soaked by the time they catch up with Franka and Melanie. He comes to a standstill with his nose practically pressed up against the door, whose green paint is peeling off in dismal strips. Franka's hand comes into his field of vision, the hand with her wedding ring on it. She grasps the rusty bolt and slides it open. 'Is there any light?'

'No,' says Melanie. 'No, madam.'

'Move your butt, Phinus,' says Astrid jovially as she pushes him across the threshold.

He can smell the mould and the damp. It isn't just the floorboards creaking under his shuffling feet, it's also the crunching of the carcasses of small animals, ancient newspapers, polystyrene cups. It's only a couple of steps from the paltry hall into the main room.

'Here's the bed,' says Melanie, gingerly picking her way through the mess that betrays the fact that this must be a favourite haunt of the young people of Aduard, who often light fires here.

In the middle of the room stands a blackened bed frame.

'Lie down,' Franka tells him.

Pain like a fountain of sparks crackles through him as he lowers himself onto the bed. He stays on his side, incapable of turning over by himself. He hears Franka giving instructions. Hands far from gentle flip him onto his back. Someone tugs at his legs. He gives an agonized groan.

'OK,' says Franka after a few moments, 'let's stop now. If it doesn't work right away, it'll never work. Is there a doorframe somewhere that he could hang from? At home we have a stretching bar.'

'Everything's pretty low around here,' answers Melanie.

Phinus works himself into a sitting position. Red-hot knives drill into his back. He looks around, in a fog. There's not much to see. The room contains no furniture besides the rickety bed. Franka, standing on one leg, is leaning against a wall in which two small windows show up as pale blocks of light. The two piranhas are standing at the foot of the bed, legs planted wide, arms crossed, scrutinizing him.

'Well, here we are then,' fumes Franka.

'You're always *some*where, aren't you,' Astrid opines. She yawns.

'Can you drive?'

'No,' she admits reluctantly.

Melanie says, 'That isn't allowed, madam, is it, if you're not eighteen yet?'

'Then I'll have to ask you to go for help on foot.'

The girls exchange glances.

'Come now, one good deed for your fellow man won't kill you. And it'll give you a good story, too, to tell your parents, why you're home so late.'

Astrid says, 'In the pissing rain?'

But Melanie's eyes light up. She grabs her friend by the sleeve. 'Come on, let's go.'

'How long a walk is it to the village?'

'Fifteen minutes, half an hour maybe.'

Franka takes Phinus's watch out of her pocket. 'Excellent, so you'll be back within the hour. I nearly said, no talking to strangers out there.'

Astrid laughs. Melanie doesn't. She purses her lips, which are pale and thin. 'Well, so long!' she murmurs to Phinus in a chummy tone.

As soon as the door has shut behind them, he tries, with the subtlest of movements, to find a less excruciating position. He avoids looking directly at Franka, all the while keeping a close eye on her. She is still holding his watch in her hand. She looks at it as if it's some obscene object, instead of a gift she once picked out for him with love and care. Then she hurls it to the ground and bangs her fist on the wall. 'Damn! We could simply have phoned! Now those girls are having to walk through the pouring rain for nothing.' She takes a step, but cries out as her weight lands on the injured leg.

'Careful,' he says, out of habit.

She throws him a dirty look, lowers herself to the floor and then crawls on hands and knees towards the front door. Franka, who is never caught off guard. Franka who knows the ropes. Franka who has cooked his goose, who has thoroughly screwed up his chances to finally get what he deserves by removing those two she-devils from the scene as if it were no big deal.

'I'm going to get the phone,' she says.

'The thing is on the blink!' That, at least, is no lie.

'You just had it fixed.'

'I'm telling you, woman, I tried to make a call with it this afternoon, and it doesn't work. Sit down, for crying out loud. The floor is littered with filth.'

'Right, that's what *you* think. And listen to your lies, I suppose. Not in a million years.' She has almost reached the hall.

'My lies? What lies?'

Sitting on her knees, she looks at him with revulsion. 'If you could have seen yourself, the way you looked with that – thing on your head . . .'

'You want to know something? You're just looking for a convenient excuse!'

'Well, and so what? I've had it up to here with you, for months now. This situation is the last straw. The very last one. You've gone totally ballistic, you're a madman! You don't have a shred of self-control left! I'm ashamed of you, do you hear me! I'm utterly ashamed!'

'But those two tarts were conning us! Believe me, they're bad news. They were out to screw us.' He has to convince her. She has got to know the score.

'Oh please. Here we go again. You're hallucinating. You're off your bloody rocker! You think everyone's got it in for you. You're a psychopath! You beat the living daylights out of a couple of kids who were just—'

'I was coming to your aid!'

'Oh, stop it,' she says, brimming with contempt. 'The saviour, galloping to the rescue. It's only because you couldn't save Jem. That's bugging you so much it's driving you half crazy! Don't you get it? But we aren't allowed to talk about that, are we! And how do you think that makes me feel? Do you ever wonder about that? I've had bugger all from you, no support, all this time . . . Do you realize that? Not a thing!'

He starts to stutter. 'But . . . those . . . two . . .'

'You'd better believe I don't wish to be married to a boor who beats people up for no good reason!' She looks as though she could go for his throat at any minute, the woman he's had breakfast with a thousand mornings, who has stood for hundreds of hours in countless post office, museum and checkout lines with him, who has thrown dozens of successful parties with him and who once told him, 'Of course I'll stay with you for ever. Whatever gives you the idea I might not?'

'You make me sick.' She turns her head away. 'I'm calling the police and I'm going to wait in the car until they get here.'

When she discovers the phone is missing, will she finally see what sort of stuff those two harpies are made of? Or will it only rouse more suspicion in her? He hesitates.

Grimly she sets herself in motion again and drags herself across the floor on all fours, through the piles of rubbish, in the sunny yellow suit that was supposed to save their marriage.

In one fierce lunge he hauls himself up off the bed. The pain is excruciating. Doubled over, he waddles after her.

'Don't you dare!' she snarls. 'If you so much as lay a finger on me . . . !' She has reached the door. She grasps the handle and pushes it down.

'Franka, come on, please! Can't we just talk about it?'

'Talk? You? Don't make me laugh.'

'Listen to me! What happened tonight . . .' But what did happen, exactly? It is already impossible to reconstruct which event led to which deed, who unleashed what and who was out to dig whose grave.

'You don't have to bullshit me. I was there.'

'You were asleep, goddammit, you didn't notice a thing!'

'I was certainly wide awake on that bridge. I can still see the whole thing before me, plain as daylight. And

I won't soon forget it, either.' She puts her shoulder up against the door and gives it a push.

'But I'm telling you, at that point I thought you were in danger! Don't we run into the same sort of thing when we're working on a puzzle sometimes?'

She gazes at him in disbelief.

'That's right, a jigsaw puzzle. When you decide a piece belongs to the sky and I think it's part of the sea. When we'd both swear—'

She raises her hands. She lets them fall again. 'I am not even going to dignify that one with a reply. I'm going to make sure I don't waste any more of my time on someone who deliberately sticks his head in the sand.' Her nostrils dilate, her teeth are bared. 'So long, Phinus.' She yanks at the handle. She pushes and she pulls. Finally, with an oath, she throws her full weight against the door.

He suddenly has an unpleasant hunch. He hobbles closer, pushes her out of the way and tries the door. It is bolted tight.

Briefly, they share at least this much: the shock.

Just a few hours ago, he had thought everything would turn out all right if only he could have her all to himself again. Now here they are, alone together at last, and by the look of it, they may be so for a while.

Outside, in the first grey morning light, a blackbird begins to sing.

PART II
Miss a Turn

What Franka concludes

The girls must have bolted the door by accident. They'll be back within an hour. There is nothing wrong, nothing at all. She isn't inclined to take Phinus seriously, not even for half a second. She has lowered herself to the floor, her back against the door, the swollen leg stretched out in front of her. Her jaw is clenched. She would sell her soul to the devil this very minute in exchange for being rid of that raving maniac sitting across from her. Anything, anything is preferable to having to get another hour older in his company, in a space so confined she can practically smell his breath.

It's too bad that the devil has never shown any interest in her soul. She has always invoked his name in vain, until now. She was still very young the first time she tried it. 'My husband is dead.' Her soul, for his return. But at which ticket window were you supposed to hand in your soul, along with the jam pots of tears, the jars brimming with the proof of your love? Who showed even the slightest interest? Or perhaps it simply didn't count if you came to turn yourself in, perhaps the devil didn't care for goods that were free for the taking, for souls voluntarily surrendered. What good were they to him anyway, mortals who presented themselves at the gates of hell of their own free will, thus offering no great opportunity for further defilement? And you couldn't exactly get huffy with the devil either, or insist on your rights. 'Rights? Come on, we haven't signed a contract, you people and I! We don't have staff committees here, farting around with memos!' Or perhaps the devil simply didn't exist. Otherwise you'd have expected him to show up right after Jem died, surely. At that time her thoughts alone should have summoned him to do his duty immediately: suicides, after all, were right up his alley. Or hadn't she meant it seriously? She had brought up the subject often enough anyway, in snatched whispers, with her women friends. At home there had been no point even mentioning it, at home was the man who acted as though life went on regardless. Her friends had reacted with sympathy. Of course you're having those thoughts now, they said, it's only natural, but what good will it do you? They were practical. They said she should eat, to keep up her strength. They brought over casseroles wrapped in foil. They addressed the death announcements Phinus and Franka couldn't even bear to look at. Taking turns with her relatives, they plumped up cushions, they brewed tea and poured gin and made soup and answered the phone and tied up overflowing bin liners and discreetly flushed Jem's goldfish down the loo and spoke to the undertakers and to Jem's tutor at school and the little girl from next door, only ten years old, who turned out to have kept a journal entirely devoted to Jem. The friends were good deeds personified. Nothing brings out so very much of the best in people as a bereavement. Except in the immediate survivors, of course.

When the doorbell rang at half past two in the morning, she'd thought Jem must have forgotten his key. She stumbled groggily down the stairs as she shrugged on her dressing gown. He'd be standing outside the door grinning sheepishly, with Sanne, for whose sake he had left his baseball cap at home. To have to rouse your mother from her bed was pretty mortifying.

Two police officers stood on the threshold.

'Oh heavens,' said Franka automatically; her entire roster of juvenile clients flashed through her head. *Now* who was in trouble? She put on a professional expression, patted her hair and said, flipping through her files in her mind, 'What can I do for you?'

'Mrs Vermeer?'

She nodded impatiently, wide awake now. Phinus always hated it when they were woken up in the middle of the night.

'May we come in for a second?'

She walked ahead of them to the living room, hoping they would lower their voices. She turned on the light. She gestured to the chairs around the dining table.

The men remained standing. 'Is your husband home?' asked the taller of the two.

'Yes,' said Franka, 'he's sleeping, so perhaps we could keep our voices down.' She pulled out a chair, sat down and mechanically started moving some things around on the overflowing table. A newspaper, a coffee mug, a library book about dinosaurs that belonged to Jem.

131

'You had better wake him up.'

She felt the urge to laugh. Phinus would rather . . . why should Phinus . . . Then her stomach did a somersault. 'Jem? It isn't Jem, is it?'

There was from the outset an invisible script, with a clear division of roles. Franka was the Mother. Phinus was designated the Spouse. Jem, the Victim. An important supporting role was reserved for Sanne (the Witness). It was just like a game of Cluedo, except that it was real.

The Mother and the Spouse first had to identify the Victim. The Victim had been shot through the head, three times at close range. There was nothing left of the eyes that used to look out at the world full of interest and trust, he was now someone without a smile on his lips.

The Mother said, frantically, 'It isn't him, is it, Phinus? It isn't him, it's only someone wearing his clothes.'

'Right, they could have been stolen,' said the Spouse. 'He was mugged in an alleyway by a junkie or something . . .' His voice died away. His shoulders were shaking.

'Look,' said the Mother. 'He's got gel on his hair. Gel! That can't be Jem.' She grabbed at a lock of hair on the side of the bloody blob, she licked her fingers and mumbled, 'Gel! That's made from bones! Our Jem would never . . .' She jerked her head round, towards the watching, set faces. 'Our Jem would never . . .'

The Spouse, standing in the corner, was shaking his head, stupefied.

After that they were both given a cup of coffee.

They signed forms.

They were taken from the hospital to the police station. There they sat on identical orange bucket seats in a neon-lit space that was pretty much identical to the first, waiting for more business to be conducted behind their backs. They held each other's hands and let go again. They began sentences which they never finished, while in their thoughts they frantically tried to reconstruct the Victim's face, to piece it back together out of the pulpy mush they'd just been shown, to fashion a face with a name and a history out of it once more, but then they'd be left gasping for breath. The Mother desperately dreamed up one rescue scenario after another, all quite futile now. For instance, she thought, if only I'd been wearing my tracksuit tonight. That's the kind of outfit that will notify fate that you're alert, that you're on your toes, that in an emergency you won't let a second go to waste. Why oh why didn't I wear my tracksuit? She said, elbowing the Spouse in the ribs, 'Why didn't I wear my tracksuit?'

The Spouse was sitting slumped over in his orange bucket. Instead of answering, he repeated for the twentieth time, 'Have I understood correctly? Have I understood correctly that he was trying to intervene when that crazy nut suddenly started shooting?'

The Mother was silent. She bit her nails. What else had she been remiss in or neglectful of tonight? In what thousands of other ways was she responsible for the Victim's death?

A policewoman brought them another cup of coffee, in corrugated disposable cups. She told them that the interrogation of the Witness was completed. Perhaps the Mother and the Spouse would like to have a word

133

with her as well? The policewoman looked at them questioningly. She was small and slim, but there was also something tough about her. Not a woman who'd allow her child to be shot dead just like that. You could tell she'd be the type to throw herself bodily in front of any approaching danger. Like some kind of Superwoman. The bullets would bounce off her chest.

'Yes! Yes! Of course we want to have a word with her!' Distraught and dishevelled, the Spouse got to his feet.

'Who?' asked the Mother.

'That . . . that little slut! Who just stood there, while . . .'

Superwoman seemed to swell a little. She said in a warning tone, 'The girl is extremely upset. I won't let you speak to her if you can't be reasonable.'

The Mother said, 'Actually, I wouldn't mind a hot dog first.' The reasonableness of this request gave her some modest satisfaction.

'With mustard?' asked Superwoman. 'On a roll?'

'With chips,' decided the Mother. Really, she'd never been so hungry in all her life.

'*Bon appétit*,' said Superwoman. With a flourish she drew a plate out of the air, heaped with hot dogs and chips, and handed it to the Mother.

The Spouse knocked it out of her hand. 'Say something! Don't you want to talk to that Sanne girl too?'

'Sanne?' She blinked. 'Yes, yes of course.'

'Sanne's father is also here,' said Superwoman stiffly to the Spouse. 'I advise you to keep calm.'

The Mother and her Spouse followed her through an endless labyrinth of corridors with worn linoleum on the floor. Doors that could use a coat of paint flashed by, with murmuring voices behind them. I'm coming,

Jem, I'm coming, thought the Mother, matching the words to the cadence of her footsteps. Such a sweet, sunny baby. Never any trouble at all. No tantrums, no crying through the night, no nappy rash, no nasty business with teething. She had often thought that other mothers went about it all wrong. That they did too much of this, not enough of that. When it was so simple to have a calm baby. Like Jem. Determined to please his mummy, little as he was. As if he knew he had to compensate for the loss of his daddy. A wise, thoughtful infant.

A door was flung open.

Already she had her arms open wide. But instead of Jem, the bare room held only the girl in whose company he had gone to meet his unhappy fate. Her father was standing behind her with his hands resting on her shoulders, a small, portly man, his face twisted with shock. He opened his mouth and closed it again. Then he looked down at his feet.

The Mother sat down on the first chair within reach, equally incapable of speech. The Spouse remained standing. Superwoman settled herself on a stool by the door. Her attitude implied, I hear nothing, I see nothing, I say nothing. But her eyes were wary.

Somebody had wrapped a blanket round the Witness. Her red hair was plastered to her skull. Her cheeks showed pink traces of tears. Her fingers plucked at the hem of her dress, and from time to time she shivered so vehemently that her whole body shook.

Looking at her, the Mother suddenly felt herself grow incredibly clear-headed, as if her consciousness were straining to make room for the realization that this little face must have been the very last thing her son had seen before he lost his life. It filled her with a monstrous, spitting envy. 'Is that his blood?' she asked, nodding at the tracks on her cheeks. What she was thinking was, if so, it's *my* blood.

The Witness turned her gaze on her, dull and skittish at once. 'It sprayed all over the place,' she said, nearly inaudibly. 'We were dancing, and then . . .' She began to cry.

'She's only fifteen,' muttered the girl's father. 'How is she ever going to get over this?'

'There is Victim Support,' said the Mother on auto-pilot. She had used that line so often that she could recite the telephone number with her eyes closed.

'Sure, for the living,' snarled the Spouse.

The girl's father said hastily, 'We are so terribly sorry for your loss. What a tragedy. I simply don't know what to say. I—'

'Why didn't you stop him?' the Spouse interrupted him in a tight voice. 'Why didn't you *do* something?'

'Surely you don't mean that! Sanne can't help it if—'

'Oh no? Jem wasn't the type of kid who plays the hero. He let her egg him on!'

The Witness cringed. 'Someone suddenly started shooting,' she stuttered. 'Just like that. The music was so loud, nobody noticed, and you couldn't see very well either, the light show, the crush. We didn't know anything was wrong at first, but all of a sudden he was standing next to us, like this.' She raised her arm in the air and pulled an imaginary trigger.

'So he was shooting at the ceiling?' asked the Spouse. 'At the ceiling? Not at people?'

'Yes, in the air, and Jem said something to him, Jem said something, I couldn't hear what he said, and next thing I knew . . .' She burst into tears again.

136

'Jem got it between the eyes?'

'But what did Jem say?' the Mother cried. She clenched her hands together.

'I couldn't hear it!'

Superwoman got up from her stool. Calmly she said, 'The music was loud. You know how it is, in a club.'

'No we don't know!' said the Spouse. 'God Almighty! And what's the story, anyway? Don't they check for weapons at the door?'

'There's no anticipating an event like this one, Mr Vermeer.'

'No, you'd rather be handing out parking tickets, wouldn't you!'

Superwoman sent the Mother a meaningful glance: if your husband keeps this up, we'll have to end this conversation.

But she was barking up the wrong tree in appealing to the Mother. As far as she was concerned, every word the Spouse uttered was true, relevant and carefully chosen. She grabbed his sleeve. He was her champion. She felt his hand slide round hers, as feverish as a glowing ember. Strengthened by this, she said, 'Something like this doesn't just happen out of the blue, surely? You can see it coming, can't you?'

The Witness jumped up so abruptly that the blanket fell from her shoulders and her bloodstained dress was revealed. 'We were just dancing, nothing was going on, nobody was fighting or anything, it was—'

'So tell me,' said the Mother, 'why was it so important to drag Jem to a club?'

'I propose,' said Superwoman, getting to her feet, 'that we leave it at that.'

'He asked me!' screamed the Witness, her head jutting forward.

Her father, behind her, grabbed her round the waist and pulled her close. 'We're going. Come on, darling, we're going home.'

The hatred that welled up in the Mother was so intense that she felt her hair and nails shrivel up; *her* arms would remain empty, *she* would be going home without a child.

The Spouse shouted, 'You'll be hearing from our lawyer!'

Superwoman shut the door behind the Witness and her father. Her eyes were fixed on the floor. 'Do you have any more questions?'

The Mother couldn't think of anything to say for a long time.

The Spouse finally remarked, as if a completely new thought had just occurred to him, 'And the culprit? You have caught the culprit, haven't you?'

'We are looking for him now. Dozens of witnesses saw him. He got away in all the confusion, but rest assured we will have him in custody within the next twenty-four hours.'

The Spouse kicked at a chair.

'You may want to get some counselling from social services,' said Superwoman. 'And would you like to be driven home, or would you rather make your own way?'

'We'll walk,' said the Mother, snatching at a last hope, that by leaving this place she might cancel out everything that had happened.

They walked back through the labyrinth. It was quieter in the corridors than before, as if all the people behind the closed doors fell silent as they passed by.

There was no sound of voices or footsteps. A young officer sat dozing behind the counter in the front hall.

Outside, it was even quieter. The trams and cars had long stopped running. The Spouse said, 'It's safest in town after four a.m. That's what Jem told me.'

The Mother asked herself how her son had known that, and what other notions he'd had which she would now never get to hear about. She took a deep breath to ward off a dizzy spell. You could smell the approaching autumn, the very first season that would now have to manage without Jem, without his hollowed-out pumpkins, his pockets filled with chestnuts, his mushroom obsession. How were the trees supposed to know it was time to let go of their leaves, now that he wasn't there with his red cheeks to rake them up? How would the hedgehogs know it was time to hibernate?

Behind her she heard the Spouse keening softly to himself. But she had no room for his grief, she was crammed up to here with her own. She rushed on blindly. She was trying as hard as she could to walk away from this terrible moment, to leave it behind, but it was wrapped round her ankle like a stubborn piece of elastic and she was dragging it along, all the way home, where Jem's baseball cap hung on the coat rack, next to his Salty Dog jacket with the broken zipper which she had promised to replace weeks ago.

And from that moment on, the minutes stopped being minutes, they lasted for centuries, and because of that, an hour now covered a time span that was longer than the entire history of the world. The only thing you could concentrate on was getting through the seconds, those tedious, sluggish moments which time doled out

139

once every so many years. Once you had completed one second, you'd start grimly on the next. The hands of the clock were the bars of your prison cell. They gave you no chance to escape. The things that were unbearable would therefore remain so for ever, for how could time heal anything if time itself was sabotaging the whole affair?

Franka's women friends came and paid their respects with their casseroles. With strained faces they, too, waded through the syrupy sea of senseless time, while seeing to the countless futile transactions that life does, after all, insist on. Pooling their strength, they just about kept the world turning.

The Spouse meanwhile was on a mission of his own. He threw himself into the hunt for the gunman. He went to the club, he interrogated the staff, he posted himself at the door and until late at night he waylaid everyone trying to enter with the question, had they been present at the shooting? He took down names and phone numbers and spent hours at the police station, where he raged at the detectives.

'It gives him something to do,' said the friends indulgently. 'Just let him be.'

She, however, thought he ought to have something else to do. He ought to be with her and do his mourning here, at home, with her, at the very bottom of stagnant time. He ought to be helping her keep the memory of Jem alive. Jem, whose undamaged face she was having a hard time recollecting. Who or what the perpetrator was left her as cold as Siberia. Knowing wouldn't revoke Jem's death, no matter what.

On the morning of the third day, the doorbell rang. She was home alone. She had been on the point of pouring herself a cup of tea from the pot which considerate hands had prepared for her. Absent-mindedly holding the empty cup in her hand, she went to the front door.

On the front step was Sanne, in jeans and a bright blue sweater, pale, white-lipped, which made her hair flame twice as red. She asked, uncertainly, 'Is this a good time?'

Franka wanted to say, how could you even think you'd ever be welcome here, child? but she was too astonished to do so.

When there was no answer forthcoming, the girl bit her lower lip. She said, 'I couldn't stand it at home any more. Really! They keep trying to cheer me up and I got a new bike.' She nodded at the bicycle on the front path.

'I see,' said Franka, for want of something better to say.

'They keep saying, they say' – tears welled up in her eyes – 'that I should try and forget as quickly as possible.' Testily she wiped her cheeks.

'That isn't very good advice,' said Franka slowly.

'No, it isn't. That's why I decided I'd just come and spend an hour or so with you.'

'An hour?'

'Yes, if that's all right.' She sniffed.

Franka stiffly stepped aside, waving her teacup to motion the girl inside.

In the living room they sat down across from each other at the dining table. 'What a lot of flowers,' remarked the girl shyly.

'Do we really have to talk?' asked Franka.

Startled, Sanne shook her head. She sat there look-ing helpless. After a little while she whispered, 'Maybe we could look at some pictures.' Her eyes filled up again. 'Jem said you kept two photo albums, one for yourself and one for him, for when he leaves home. So that he could take the whole of his old life with him.'

'That's right, I always had everything printed double,' said Franka, without thinking. She finally put the cup down on the table.

'If you have any spare pictures, then I wouldn't mind if, then I'd . . .'

'How long has this been going on, anyway, between Jem and you?'

'Five weeks.' A faint flush appeared on her cheeks. She stared straight ahead. 'But you wish he hadn't fallen in love with me, right? 'Cause now you keep wondering, why is *she* still alive and he isn't.'

This last point was a whole new way of looking at the situation. 'Is that what your parents say?'

'Yes, because your husband and you were so mad at me.'

A shadow of her former self, Franka said, 'Well, in that case you have certainly ventured into the lion's den.' She took the teapot and filled her cup. Then she said, with great self-control, 'I'll go and get Jem's scrapbook.' No one else had suggested going over Jem's history with her yet.

His photo album was lying in the drawer, on top of hers. She had never known Jem to show the slightest interest in it. But, when time had still been on her side, she'd often thought to herself, just you wait, later, later you'll thank me. Here you are walking with Mummy in the park; you had to hold on to your pushchair. And in that one, you're wearing the tiara you bought with Phinus. And look at this, Jem, look: it was your seventh birthday, and we gave you seven mice, white ones with little red eyes, Phinus had written numbers on their backs with a felt tip pen, they were all males, on purpose of course, but you kept hoping for babies ... The things we do to our children, for their own good, but especially for ours, let's not forget that. We fool and we cheat them without batting an eye or even blushing. As it happened, those mice lived quite a long time. When the last one turned bald around his snout and began biting his own tail out of sheer loneliness, Phinus had suggested taking it to the vet. 'That way we'll just let him quietly go to sleep, see.' Jem had been in tears as he said his goodbyes. But on the way to the vet's, Phinus had, as he confessed to Franka later, suddenly felt himself to be an awfully big man with an awfully small mouse. He had accordingly taken matters into his own hands, and had crushed the decrepit rodent under his heel on the grass.

'This is Jem on his seventh birthday,' she said. She placed the open album in front of the girl.

'Oh, he had glasses even back then!' Perking up a little, she rubbed a thumb over the photo. Then she slowly turned the page.

Franka looked on, over her shoulder. For the first time, a kind of peace came over her. Here, at last, was a moment she didn't have to try her hardest to ditch, here time could stand still for as long as it wanted, here, where Jem was playing with his tortoise, where Jem was lying on his stomach beside a canal edged with flowering cow parsley, Jem on a small, squat pony at Slagharen Amusement Park, Jem for ever seven years old. At that age your child still belonged to you and you alone. Later on you had to share him with the rest of the world. That just couldn't be helped.

Sanne asked shakily, 'Do you have a tissue?'

Franka walked to the kitchen and tore off a piece of paper kitchen roll. Pensively she folded it in half. She went back to the living room and said, 'To get back to what you were saying, Sanne, you mustn't think we're blaming you. It may have seemed that way, last time, but at that point we were utterly beside ourselves.'

Sanne swallowed. With difficulty, she said, 'But it is true that I . . . that I . . .' She pushed her chair back, and stood up. In the middle of the room she turned her back on Franka and wiggled her behind, one arm up in the air. 'Look at, look, this is the way we were dancing. And then, I don't know why, really I don't, then I turned round, and that's how Jem and I suddenly changed places.' She turned back, her arm still over her head. Tears were beginning to stream down her cheeks. 'And at that moment, I suppose, he saw the boy with the gun. If we hadn't changed places, then it would have been me seeing that bloke. And then it would have been me telling him, hey, man, hey . . . And then Jem would still be here.'

'Oh, stop it, for crying out loud,' said Franka. 'It's not as if that's going to help anyone. Blow your nose.'

Sanne blew her nose into the piece of kitchen roll. 'I didn't dare tell anyone,' she said.

'You can hardly dance without turning round occasionally. Nobody can blame you for that.' The fact that a random move should have sealed Jem's fate was pretty hard to digest. But hadn't the entire situation been due to a freak stroke of bad luck? At that thought, she had to brace herself for a new wave of horror. It felt as if she were being hammered by pounding fists. She thought to herself, I can't keep this up, I can't keep it up.

She let herself fall heavily onto her chair and buried

her head in both hands. If only she had been allowed to have him here with her, at home. If only she could have calmly sat with him, the way she used to sit by his cradle, then it might have been just a fraction easier to bear. She could still have done all kinds of little things for him. Press coins for the ferryman into his palm, smooth his hair down, adjust his shirt, put a shell from his collection beside him, turn the refrigeration coil beneath the casket on or off. She'd have been his mother for just a little while longer. But when a crime has been committed, the police keep the body for five days. The body, she thought. The body! Her son had been reduced to a stiff bundle of tissue. They had robbed him of his dreams and ambitions, his predilection for comics and his inability to throw out his old Disney videos, his habit of leaving scribbled notes on the fridge door, his customary, unique Jemness. What would she have done with a body, anyway? Held it on her lap, in a pietà pose? Maybe it really was better off in that cold vault than in here. Out loud she said, 'I just don't know any more.'

'I'd so very much like to organize a silent vigil.' Sanne looked at her expectantly. 'Shall we go to the club and ask if they'll help?'

It was a question coming from some other dimension, she had no idea what the girl was talking about. Bewildered, Franka rubbed her temples.

'To commemorate him,' Sanne clarified.

To her astonishment, Franka found herself outdoors a short while later, crossing canals and city squares, with Sanne sprinting impatiently ahead of her. It was a lovely morning. Soft autumn light enveloped them, the temperature was pleasant, the flower stalls were doing a good business.

'Wait a minute,' she said, stopping before a display of blooms, growth, life. Without knowing quite what she was doing, she picked up a large pot of purple asters. Actually, pansies had been his favourite flowers, 'they're just like Chinese children's faces'. Well, he shouldn't have died in the autumn, then. Stupid boy! Silly yob! Why did you have to go clubbing? You could have stayed at home! With me! We wouldn't have sat around yawning over some dull game of Scrabble, believe me. We'd have installed ourselves on the sofa with a bowl of crisps between us, you with your head pointing north, me with mine pointing south, doing lame imitations of the commercials while waiting for the late movie to start.

'Or else that one.' Sanne pointed at a chrysanthemum.

'Excuse me?'

'Well, you know, that one's Jem all over.'

Shaken, she paid for the plant. How much could you get to know about someone in five weeks? What had they talked about, those two — and what had they done together? She thought to herself, I should have paid more attention, I never noticed anything was up with him. It had been a busy time for her at work. Come to think of it, maybe Jem *had* dawdled around her with a face that indicated he wanted to tell her something a couple of times. Mum, I'm going out with someone. Listen, Franka, I'm in love. But she'd been too preoccupied with other things. And besides, hadn't she decided that he wasn't ready yet for girls? Or the other way round: had she decided that girls his age had no use for a shy beanpole who'd only just had his braces off? 'Jem's a late bloomer,' Phinus always said.

She plodded along behind Sanne without knowing where she was. At last she found herself in a square, standing in front of a building daubed with riotous graffiti. Through this door Jem had gone to meet his death. Unsuspectingly, he had crossed the threshold, thrilled in his own calm way at the prospect of a night out.

'You know,' said Sanne, 'he had this big grin on his face when we switched places when we were dancing. He was just, he was just – *happy*, you know?' She pronounced the word as if she had just invented it, and could hardly comprehend how she could possibly have come up with such a fitting term.

It's because he was with you, my girl, thought Franka, but articulating that thought required more magnanimity than she could manage just then.

'Do you know why he was so pleased? Because he couldn't believe you'd said I could stay the night.'

'I'd rather you did it under a familiar roof than in a doorway somewhere.' She said it as if she was addressing one of her clients. But . . . actually, hadn't her suggestion that Sanne could sleep over been made quite thoughtlessly, out of motherly habit or, rather, with the deliberate calculation of a mother who never lets a chance go by to invite her kid's pals to stay the night, so that he might consider himself popular?

'He'd already bought condoms, in the loo here, and put them in my bag.'

'Sanne,' she said, 'that's none of my business.' She couldn't by any stretch of the imagination picture Jem in front of a condom dispenser.

'Oh, if only we'd gone home sooner!' Sanne exclaimed.

'Yes.' And then the next morning, she'd have heated up two croissants for them, no doubt, and made orange juice, and innocently chatted about this and that, not suspecting for a minute that a momentous milestone in Jem's life had just been passed. Or would she have noticed something different about him after all? She squatted down, with the chrysanthemum. With a lump in her throat she said, 'For my big boy Jem,' and set the pot down by the doorpost, up against the defaced wall.

To her alarm, Phinus nearly exploded. A horde of halfwits waving candles and white roses singing 'Bridge Over Troubled Water' with their arms round each other, declaiming poems by Toon Hermans with tearful faces: that was definitely the last thing either of them needed right now. That kind of uncalled-for outpouring of sympathy from hysterical strangers — it wouldn't happen. Ever. Over his dead body.

'I think Jem might have liked it, though,' she said uncertainly. 'After all, it would also be an anti-violence demonstration.' They were standing side by side in Jem's room, with the huge poster of the Red Hot Chili Peppers on the wall and the chart of the solar system. On the floor was a Star Wars kit and a piece of bent wire whose function nobody would now ever be able to figure out. They were standing in front of the open wardrobe, incapable of choosing the clothes the undertaker had asked for.

'You ought to have your head examined,' said Phinus. 'Never in his life would Jem have wanted that kind of attention. Not from a pack of sensation seekers, that's for sure.' He picked up a shirt that had fallen off a hanger and hung it up again.

The question of who had known Jem best had never before presented itself. Phinus and she had always agreed on all the big as well as the little decisions concerning his upbringing. Bedtime, choice of school, punishments: they had always arrived at the same place effortlessly. It dismayed her, to think that his death would now mean the end of that accord. As if, for all that time, it had only been Jem's accommodating nature that had made it so easy for them. 'Oh, look at that,' she said, to mollify him, 'the thing you made for him, for St Nicholas.' She pointed at the papier-mâché seal in the corner, all dusty and dented. 'It was such a good idea of yours, to use ping-pong balls for the eyes. There's a reason Jem kept it all this time.'

'It's over.' Phinus grabbed a pair of trousers from a pile in the wardrobe, and immediately put them back again. 'We are going to put him in the ground properly, without any hoopla or cameras.'

She bent down to pick up a sweater from the floor. She pushed her nose into it. Jem's smell. You'd think, wouldn't you, that the dead would be pleased to know they were being mourned by an entire community? And wouldn't a deluge of tears, shed by strangers, launch the departed straight up to heaven? Surely all that grief would move the Almighty; surely He would open His arms wide to someone who had touched so many hearts. Jem's entire future in the hereafter was at stake. 'I want it,' she said. 'Jem was worth it.'

'You're going to regret it. Regret it terribly.' He pulled out a pile of T-shirts and proceeded to smooth them flat one by one, then fold them.

'We don't have enough tears by ourselves, Phinus.' Her heart was palpitating painfully. It was dangling, horrified, from a parachute that refused to open. She tried to convince herself, this is Phinus. He's the one who has always, always, been on my side, who has always wanted the best for me, who has been unconditionally there for me, to the point of absurdity.

149

Or . . . or was she simply too tired and too drained for a fight? 'I don't think I want us to quarrel about Jem's funeral,' she said shrilly.

The hostility only barely faded from his face, he said, after a short pause, 'No, you're quite right there.' He was done with the T-shirts. Next he started on the gaudy collection of socks and underwear.

'What the hell are you fussing with his stuff for like a maniac?' she yelled. 'There's no need to tidy up in here any more, is there! All we have to do is choose the clothes in which he's going to disappear so properly in that casket of yours!'

Phinus rolled a pair of socks into a ball and tidied it away in the wardrobe. 'If you're going to get all emotional, I'm not staying around to listen.'

'Me, emotional? And what about you, then? You're shaking with rage! Isn't that an emotion?'

'You allow yourself to be ruled by your emotions, whereas I—'

'And besides, don't I have a say in how we say good-bye to Jem?'

'Whereas I stick to the facts. Jem didn't just die, he was murdered! OK? Do you follow me? Murdered by some uncivilized brute! Who can't be found! The police are incompetent baboons! *That* is what it's about! And as long as the murderer's still on the loose, we are not going to whoop it up with a . . . with a . . .' he spat the words out with distaste, 'with a *silent vigil*! We have to establish our priorities! That piece of shit deserves to be locked up for life!'

She thought the wiring in her head would short-circuit, that's how overwhelming it was, her inability to make him see what she meant. She desperately wanted to be left in peace, to be left alone with her pain. To sit quietly and breathe, her hands resting on her abdomen. She stared glassily at the socks that Phinus was now sorting by colour. She remembered traipsing, pregnant, through the Hema department store fifteen years ago. She had bought nothing for Jem's layette except some little socks. The loss of Jem's father had so shattered her that nappies and dummies were completely beyond her. She purchased nothing but socks, sometimes as many as ten or twelve pairs at once. One time, in an attempt to seem somewhat normal, she told the saleswoman she was expecting twins.

A troubling thought occurred to her: if only she'd done a better job of preparing for Jem's arrival on earth back then. If only she had marked his rightful place among mankind more clearly, with flannel baby-grows, a supply of baby oil and talcum powder, rattles, sleepsuits, plastic pants and a rubber dolphin for the bath. She had neglected to announce that he belonged here, right here with her, and not there, wherever and whatever 'there' might be, the 'there' where you waited before living and after dying. Out there they may have been thinking, she isn't making him very welcome. During all the time that Jem was with her, they may have been keeping their invisible tentacles stretched out towards him protectively, ready to take him back at the first sign of incompetence on her part. 'Mum, I'm going out with someone.'

The next morning they buried Jem, in a tight circle. No one waved roses or launched into 'Bridge Over Troubled Water'. Friends and relatives, not yet over the shock, stood wordlessly around the grave, hugging themselves. Their wretchedness was more comforting than any stammered word would have been.

Sanne and her parents stayed at a respectful distance.

And only the little girl from next door, of the diary, had brought a white balloon.

Franka had wanted to lower the casket into the grave herself. But when the time came, as she stood there next to the undertakers, holding the rope, she simply didn't know how she could manage this task. ('We'll be counting slowly to ten, Mrs Vermeer, and at each count you'll let out the rope a little, hand over hand.') She waited for Phinus's hand on her back, to give her strength in this ordeal. His support, however, was not forthcoming.

And after that she gave herself over to mourning and, no longer able to sleep, came to know the night. The night that was without mercy, without comfort or security, just like the black hole of eternity into which the dead disappear. Week after week she sat alone in the dark. All right, she had wished for nothing more fervently than to be left alone. But it still upset her. Once or twice, when his expression happened to be a little less forbidding, she tried to share with Phinus what was going on with her. Did any of it get through to him? He could look at her as if her inner life meant nothing to him, absolutely nothing. As if it didn't even exist, and perhaps it was indeed so, now that her deepest thoughts were no longer heard or shared. Increasingly she had the sinking feeling that she was nothing but an empty shell.

He had just switched her off, like a radio. And in every shrug and brush-off, each evasive glance, she could see that he would do his utmost to muzzle the voice of her grief. He would turn a deaf ear to her, and as long as he managed to do so, she was condemned to muteness. Nothing would ever be heard from her again.

What incited the culprit

Two days after the funeral, the culprit was caught. He was sixteen-year-old Marius H., from Aerdenhout. Nothing in his past history or personality could serve to explain the tragedy he had caused, let alone to excuse it: father, accountant; mother, gardener and interior design consultant to her circle of friends; a younger sister who loved Marius at least as much as her pony; acceptable, average grades, the best batsman on his cricket team; lover of orchestrated Beatles arrangements ever since his girlfriend Joyce had introduced him to 'I Am The Walrus' with violins in the background; proud owner of a mountain bike; possessed, furthermore, of the engaging habit of sending both his grandmothers a Valentine's Day card; objector to dog dirt on the pavement; gifted editor of the school newspaper.

His lawyer (with the advent of the Culprit, an entirely new team of players made their entrance, such as Lawyers, Court-Appointed Psychiatrists, Prosecutors and, let's not forget, Journalists) was to refer often in court to his client's stable, respectable background. The Lawyer had a thankless job ahead of him. The only thing he had going for him was Marius H.'s blank police record, his age, and the fact that he was blessed with everything necessary to develop into a model citizen, the incident in question notwithstanding; the chances of his re-offending were less than nil. The Culprit was neither deranged nor a psychopath, the Court-Appointed Psychiatrist would attest to that. Marius H. had not been out to make trouble that fateful night. He didn't have a motive. He had tossed down twenty beers, that was all, because his cricket team had suffered a humiliating defeat that afternoon and it had been his fault. The weapon he unfortunately happened to have on his person was a 9mm pistol of Belgian origin. Earlier that evening, a teammate – whose father was a collector of antique and not-so-antique weapons – had lent it to him for some tin-can target practice that weekend.

Why he had taken it out of his pocket in the disco and fired a few rounds in the air, Marius didn't exactly know. After twenty glasses of beer, amnesia is not all that unheard of. At that moment, he didn't even remember which of the opposing team's bowlers had taken his wicket, and so he certainly didn't know what had been going through his head when one of the clubbers, some tall, skinny kid with glasses, had lunged at the hand holding the pistol and yelled at him something along the lines of, 'Hey, man, what are you doing?' He could only make a wild guess. He'd been pissed off enough over losing the match in the first place, and then on top of that some prick was bugging him and trying to stop him from unwinding a little. It simply hadn't been a good moment to mess with him.

The newspapers discovered 'a new dimension to the concept of senseless violence'. On television, deeply concerned Experts deplored the younger generation's declining tolerance for frustration; others were questioned about the rise in juvenile alcohol consumption. And somewhere in the eye of this storm hovered the Victim: robbed of his life because the Culprit couldn't stomach losing some game. It was just too painful and too absurd to think about.

The Victim hadn't even done anything heroic.

He hadn't had the chance.

Just think if it had been your own child: dying for no reason, just pure bad luck.

The Prosecutor had, during the preliminary investigation, tried to prepare the Spouse for all of this. But how could Phinus have anticipated the impact of the publicity, or the indignation of the media, which, like running water, always tends to seek the lowest level? To him, the fact that the shooting was almost immediately termed a 'sheer fluke' added insult to the injury, it was an extra violation, an extra desecration of Jem. Every other death had a reason, a cause, a background, lending it a certain dignity. But Jem had been shot 'just like that'; it could have happened to anyone, in other words. Didn't that make him, somewhat disparagingly, more or less a minor player in the whole drama?

The Prosecutor did what she could to give the Spouse the opportunity to let off steam. She was always available for him, patiently talked things over with him, and referred to the Victim as 'Jem'. She listened to Phinus's tirades. She answered his questions. In short, she acquitted herself in an exemplary manner. But she was nevertheless, time and again, the bearer of tidings he couldn't stand to hear.

'Mr Vermeer,' she said for instance, as briskly as she could, 'as far as the sentence goes, you will have to prepare yourself for the likelihood that opposing counsel will plead the defendant's age as an extenuating circumstance. The maximum sentence for juvenile offenders is twenty-four months.'

'You've got to be joking! *Two* years?'

'On the other hand, I will set against that the enormity of the crime. An adult felony has been committed, which calls for a commensurate punishment. Hopefully the court will be receptive to that argument. Nor will the fact that alcohol was involved be considered a mitigating factor: a sixteen-year-old is considered old enough to be responsible for his actions, including his state of inebriation. Moreover, carrying a gun is against the law.'

'He'll get life, surely?'

'Not for manslaughter. We had better count on—'

'Wait a minute, wait a minute! Because it happened to Jem by a *sheer fluke*' – the words stuck in his craw – 'it isn't murder?'

'The law does make that distinction, whether we like it or not. There was no question of premeditation here. The most we can count on is four to six years. Less time served, of course. And I'm afraid I must also point out to you that here in the Netherlands it is standard practice to be granted parole upon completion of two-thirds of one's sentence. I am sorry.'

When Phinus left the Prosecutor's office, he felt

hollow, crushed. He couldn't reverse the damage the deadly bullets had done, but surely some influence could be brought to bear upon the course of justice? In the car park he sat in his car, his head resting on the steering wheel. *A letter to the Queen. To the Prime Minister. Those people had children themselves.* They would consider it less devastating for Phinus, because he was only the stepfather. Franka would have to write those letters.

He drove home so fast that he was trapped by the flash of a speed camera. Red lights, amber lights, clanging signals at railway crossings . . . *Shut your eyes, Jem, quick, we're in a hurry.* Jem in the back seat, and later up front next to him, getting picked up, being dropped off, something he'd made at school clenched in his little fists, his Sesame Street backpack full of uneaten apples, and, later, long animated tales about the sperm whale (not to be confused with the orca), questions about the properties of the Magdeburg hemispheres and opinions about television programmes. All those little moments that never got the attention they deserved, because you thought they were infinite in number, and would always be. All the irritations too — *Wipe your feet before you get in the car!* or *Keep your hands off those dials, I was trying to listen to the news!* — even the aggravations had been essential. Because every one of those moments had added a fresh strand to the fabric of their joint history. A fabric which, over the years, had wrapped itself round Phinus, a space-suit that had made it possible for him to remain inside Jem's orbit.

He opened the sun roof, it was so suffocating in there.

Finally he arrived at the house where Franka, Jem

158

and he had lived together for such a short time, really.

'Franka!' he shouted, shrugging his jacket off in the hall with the cracked floor tiles.

She emerged from the kitchen. She was wearing a tracksuit. Her unwashed hair framed her grubby face in matted tangles. Her skin was greasy. She was holding a tea towel in her hand.

'There's work to be done, darling,' he said, grabbing her by the upper arms. She looked so distracted that he had to suppress the urge to shake her. Putting emphasis on every word, he began explaining his plan to her, trembling with the desire to get started. While the words were still tumbling out, he was already turning on his laptop in his mind. At last, something concrete to do.

'I don't understand,' was the only thing she said when he was done.

'Then listen to me! We have the law against us, so we'll have to come up with some other—'

'But surely we're not going to get Jem back that way.'

'No, we won't get Jem back that way, oh no. Goodness me. You're right about that. You've hit it right on the nose, in fact. By God, what was I talking about?'

'I mean . . .' She brought a hand up to her forehead. 'Couldn't you be a little less aggressive? I mean that I don't understand why we can't be satisfied with the usual sentence. What are you really after? Do you want to deprive that boy of the rest of *his* life as well?'

He tried to catch his breath. 'And why not?'

'Because you won't get Jem back that way. So what's it to you?' She shrugged, dropped the tea towel on the floor and walked into the living room.

He was still standing by the coat rack. He stood

159

there for almost a full minute, incapable of moving, feeling he was about to implode. Then he followed her, first stooping to pick up the tea towel. 'Are you on Valium or something?'

She was sitting on the sofa, bent forward, the sleeves of the grubby tracksuit pulled down over her hands. She was surrounded by old newspapers, dirty coffee cups, a pizza box, clothes left lying around. Tears were streaming down her cheeks.

'I asked you a question, Franka.'

'I have one for you, too. Why do you want to see that boy hang? What's the point, Phinus, what's the point of it, what's the point?' She was crying so hard now that her whole face was contorted. It was a terrible sight, that sudden splitting asunder of the map of her face, a territory he'd thought he knew like the back of his hand. '*Another* life down the drain! Isn't it enough for you that he'll be locked up for four years? Isn't four years an eternity when you're sixteen years old? Jem considered even twenty-year-olds ancient!'

With as much self-control as he could muster, he said, 'So I take it you don't agree?'

'No, and I don't want you to do anything! I let you have your way about that silent vigil, and now you've got to let me have mine. That boy will have to find a way to live with this from here on in, with every breath he takes. He has given himself a life sentence. There's no need for us to interfere. And we don't have to pile any more on, either. Think of his parents!'

'Oh, right! As if we even know those people!'

'This is about the life of their child, Phinus! Can't you put yourself in their shoes?'

'Well, well,' he said slowly. That certainly let the cat out of the bag, and most unexpectedly and nastily too.

In pretending to appeal to his compassion, she was really having a dig at him: how would *you* know what this kind of thing means for a parent? This falls totally outside of your field of expertise, you fool!

He spun round on his heel. He walked out of the room. He grabbed his jacket from the coat rack. He went outside. He got into the car, its cooling motor still ticking softly. Just a while ago, when he had shut the door of the Public Prosecutor's office, he'd thought, it can't get any worse than this. But he had been wrong about that.

Half an hour later he found himself on the outskirts of Aerdenhout. On a whim, he turned off the highway and drove into the leafy suburb. Here lived the rich folk of the Netherlands, inside monstrous piles, behind tall gates with electronic surveillance. Deep in grim thought, he drove for a while down the elegant lanes. Then parked somewhere at random and got out. It was already October, but it was as if the happy scent of fresh-mown grass still hung in the air around here, as did the hissing sound of sprinkler systems and the thumping of tennis balls on a court hidden behind one of the houses. But if you were a small, gutsy conservationist and you arrived in this neighbourhood hoping to sell door-to-door the biscuits you'd baked with your dad to save the crested lark, then you'd be in for a disappointment: the houses were spaced miles apart, their driveways of spotless white gravel were endless, and, by the sound of it, every property had a watchful guard dog.

There was nobody out on the street. It was as if all Aerdenhout were hiding in shame indoors, every resident stiff with dismay, suddenly made painfully conscious of what happens if you raise your children to be spoilt brats. Compelled to skulk for months behind drawn curtains, when you could be sitting on your own terrace, under your own hemlocks, in your own wicker chair with a glass in your hand, relaxing and enjoying the year's unusually mild autumn evenings. Would the citizens of this privileged community still have the nerve to invite guests for the upcoming Christmas holidays? Would they venture outside on New Year's Eve to set off fireworks? Or didn't they care what the world thought of them? Were they simply continuing to fork out enough pocket money for their kids to get stoned during every free period at school, and to hang out pissed in clubs every weekend while sending text messages on their Nokia mobiles to their mates, whom later in the evening they'd challenge to a bout of Unreal Tournament, or Half Life, or some other video game revolving solely around killing everyone they can? With a Davidoff dangling from their lips, a Saab convertible already parked in the driveway at home in anticipation of their eighteenth birthday, and a good story or two about how they mashed some first-year nerd's sprout sand-wich into his face: you casually jostle him with your shoulder, see, and next thing he knows, the prole can't see a thing because of all the mayonnaise smeared on his glasses.

Mrs Vermeer must really have wanted to take him down a peg or two, so much so, in fact, that she'd had to swallow her usual loathing of snobbery and uppity bullshit. That certainly proved something. He pounded his fists feebly on the bonnet of his car. *You have a talk with him, Phinus. I can tell from the state of his sheets that it's high time for that man-to-man talk.* He had always lovingly, and to the very best of his ability, taken those things upon himself, he had put his heart and soul into it. Just as if Jem had been his own flesh and blood. And now, suddenly, Jem was simply the child that wasn't his.

Shit, shit and super shit, Jem would have shrugged with annoyance at this point: what a hopeless pain in the neck that man is. I don't know anyone who gets offended so easily, who is so quick to feel rejected and insulted. With Dad, every trivial little thing is immediately A BETRAYAL.

Yeah, Dad, don't deny it! Or I'll tell them the story of the time that . . .

All right then, here goes. See, my father is a man who knows everything there is to know about baking and roasting. Who for breakfast can get a bacon rasher to come out so crisp that it makes Mum groan with pleasure. Who can roll perfect meatballs even with a phone cradled to his ear, while ranting on about reversed logos on the packaging of some game. At the word 'Christmas', the first thought that will flash through his brain is the magnificent joint in the oven that has to be basted every twenty minutes. He gives his butcher a run for his money. Dad always knows best, and is more than happy to provide information, both profuse and unsolicited, on how Scottish beef gets to be so tender, or the Phoenicians' method of preparing lamb's liver sausage.

From the time human beings left the trees and began standing upright, my father always says, it was the fittest of the species who supplied the tribe with food. Even back in prehistoric days they understood what was most important in life, its very point, in fact, i.e., to cudgel a wild boar to death, bleed it, stuff an apple in its mouth and then, after a few hours on the spit with some *herbes de Provence*, to serve it to one's hungry loved ones. My dad considers himself quite capable, if ever the occasion should arise, of felling a boar with his bare hands and preparing it for the barbecue. And so the shit really hit the fan when one day I left food on my plate.

'What's the matter with you?' asked Phinus.

'Not hungry any more,' said Jem neutrally, pushing what was left of his meal away from him.

'Oh, pass it over here, then,' said Franka. 'I always have room for more of Phinus's steak tartare.' She reached for his plate, unconcerned.

'You don't know what you're missing, Jem,' said Phinus, disappointed.

'It's simply out of this world,' said Franka with her mouth full.

His heart melted, and he let it go.

But the next day Jem again finished only half his plate.

'Doesn't it taste good?' asked Phinus. 'Or aren't you feeling well?' He scrutinized Jem closely. Hadn't there been an outbreak of glandular fever at his school? Or, wait a minute, anaemia, that could be it, these kids grew so fast. When had Jem last had anything wrong with him? He'd make sure to look it up this evening in the folder labelled 'Jem'. His inoculations, his measles, the dosage of his citrus allergy medication, his spectacles prescription. Record-keeping was safe-keeping. And safeguarding. Every time Phinus made some new entry in this dossier, he mentally addressed all of Jem's cells and blood vessels, urging them on to perfection.

On the third day, too, Jem left part of his meal untouched.

Phinus's concern was now mixed with irritation. 'I haven't been slaving away in the kitchen an hour for nothing, you know.'

'It's a free country,' said Jem.

Franka had to laugh.

'Yeah, Dad, don't you cook because you like to cook?'

'Oh, in which case a little appreciation isn't necessary, I suppose.'

'We do revere you greatly,' Franka remarked laconically, 'but Jem's right.'

'How many other families, do you think, are having such delicious braised veal for their supper tonight?'

'Dad,' said Jem, 'I've just turned vegetarian, that's all.' He said it nonchalantly, as if he saw nothing wrong with it. He was, it seemed, briefly deserted by that sixth sense which nature has so mercifully bestowed upon children, the sense which allows them to surmise from the mere raising of a parental eyebrow which way the mood will swing, the sensitivity that makes them able to put themselves in their parents' shoes at every turn, so that they may anticipate their parents' every move. When this crucial sense is missing, things often go wrong; after all, parents blindly trust that it will keep working without fail, in the interests of all concerned.

'Vegetarian?' demanded Phinus.

'It's preferable to anorexic, anyway,' said Franka. 'But in that case, will you please start eating more nuts and cheese, Jem? Or do you want Phinus to make those, what do you call them, those soya thingies for you?'

'Soya!' Phinus's voice rose. 'Meat is my forte! Even if I say so myself.'

'Meat is murder,' said Jem peaceably.

'Do you think' – seething, Phinus stuck his fork into the veal on Jem's plate – 'that this piece of meat gives a shit whether you eat it or not? Do you think the entire food-processing industry will go belly up as a result of your little whim?'

'But Phinus, don't you always buy your meat at the free-range butcher's?' asked Franka. 'Surely this isn't one of those penned-up calves packed with hormones?' She was peering mistrustfully at her plate.

'It's one hundred per cent organic!' He waved his fork in the air. 'So no one in this house has got the first reason to be a vegetarian.'

'It's up to everyone to decide for himself,' said Jem without getting excited.

'And what about hamburgers, then? You love them. Don't deny it.'

'I'm not doing it because I dislike it, Dad.'

'What about sausages on the grill? Aren't those delicious, or what?'

'It's about the principle,' said Jem with the insufferable self-righteousness of the idealist who gladly sacrifices himself to a nobler cause.

Phinus, however, had his own principles. And one of those held that the sacred business of cooking deserved some respect, as well as the grateful mastication of jaws. In other words, stabbing the cook through the heart would not go unpunished. So he dug in his heels and began a counter-offensive. He cooked and chopped until his hands were raw with blisters, and filled the house with tempting smells of superbly seared fillets of beef and his irresistible satay. All the food that Jem used to love was served. But Jem did not succumb.

'Maybe it's just a phase,' said Franka in bed, at night. 'It isn't the end of the world, in any case.'

'He needs his proteins. You said so yourself. He has to eat properly.' Phinus hadn't yet been able to bring himself to record in the folder that Jem had switched diets. Writing down those words implied something larger, something unmanageable, perhaps even something irreparable.

'We should have seen it coming, Phinus.' She let out a burp that reeked of browned butter. 'Oh, excuse me. It was obviously on the cards. You ought to be happy he didn't become a vegan. At least we can still get him to drink the odd glass of milk.'

'You always take his side,' said Phinus, rather unfairly, but he felt entitled, under the circumstances.

'We can't force him. And if you didn't have to make it into such a big thing, the atmosphere here at home would be so much more pleasant. Actually, I think it shows guts. Is it the fact that he's made this decision all by himself? Is that what's bothering you? Well? Say something!'

'It isn't what *I* think about it, it's what Jem's doing to himself.'

'The more you resist, the more obstinately he'll stick to his guns. It's called adolescence.' She gave him a peck on the cheek and rolled onto her side. She was wearing his favourite pyjamas, the light blue ones with the little white clouds, the pyjamas which made her look like a little girl in a safe, orderly world. What if Jem's behaviour ended up being contagious? He wouldn't put it past her, she might very well decide that meat was, ultimately, an unnecessary luxury. One moment you still had a happy family, one hundred per cent guaranteed; the next you were sitting in the

167

smouldering ruins. He would have to try and bring the adolescent to his knees.

But Jem had inherited Franka's imperturbable nature. He passed on the shish kebabs, the stuffed beef rolls, the Bolognese sauce, without giving them a second glance. Phinus's final defeat came on the afternoon he found Jem in the kitchen consulting a cookbook opened to a page of vegetarian recipes. 'Hey, Dad. I'm going to try making a lentil pâté,' he said cheerfully.

'I need all four burners,' snarled Phinus, immediately a nervous wreck at the prospect of someone poaching on his territory.

'Oh, no problem, this has to go in the oven.'

'But you're in my way.' As if they hadn't stood side by side at the counter hundreds of times in happier days, chopping and sifting in total harmony. Together in this kitchen they had baked unsurpassed crumpets, and in the winter they'd cooked up great pots of sauerkraut and pea soup. This was where, over the years, the most intimate exchanges had taken place as they waited for the dough to rise or for the sauce to reduce. Suddenly their shared territory had become a battlefield. And he was losing ground awfully fast.

'Why don't you just give it up?' he asked, slamming pans down on the stove at random. 'The minority has to give in to the majority. That's the way democracy works. Don't they teach you kids anything useful at school any more?'

Jem was weighing his lentils. 'There is such a thing as freedom of speech, isn't there? And freedom of belief?'

'Only for those who have reached the age of reason, smarty-pants. Until that time, your parents decide what's good for you.'

'You're not going to tell me that torturing and killing animals is a good thing, are you?'

It irritated Phinus no end to see the deft manner in which Jem stripped an onion of its skin. He should never have taught him to cook. Here he was, hoist with his own petard.

'Why don't you just say it? You don't think it's such a good thing either!' Jem sent him a defiant look.

'Whether something is good or bad depends, quite simply, on your point of view. You maintain that it's noble to be a vegetarian, I say it's just a great big hassle for us.'

'Yeah, but that's only because you're such a tyrant. If you'd just let me do my own thing . . .'

He had the sensation of collapsing, clicking shut like a telescope. 'Me, a tyrant? All I've done is cook delicious food for you as far back as you can remember. Day in, day out. I put my whole heart and soul into it. And you don't give a shit. It doesn't mean a thing to you. You're flinging everything I've done for you back in my face . . .'

'Oh, bullshit, man! I'm just not eating meat any more. That's all.'

A sobering silence fell between them.

'Face it, Dad. You're making an ass of yourself.'

Phinus picked up a paring knife and, in an attempt to recover his dignity, mechanically began peeling potatoes.

'Do you need this?' Jem was holding up a baking dish.

He shook his head.

Jem took out a bottle of olive oil and began greasing the pan. Under his partially rolled-up shirtsleeves, his wrists were bony, his hands large.

169

One minute they were standing next to you, at hip height, carefully pressing the pastry into the tin, after each step waiting for new instructions and another pat on the head, and the next thing you knew they were beanpoles nearly six feet tall, who reckoned they didn't need you any more.

'Here,' he said curtly, grabbing a leek. 'You'd better put some of this in it, otherwise that lentil thing of yours won't amount to much, I can tell you that right now.'

And later on he couldn't think back on this episode without cringing with shame and remorse. For this one example said it all, it told the entire story. He had ordered Jem to go clubbing that last night in exactly the same way . . . No, no, no! It was unbearable.

Forget it!

But forgetting is hard work. Infinitely more difficult than remembering. He soon noticed that it's almost as if some things absolutely refuse to be forgotten, resisting tooth and nail, with might and main. They don't understand why you'd want to get rid of them, they are as attached to you as your own shadow. With arms outstretched they wait for you, in the strangest of places and at the most inconvenient of times. They are implacably chummy: we belong together, their thinking goes . . . And not without reason.

He was sometimes afraid Franka suspected what was fermenting and rotting inside him. Because she never missed an opportunity, by means of subtle, vicious digs, to let him feel there was no place for him any longer in the parental arena. From that very first night at the police station, hadn't she disqualified him as a father? In this game, when it came right down to it, was there a role left for him to play at all?

* * *

The preliminary investigation lasted a good two months. Phinus produced reams of comments and objections to every document the Prosecutor was kind enough to send him. Just before the hearing, she invited him to her office to discuss whether he wished to avail himself of the right to claim damages. The funeral costs, she said, would, naturally, be borne by the H. family. That had been established in negotiations with opposing counsel.

But compensation on emotional grounds? Oh dear, Mr Vermeer, I do know how you must feel, but how can we ever put a monetary value on a human life?

He slunk out of the building, clutching his sweat-soaked jacket under his arm, too mortified for words: she had decided all he cared about was the money.

Back home, Franka was seated with quotations from stonemasons and nurseries spread out before her on the table. Her pencil scratched resolutely across the sheets. There was a little colour in her pallid cheeks. 'Marble, don't you think, but not too formal-looking?'

The evident pleasure she took in this morbid task appalled him. He sat down opposite her and pretended to look over the figures. 'Shouldn't you have made a decision by now? How much longer are you planning to be so involved with this?'

'There's no other way, Phinus, believe me. The ground has to settle first. With a grave it can take months before everything's finished. And if it freezes this winter, it'll take even longer.'

Except that, as it turned out, it didn't freeze all winter. The weather was to remain pleasant and mild, week after week. Everyone would be talking about how nature seemed to be out of sorts, somehow.

'Without Jem, winter doesn't know how to be winter,' Franka would repeat every morning over a cup of coffee reheated from the night before. And just before what turned out to be a far from white Christmas, Marius H. was sentenced to five years in prison for manslaughter.

The Prosecutor implored Phinus to be satisfied with the verdict. Nevertheless, he insisted on an appeal. The circumstances, he decided, justified it. There had to have been a gross miscarriage of justice, surely, for this terrible crime to result in such a light sentence.

For the next weeks, while waiting for the outcome of the appeal, he didn't do anything but pace up and down. Franka meantime sketched little designs for the ideal grave. Nobody cooked any more, no meals were served at the table. They just grabbed handfuls of corn-flakes straight from the box. Trails of these were strewn throughout the house. On the stairs, in the hall-way. Just as in the story of the little boy who has to find his own way home. All you have to do is whistle, Jem, then we'll know where you are.

It was so atrociously unreal, that he wasn't around any more. So unbelievable.

Every time a stair tread creaked somewhere in the house, or a door opened, or a floorboard squeaked, it felt as though it was Jem walking around up there, in his big shoes. But waiting behind every door was the shock of emptiness.

Phinus would leave the house for a breath of fresh air. Run a few errands. But in the supermarket his hand would automatically reach for Jem's soft drinks ('Coke in Bert and Pepsi in Ernie') and at the till, without six pints of milk or three loaves of bread, but only a meagre ounce of this or that in his trolley, he could see the check-out girl jumping to the conclusion: a bachelor living alone.

The appeal resulted in a three-year prison sentence for Marius H.

'This was precisely the outcome I tried to warn you about,' said the Prosecutor with an unhappy sigh in her handsomely panelled office. She might as well have said, 'What a stupid oaf you are, Phinus Vermeer.' Her face spoke volumes. Three years! Three years for one human life! *One* human life? Marius H. had not only robbed Jem of his life, he had destroyed the lives of Phinus and Franka as well, and he had left deep scars in the lives of many others. In Sanne's life, in the lives of Jem's friends, classmates, fellow animal-rights activists, dozens of relatives and countless acquaintances whose hearts went out to Jem and his parents.

And, as Franka would add at this point, 'Don't forget the kid's own parents.' Their hopes for Marius's future, all their plans for him: down the drain. Besides, as an accountant, how could you face your clients under such circumstances, or who, given what happened, would still feel the need for a *Lavatera* cutting or advice on the colour scheme for the new bathroom? And how could the boy's kid sister continue her riding lessons now that folk at the stables were openly pointing her out?

All those ruined lives! You could count them on your fingers, the ripple effects, circle upon concentric circle. Marius H.'s cricket coach, his teammates, the editorial members of the school newspaper, the friends he used to horse around with, mountain-biking in the dunes; they'd have to do without his company for years, and they'd never get back the old Marius they used to love.

And Mrs Jongeling the piano teacher, who had been so delighted with the lightness of his touch.

And the Herders family, seven in all, the next-door neighbours, where Marius had practically been one of the family, and where he had spent the night so often that the guest room was known as 'Marius's room'.

And Edith Elders, the godmother who had held him in her arms at the baptismal font, weeping, overcome with emotion, and who, ever since emigrating to Australia, sent him a present every year for his birthday, a plea, really, that Marius not forget that she was his godmother, which in Edith's life was just about her only claim to fame.

And both of his grannies, who wouldn't be receiving any more Valentine's Day cards to show off to their bridge partners as proof that they still mattered, and then some.

And, last but not least, Joyce, his girlfriend. Joyce put her young, musically gifted head in the oven when she heard that Marius H. would have to go to prison no matter what, thereby setting off a fresh chain reaction of unappeasable sorrow.

All in all, quite a score for someone who just got a little pissed off because he lost a cricket match.

The second verdict had given Phinus the feeling that it was just him now, him alone against the rest of the world. Every morning when he went to work, he had to make a conscious effort to square his shoulders before he could bring himself to open the front door, for on the other side the jungle was lying in wait for him.

Sitting at his desk at Jumbo, even the colourful eco-system of Electro, Mikado, Tic Tac Toe, Jumbolino and the Flying Hats felt threatening to him, and as he read the printer's proofs for the new catalogue, he broke out in a cold sweat. Game No. 559, for ages seven and up: 'Am I a banana? Or am I a washing machine? He who asks the most pertinent questions will be the first to discover what he's supposed to be.' Game No. 488, for all ages: 'Good-Times-Bad-Times Party Quiz, the game is won if you're having fun!' It all seemed so innocuous, but how was he to know what sort of felons or maniacs might some day take out their wallets in the shop to purchase them? What kind of murderer would be opening them on their birthday, or find them tucked into their shoe on St Nicholas's morning? Every draughtboard, every game of dominoes he shepherded to market had a good chance of falling into the wrong hands. They were walking around freely everywhere, those ostensibly upright citizens of all ages, those wolves in sheep's clothing who, even if they themselves hadn't gone as far as murdering some-one for no reason, were so depraved anyway that it was fine with them if someone else did. Why insist on stiffer criminal penalties, after all? That could as easily have been you, if you'd happened to have a gun or a knife on you. Might as well admit it: everyone's got to get it out of their system once in a while.

'Where in God's name *are* we, then?' he asked his secretary, in despair, when she came in to pick up the proofs.

Bewildered, she looked around: didn't he recognize his own office any more, with its view over one of Amsterdam's loveliest canals? 'On earth?' she tried, leaving it as vague as possible.

He took the rest of the day off, but where were you supposed to go if you lived on a planet where there was no redress to be had for your deeply injured sense of justice? And where were you supposed to go if you had let the one pathetic smidgen of satisfaction that could have been yours slip through your fingers? If you hadn't merely fucked up, but had managed to screw everything up twice as bad again? He drove home in a black funk.

As he walked in, Franka was just pulling on her coat in the hall. A smile of relief lit up her face. 'Oh, Phinus! I was afraid that . . . But luckily you didn't forget. I'm so glad I waited for you a little while longer. Was the traffic bad?'

He had to dredge the depths of his memory to understand what she was going on about. The stone! Today at two o'clock the stone was to be set on the grave. Weeks ago she had insisted that they should go there together and watch. He had intended to come home late, with some excuse about a marketing meeting that had run over, or a serious crisis in product development. How could his carefully planned strategy have slipped his mind so completely?

'Here, take your raincoat. They're forecasting a storm,' said Franka. 'Shall I drive? You must be tired.'

Her concern was the last straw. Wanly he leaned against the doorframe. 'I don't know how you can still stand me.'

'You know perfectly well I never took the slightest interest in that sentencing business, if that's what you mean. I wish you'd just stop going on about it. You're always agonizing about things that aren't worth the agony.'

'You think I'm a fool.'

'Well, yes, but not because you lost your case. You shouldn't have started on it in the first place, that's all. Anyway. Just let it go, I beg you, and start focusing on the things that really matter.'

And so, under a dark February sky, they drove together to the Zorgvlied Cemetery, charmingly situated on the banks of the Amstel. At the entrance he was once again struck by the peculiar opening hours: the cemetery closed at dusk, making it impossible in the wintertime for people with regular jobs to visit their loved ones during the week. But then, this kind of establishment was, after all, run by professionals. They must have their reasons for the policy. It was their way of ensuring that the departed ones would rest in peace for as much of the time as possible.

Only the stone, he decided, bucking up at the thought. That's all there is left. Just the stone, and then they'd have closure. It would wear off. They would get used to it. You could get used to anything. Finding some kind of distraction, that was the trick. Keeping yourself busy. Not moping about, rehashing it all. What was done, was done.

He hadn't been to this place since the funeral, but Franka knew the way like the back of her hand. Turn right five rows in, left at the toppled column. She marched beside him with long strides, towards Area 9. There were rumblings of thunder in the distance.

The stone was there, lying on the grave. An unpolished piece of yellow marble, irregular in shape. 'Oh,' said Franka, in a strangled voice.

He had to look away.

'It's so final, suddenly. Strange, isn't it? All these months, yet it's only now that it feels real.'

177

'Right,' he said, with a little more warmth. Perhaps she, too, would now be able to begin to find some peace. Perhaps the worst was behind them, and it was just a question of finding a new structure for their lives. After all, she had already been through this once before. She knew that sooner or later you bounced back, that you'd be able to go on, as long as you buried the past.

She took a tea light out of her coat pocket and lit it. She placed it on the pale marble. 'Hi, Jem,' she said softly. 'It's Mum and Dad, come to tuck you in.' The wind promptly blew out the flame. A lightning bolt tore across the sky.

'It's going to start raining cats and dogs,' said Phinus, taking her by the arm.

'Remember? You used to tell him he couldn't go outside in a thunderstorm because the fillings in his molars might attract the lightning. Not that he had any cavities; after all, he was one of the fluoride generation.' She smiled fleetingly, *just unbelievable*.

They stood in silence for several moments.

'But the stone is quite lovely, don't you think? And what if we planted hydrangeas at the head, and some trailing ground cover to fill in the rest, periwinkle maybe, some wild strawberries perhaps . . .'

'Did you intend to come here to garden every weekend, then?'

'Yes, I think I'd like that.'

He cleared his throat. 'In that case let me tell you right now that I'm not one of your grave-sitters. Not my sort of thing.'

She jiggled the car keys in her coat pocket for a spell. Then she said, in a voice suddenly ringing with exasperation, 'Then I'll do it by myself, as usual. But on those days, you might cook something Jem used to specially like, so that afterwards together we'd . . . a kind of ritual, you know?'

Over his dead body would he start cooking – *cooking, of all things*! 'Right, and why don't we have that Sanne girl knit a few cosy sweaters for him as well?'

'Phinus!' she said, indignant.

'I'm sorry, but I really don't understand you. On the one hand you're constantly going around bleating and snivelling—'

'Bleating? Sniv—'

'OK, no need to get hung up on every single word! I mean, *nice* stone! Hey, hydrangeas all around. Let's all dig and hoe! A nifty little garden he's getting, that Jem of yours. Just add a barbecue, and you—'

'That Jem of mine was also *your* Jem.'

'Oh, woman, everything I did was wrong, down to the fillings in his teeth. You never let me forget it.'

'But that isn't true! It's not!' She frowned. 'But is that why you've been acting so, so . . . Because you think you've done something wrong? Oh, Phinus. I've been thinking the very same thing – about myself, I mean – I've been getting the craziest notions in my head, things I should have done or shouldn't have done, but all that is, really, is paranoia – am I glad we're finally talking about it! Listen to me, we could never have confronted fate, we haven't got a thing to reproach ourselves with, it isn't our fault that Jem's dead. It isn't yours, and it isn't mine.'

'*How much do you need, Jem? Do you know how much it costs to get in, and how much the drinks are?*'

'*We could go to the Eko-café instead, Dad.*'

'*But you told me yourself she wanted to go clubbing. Remember, Jem, if you want to impress a girl, always*

179

let her have her way. Jesus, you kids of today don't even know the most basic rules of the game. Back in my day . . . well, OK, never mind that. Here, take it. Go on, spoil that girl rotten, take her to the joint she wants to go to. You'll thank me later.'

'We never wanted anything but the best for him,' said Franka. She was talking so fast she had to catch her breath. 'We always . . . Phinus! Phinus! Stay here!'

Along the zigzagging paths he ran, among the tombstones. Sparrows chirped on tree branches that were still bare; the snowdrops were almost finished. He noticed all of it, oddly enough, as he got himself trapped deeper and deeper in this labyrinth of the deceased. Were they lying down there in their graves just tickled to death, the dearly departed? Just try and get yourself out of this one, Phinus Vermeer! Go on, keep running in circles, with your heart in your mouth and a stitch in your side!

He finally sank down on a bench, panting.

The most precious thing in his life was lying somewhere around here under a slab of marble, all because of him. There were going to be hydrangeas planted all around. Beneath their roots, nature would go about her imperturbable business for as long as it took for a kind-hearted boy brimming with plans and projects to be reduced to nothing but bones. Phinus himself should be lying here. Year in, year out he ought to lie here, fully conscious, while being taken apart, slowly and methodically, by God's lowliest creatures, and turned into compost.

He heard footsteps approaching, and looked up, startled. Had Franka followed him?

It was Sanne who came along, carrying a white rose.

Her cheeks grew flushed when she saw him sitting there. 'Hey,' she stammered. She was wearing an open fur-collared jacket over flowery leggings.

When he didn't say anything, she managed with some difficulty, 'Your wife told me the other day' – shifting her weight from one leg to the other – 'Franka said, Franka said that the stone-setting would be today. I just wanted to have a look, if that's all right.'

'But of course.'

'Have you already been, or are you on your way there?'

'I was just sitting here to catch my breath.' Afraid she would come and sit down next to him, he stood up with the decisiveness of someone resuming a stroll.

'Yeah, I often sit down here too. It's such a pretty spot, and you can see where Jem lies from here.'

He followed the direction of her gaze. He must have jogged in a circle; he was back in Area 9. There was no one else in sight. Franka must have gone home, angry and upset.

'Did it come out nice?' asked the girl, starting to walk.

'Oh, I'm no expert,' said Phinus, automatically falling in step with her.

When they arrived at the grave, she squatted down and laid the rose on the stone, right under Jem's name. 'It's still looking pretty bare.'

'There are going to be some hydrangeas over there.' He had to swallow. 'And there . . . something else.'

'Oh, good idea.' She got up.

They stood next to each other awkwardly. Finally she said, pushing her hair to the side in that unique way of hers, 'Well, what's there to say, in this situation?'

'I'm having the same problem,' he said, thawing slightly.

Again came the rumbling of thunder, closer now.

She shrank. 'I'm always scared to death of—'

'A little thunderstorm won't hurt you,' he said. 'As long as you don't have any fillings.'

'Fillings?' She stared at him, puzzled. At that moment a crackling bolt of lightning right above their heads lit up the sky. The flashing light strobed over Jem's headstone, flickering like an old black and white horror film. The girl let out a scream. And Phinus automatically opened his arms wide.

PART III
Move Directly to Jail

What Phinus leaves behind

Slowly the sun comes up over Groningen's fields of germinating wheat and budding rapeseed. Beams of dusty light stream in through the windows of the old day-labourer's cottage outside Aduard. Wide gaps in the floorboards come into view, crawling with woodlice and earwigs. The wall between the hall and the living room displays deep cracks. The plaster is so crumbly that the red brick behind it shows through in many places. The lathing is sagging down through a hole in the ceiling. Here and there woody shoots of ivy have bored their way in through the walls.

Phinus, lying on the mattress, scratches the stubble of his chin. He feels like a mole, or some other subterranean creature whose coat is crusted with dirt. It doesn't bother him. He hardly notices the musty, almost rotten smell any more, he's stopped flicking the fat sluggish spiders off his trouser legs. If his bladder weren't bursting, he'd almost say he was a contented man right now, marinating in filth.

Franka is sitting on the floor, with her swollen ankle

in the torn tights. From time to time he hears her teeth chattering from the cold. She's keeping her eyes fixed on his watch lying on the floor. But surely it's clear as daylight to even Franka by now, gullible and pig-headed as she is, that he was right: under their cosy quilt at home, Astrid and Melanie must be rolling around in stitches right now – 'Did we ever teach that loser a lesson!'

'What's keeping them?' he asks sarcastically. He sits up and with both hands pushes himself up to a standing position. He jackknifes his way to one of the low windows. He can hardly see out of the filthy glass. From the mere fact that it's light out, one can surmise the world outside still exists. Another new day.

'I want to get out of here,' says Franka. It's the first thing she has said in hours.

'Oh, aren't we going to wait for your pals?'

'Just do it, break the glass. Or did you want to go on standing there on the lookout?' Her voice is icy. She kicks off a shoe and tosses it at him.

He'd have done better not to provoke her. Now he's going to have to actually do something. Reluctantly he picks up the pump. As he attempts to straighten up, seeking support from the crumbling remains of the windowsill, his hand plunges right through the rotten wood with a loud pop. He loses his balance and smacks his face against the window frame. The taste of blood fills his mouth. He swallows, and presses his sleeve against his lip. Then he bends down again, picks up the shoe from the floor and bangs it awkwardly, sideways, against the glass. With a brisk crack, the heel snaps off.

He turns round. 'Here, give me your other shoe.'

'There's blood all over you!' Franka exclaims. 'How

186

do you do it? The window's still in one piece, and you're in smithereens!'

'That's right. Do you want to get out of here or not?'

That puts an end to her mirth. 'I'll do it myself.' She takes off her other pump. She limps across the wrecked floor, arms flailing. The floorboards squeak dismally; dust billows up out of the cracks. When she gets to the window she assumes a combative stance, then takes a swing at it. The glass shivers and breaks. 'There now,' she says grimly, pulling the shards out of the sash and tossing them outside.

'Don't cut yourself,' he can't stop himself saying.

She throws him a derisive glance.

He licks the blood off his lip. 'And how were you thinking of getting out of here on just one leg?'

Without deigning to answer him she taps the last splinters of glass out of the frame. Fresh air and sunlight pour in. He all but shrinks back from it. His hours as a mole are over. He braces himself, and elbows Franka away from the window. With a mighty effort he manages to swing his left leg up. His foot narrowly misses the frame, lands on the sill and disappears, with a loud crack, deep into the wood.

'Jesus, what are you doing now? Can't you see you can't put your weight on that? Get down. This isn't getting us anywhere.'

He yanks at his foot with both hands, his nose pressed up against his bent knee. The sweat is dripping into his eyes.

'I swear, you're as stubborn and bloody-minded as the back end of a mule!' She gives him a savage shove. It feels like an electric current zipping up his spine and he can't keep down a scream.

'Well then don't just stand there like an idiot!'

'Woman' – he can hardly breathe – 'can't you see I'm stuck?'

She bends down unsteadily to assess the situation. Her eyes glittering with rage, she says, 'Oh please, don't tell me! Now you're blocking the way out, on top of everything else! It's as if you're determined to sabotage *us*! Do you want us to stay here until we rot, then? Come on, pull your foot out of your shoe!'

Desperately he gropes for his shoe.

'You're driving me up the wall!' She tugs at his shoelace. She yanks at his leg. His foot slides smoothly out of the shoe. With a faltering hop he just manages to save himself from losing his balance.

'Good Lord!' says Franka contemptuously. She sits down on the ledge, swings her legs over the side and the next moment she's outside. With her arms out to the side, she limps over the grass towards the car, which is parked on the muddy path.

He looks on helplessly, his eyes blinking in the daylight. A thought occurs to him that's been lying in wait for him for fourteen years, like a genie in a bottle: did she only marry him, at the time, because it was easier to give in than to resist? Was it really him who softened her up, or was it her own grief? The truth is, she's never really needed him. For anything at all.

Outside she makes her way painfully through the uncut grass, the strain showing in her rigidly hunched shoulders. When she gets to the car, she opens the door and looks inside. Then she stands up again, her cheeks flushed from the effort. 'Phinus! I don't see the mobile! Is it in the glove compartment?'

It is, after all last night's rainfall, a singularly bright morning. The stand of birches in front of the cottage shimmers in the sunlight and, a little further on, the canal glints like a child's carefully polished ruler on the first day of school. Along the bank the rushes bend in the gentle breeze. It's a day that screams for a picnic, a bike ride, a long walk. The lovely weather will draw the people of Aduard outdoors as soon as they've finished their shopping for Easter. He leans out of the window. 'Someone's bound to come along sooner or later! Sit down, before you break the other leg!'

'But where's that phone?'

'Those two darling lasses must have it.'

Panting, she comes hobbling back. *As stiff-necked as a cement mixer.* 'How's that? What's going on then?'

'Why don't you ask them yourself?'

She puts her hands on her hips. 'Don't you gloat, you. It's all your fault we're in this fix. Because they had a bone to pick with you.'

He seeks the window ledge for support. 'Oh really? And why is that, may I ask? Shall I tell you why? Just because, is why! They're two nasty pieces of work, bored out of their little skulls out here. Anything's a welcome distraction. They were out to make trouble! They had the gall to leave us here locked up, the shameless bitches, when they could see perfectly well with their own two eyes that we were hardly able to walk.'

'Something like this doesn't happen just like that!' she cries. 'For no earthly reason, I suppose?'

Just like that. For no earthly reason. Jem.

'And what are we going to do now, without a phone? Wait for the Easter bunny?'

He presses his hands to his temples. *Let's see if the Easter bunny has hidden anything for us, shall we? Look carefully now. No, lukewarm. More lukewarm, even more lukewarm. Cold! Oh, look out, go the other way, Jem! . . . Yes, there! Warmer, warmer! Hot!*

How upset Jem had been when he found out that the Easter bunny didn't really exist. When, soon after that, he was swindled out of St Nicholas as well ('Remember the Easter bunny? Well . . .'), he'd indignantly sat down on the ground, and yelled, 'And little baby Jesus, he doesn't really exist either, right?'

It had made Franka laugh. But Phinus had felt a great loss. Didn't she remember the time Jem had told him the story of Christmas, when he was nearly five? The two of them together under the tree twinkling with lights, Jem on his lap. Phinus with his arms wrapped round the little tot's tummy, his chin resting on the freshly washed hair.

'Daddy! There once was a mother, and her name was Marina. And she had a father, and his name was Youssef. They had a baby together, and his name was . . .' His voice faltered. He let himself fall back against Phinus's chest. 'I don't remember!'

'Jesus,' Phinus prompted.

'His name was Jesus,' Jem resumed energetically, 'and he . . . but why was he called that?'

'They liked the name, I suppose.'

'Oh,' said Jem. 'Did they think it up themselves?'

'Yes, that's what happens when you have a baby. Surely you don't think there's an angel who sticks a gold pin into a book of names? It's the parents who get to name their children.'

Jem looked surprised. His eyes shone in the soft candlelight. 'Mine too?'

'Yes, a long time ago Mummy was reading a book from America, and she liked it a lot. There was a boy in it who was very brave and friendly. His name was

190

Jem. And she decided right then and there: that's the name I'll give my son some day.'

'And what was his father's name?'

'Atticus,' said Phinus. 'That was the name of the father in that book.' A profound and peaceful feeling of joy came over him. What a privilege, to be able to tell his little boy where his name came from.

'Bedtime,' Franka called, poking her head round the side of the door. 'Yep, it's the party pooper again. Phinus, would you please—'

'Atticus!' said Jem severely. 'You have to call Daddy Atticus!'

'What were you two talking about?' She lifted him off Phinus's lap.

Phinus said, 'About all sorts of things, and about Marina and Youssef too, who had a baby together, called Jesus.'

'Oh, that one . . . But that baby wasn't really Youssef's baby, you know. Jem, you'll never guess who Jesus's real father was.'

'Was he up in heaven?'

'Yes, because—'

'Just like mine!'

'Not quite,' Franka laughed. She walked out of the room with Jem in her arms.

Under the Christmas tree, Phinus mused: since God foresaw that he wouldn't always be able to pay attention to everything at once, he made mothers and fathers his proxies on earth. He created man in his own image, so that man in turn would keep creating new life, and there would always be children to inherit the earth. That was the purpose of life; that was what man was made for.

At the top of the tree the Christmas angel and its

gleaming trumpet had fallen over sideways, and he got up to put it right.

The angel had been a gift from Aunt Leonoor. 'Granny Leonoor,' as she called herself. A child could never have too many grannies, she maintained. 'Even if they're phony, count your blessings!'

Irmgard, who'd sooner eat the soles of her shoes than let on that she was longing to pull Jem onto her lap, angel and all, fixed the little boy with a probing stare. 'Do you know how to count yet? Tell me, how many grannies do your poor little friends have?' She held up two fingers. 'Ha!' Then she sank back on the couch, puffing.

'Jem breaks all records.' Smiling, Franka passed round the mulled wine.

Was there any child as blessed as Jem Vermeer? Heaps of daddies and grannies, he had; if that didn't prove he was born under a lucky star . . . In heaven and on earth, everywhere, there were people watching over him. Nothing bad could happen to him. The aunts just couldn't get over it, how adept fate had been at providing Jem with guardian angels to keep him from harm. 'A child is always a precious gift,' said Leonoor, taking a hearty bite of Phinus's Christmas cake, 'but in your case, even more so.'

There was a pregnant silence. As if by prearrangement, all four turned to look at Jem, who had dragged a chair over to the Christmas tree and was now engrossed in hanging up his angel. There was icing sugar on the tip of his nose, and they all smiled, just in time to ward off melancholy.

'You do make sure he eats radishes regularly, don't you?' asked Irmgard gruffly after a moment or two. 'It keeps the mind wonderfully sharp.'

'Provided you never eat it with salt,' warned Leonoor.

'We've just mastered the carrot,' answered Franka. 'And we're working hard on the endive.' Her hands cradled her plundered womb. I'm sorry, her body language said. I'm so terribly sorry, for all of us.

'As long as you get to the radish by the time Jem starts learning to read.'

'Learning to read! Do you remember, Phinus?'

'And how,' he said, resting his hand on Franka's for a second. *It doesn't matter, love.* Then he got up to heat some more wine. In the kitchen everything was in readiness for a sumptuous meal. He opened the oven door and peered at the gargantuan turkey that was sputtering seductively in its own juices. He was thinking, I have enough people to spoil rotten, really I have. There wasn't any room, in fact, for anyone else.

When he walked back into the living room with the steaming wine, Jem had apparently already zipped like a comet through his entire school career and was now about to enter university. Perhaps he would elect to study palaeontology, which had always struck Irmgard as such an interesting profession. Or else something along the lines of saving lives.

'Dear God,' said Phinus, moving from glass to glass, 'I hope you didn't have the same kinds of aspirations for me, because you must have been so disappointed.'

'Oh, child,' said Irmgard tolerantly, 'we used to tell each other, when you were just Jem's age, he's never going to have a head for books, that one.'

'Daddy is the boss of Jumbo, you know!' cried Jem. He was sitting on the hearthrug, his stockinged feet drawn up under him. His face was indignant.

'Life is full of strange surprises,' Irmgard allowed.

'It's a most respectable profession,' said Franka loyally. 'Jem and I are very satisfied with it.'

'And that's what it's all about, isn't it? And, fortunately, orphans are always tenaciously hard workers,' Leonoor decided. 'Granny Irmgard is just an old sourpuss. There's no use complaining, because in life, things are the way they are, and hardly ever the way they ought to be.' She sent Phinus a meaningful look over the top of her glass.

He coughed to cover his emotion. Come to think of it, had he, over the years, made it sufficiently clear that he loved his aunts? Tirelessly they had cleared for him a path through life, in their sensible sandals, their beige cardigans, and the festive scent of 4711 Cologne on special holidays. They had been fretting about his future when he was only four. And all the while, he thought to himself, they were looking forward to the time when I'd phone them in the middle of the night to tell them, 'It's a girl, and we're naming her Irmgard Leonoor!'

'But we *still* don't know,' said Irmgard indignantly. 'Speak up, Jem, what do you want to be when you grow up?'

Jem considered, his thumb stuck in his mouth, said appendage rapidly pulled out again on seeing Phinus's raised eyebrow. 'I wouldn't mind being in the aquarium,' he announced at last.

'He was allowed to pet the sharks' bellies there this summer, in Scheveningen,' Franka explained. 'When I was in the hospital.'

'No, Mummy! You're not allowed to touch the sharks, or else they'll die. Right, Granny?' Jem jumped up and threw himself upon Irmgard.

'Yes indeed, that's common knowledge.' Irmgard clamped the child's shoulders with her gnarled fists. She was beaming.

'Let's be clear,' said Leonoor. 'Everything dies. Everything and everyone. We won't be coming to buy entrance tickets from you, you understand, when you're working in that aquarium. We'll have long since kicked the bucket by then.'

'But there's lots of beddy-byes between now and then,' snapped Irmgard. She pulled Jem onto her knee and planted an awkward kiss on top of his head. There was no child in all the world who was loved as much as Jem, nor any child who had as bright a future.

'Well?' asks Franka, standing on the other side of the broken window, her chin raised aggressively. 'You can't drive, and neither can I. I did tell you we'd do better to get an automatic, but you thought it was for old fogeys.'

He scuffs his feet on the floor. 'Just open the door, for Pete's sake. I've been needing to pee for hours.'

'I might just leave you here.'

'Whatever.'

'Bastard.' She's close to tears.

As soon as he hears the rasping sound of the bolt being pulled back, he scurries out of the cottage as fast as he can. Facing the mossy gable wall, he fumbles for his fly. But his stomach is in the way, drooping over his waistband. He tries to raise his torso a notch, gives up, pulls at the zipper and gropes for his member. Two useless balls and a panic-stricken prick that's shrunk in on itself. He has to fish around for it, goddammit. *Oh, deliverance, deliverance.*

'Ah,' he sighs as the clattering against the bricks

starts up. You can launch a hundred new games a year, but all of that pales in comparison to the joy of taking a leak when you're ready to burst. He stares at the steamy torrent with growing self-confidence.

'I have to go so badly too.' She sounds desperate.

Relieved, he zips up his trousers. He's a new man. Hands pressed into his sides, he hobbles over to her. She is sitting on the window ledge.

'Do you need help?'

'If you're thinking even for one second of taking advantage of this, I'll shoot you in the kneecaps. I swear.' She jumps down from her perch nevertheless.

The next thing he knows, he's standing with his face more or less crushed up against her stomach. He reaches perfunctorily under her skirt, strips off her tights, pulls down her pants and yanks the lot over her dangling foot. The briefs are satin, navy blue. *Brand new. Purchased specially for him.* He feels himself grow warm. From embarrassment, but also out of sympathy. He suddenly feels terribly sorry for her.

'Oh, I've kept it in much too long!' Her voice dies away. Just inches from his nose, the smell of her urine wafts up. Here he is, somewhere on planet Earth, he has no idea of the exact coordinates, holding up his wife's skirt while she gushes like Niagara Falls. He is suddenly overcome with nostalgia. He wishes, how he wishes he had to fight the urge to stick a hand between her legs, to catch her warm urine and rub it all over his face!

'Do you have a tissue on you?'

'No, I don't.' He grabs her pants, wedges her other leg through again and yanks it halfway up her thighs. 'What about your tights?'

'Don't bother.' She lets go of his shoulder and

adjusts her clothes. Without deigning to give him a second look, she hobbles to the car and flops down in the front seat.

He remains standing a while on the reeking grass, peering down the deserted embankment and towpath. The sound of ducks nattering in the rushes, and of the water peacefully lapping in the canal. A perfect spot for lovers. Haven't they themselves often ripped off their clothes in a place like this? There was a time when, driving along a quiet country road, they had only to glance at one another to find themselves moments later entangled in an unruly jumble of arms and legs on the side of the road, or in the back seat of the car. It always happened as quickly, he liked to say, as the frying of an egg: one moment it's only an intention, the next it's already sputtering in the hot butter. There are very few actions that take as little time as the frying of an egg: one crack on the edge of the pan is all it takes.

He thinks: I wouldn't now, not even if you paid me a million.

He feels a stab of regret for his lost desire. And then remorse because, obviously, it didn't simply slip away just like that.

The sun is steadily climbing higher in the sky. It must be coming up for twelve noon. He is lying in the back of the car with his knees to his chest, seething with impotence, on the upholstery which to this day holds the faint aroma of his semen.

A fly has come in via the open door and is now ricocheting, buzzing wildly, from seat to seat.

He stares at it.

In the front Franka, with a sigh of agony, shifts in her

197

seat. She mutters, 'I just don't know what to do with this leg.'

'How about trying to—'

'I wasn't talking to you.'

He is no longer the one tending to her comfort. His advice is no longer welcome. And immediately he sees before him an endless parade of umbrellas: year after year, from sheer force of habit, every time bad weather is forecast another umbrella will be added, until his head finally explodes. What's the point of traffic reports if he can't warn Franka about traffic jams? What's the point of vitamins, which must be swallowed at the right time *and consistently*? Socks that haven't been rolled up, tea that's allowed to get cold, jam in the corner of her mouth: all those everyday things that he won't be able to put right any more, and which will pile up into inconceivable mountains inside him. He clears his throat. 'What do you see happening, exactly, once we—'

'We're still stuck here for the time being.'

The fly whirls out of the car, buzzing.

The temperature inside the car rises steadily.

Birds chirp.

The grass grows.

Franka shifts her position again. She leans forward and honks the horn insistently.

He sucks on his injured lip and listens to the sound of an airplane, impossibly far away. Seen from the air, the landscape must look empty and bare, the tumble-down cottage with the car parked next to it less significant than two dots. The little man and woman at the windows aren't visible at all. They've been erased, absorbed into the patchwork quilt of fields and meadows.

'What if nobody comes?' she asks angrily.

'Hey listen, what am I supposed to do about it? It's in the hands of fate, there's no one out looking for us.'

She turns her head and her eyes bore into his. 'Our coats are still at the hotel. Our beds haven't been slept in. And those friends of yours, too, must be wondering ever since breakfast where we are. We must have caused quite a commotion by now.'

He is somewhat taken aback at this. 'Oh, of course. Yes, naturally, that's it. You're right.' So they couldn't have fled the scene without leaving a trace, as he'd been hoping to do last night. How could he have made such an error of judgement?

'What's this?' she exclaims. 'Did I hear "You're right"? Were you saying it just to humour me? "You're right"! Well, I'm amazed, coming from your lips, that's as unheard of as "I don't know"!'

'You don't have to drag up all that other stuff again,' he says, suddenly in despair. 'Besides, there's no need to make me out to be such a monster.'

She is quiet for a moment, visibly disconcerted. 'Is that what I do? Well, I might need a little time to think about that, if it's all right with you.'

With a sigh he sinks his shoulders deeper into the upholstery, staring at her profile with escalating anxiety. What would happen if she wasn't around any more to help him sift sense from nonsense?

All of a sudden she says, looking straight ahead, 'Do you know that I'd been wondering, of late, if we shouldn't adopt a child? Fatherhood always did bring out the best in you.'

Shocked, he wrenches himself into a sitting position.

'I was thinking about it the night Jem died. How

199

good you were to him. As we were walking to the front door, he took out this whole wad of cash. You'd given it to him. You were always so sweet to him. Always, just sweet and wonderful.' She runs a hand through her hair. Her fingers twist a tuft of hair in her neck into a tassel.

He sits there paralysed. *She knew.*

Her hand slips down off her neck. 'You buried the best part of yourself with Jem. And without that part of you—'

'You knew!' he yells. 'You knew all along and you never said a word!' Before he knows what he's doing, he's fastened his hands round her neck.

She screams. She's waving her arms around.

'Why didn't you *say* something?' He's shaking her.

Wheezing, she squeaks, 'What's got into you? Let go of me!' With a throttled cry she dives to the side, but he catches hold of her by the hair. He yanks her head back against the headrest.

'Stop, Phinus, stop it!'

'Oh, and wait a minute!' He is foaming at the mouth. 'So that's why you didn't want a harsher sentence for the perpetrator! Because you knew who the *real* culprit was!'

Groaning, she manages to twist herself free and throws herself out of the open car door.

He bangs his forehead against her empty seat, panting with frustration. It takes several seconds of manoeuvring for him to get his legs outside the car.

She's already dragged herself a good distance on hands and knees, she's almost reached the beech trees, her hands clawing, her legs scissoring. She's trying to get away from him! But she has never managed it before, and she's not going to do so now. Not until he has finally settled the score.

Stumbling over his own feet, he runs after her. He is crying, he is bawling, with long drawn-out howls. 'You knew it was my fault! Don't you dare deny it!'

Her foot catches on a root and she smacks headlong onto the grass. 'Help!' she screams. 'Is anyone there? Help me!'

'Let's settle this once and for all! Come on! Haven't you been waiting for this moment all this time? I'm on to you!'

'Help!' she screams again.

How can she hear what he's saying when she's making such a row? *Listen to me!* In his panic he almost trips over a brick. At his wits' end, he picks up the brick and throws it in her direction, to get her attention. It hits her on the shoulder.

She howls at the top of her lungs.

'Franka! Is that you?' comes a voice from far away.

Stunned, he stands still. He tries to straighten up. His head is pounding.

'Franka! Where are you?'

It's true: in the distance, someone is calling her name.

'Over here!' Franka calls, sobbing. 'Over by the cottage!'

Two people come into view round a bend in the towpath. He immediately recognizes one of them by her straw-like hair.

'Oh my God! We were just about to turn back when we heard you shouting. Really! We've been looking for you all morning, haven't we, Mark? Franka, come, what's the matter, can't you walk? Tell us, Phinus, what happened? How did you end up here? Look, Mark,

201

they spent the night here! In this romantic little cottage! Don't you hear what Phinus is saying? Last night, after dinner, they went out for a . . . and in the dark it's easy to lose your way. And then, well, OK, it's simple, Franka twisted her ankle and Phinus put his back out. What a lot of excitement, eh?'

Mark's sardonic smile.

Katja says she's in seventh heaven, really she is, because who'd ever have thought that she and Mark, of all people, would find themselves in the role of angels of deliverance, you'd better believe this story will impress her kids this evening, they think all their mum is good for is cleaning up their mess, and their dad for . . . well, OK, it's not as if they see that much of their dad . . . so she's really looking forward to telling them about this adventure and getting a little respect for a change.

'Are you going home today, then?' Franka's voice is shaking. She rubs her tear-stained cheeks, like a little child.

'Yes, of course. We have to hunt for Easter eggs in the morning.'

'Do you think we could drive back with you? Or . . . we could go home in two cars, couldn't we?'

'Of course, dear girl, we have to get you to your doctor as quickly as possible, and after that we'll make you comfy on your sofa with a pot of tea. No problem. Hop in.' She invitingly holds open the door to Phinus's car for them.

Once again he ends up in the back seat. Next to him, wound tight as a spring, Franka looks stubbornly out of the window. He, too, on his side, is studying the stern poplars without really seeing them. His hands are clasped round his knees in an attempt to keep himself together.

'Do I turn left here, or right?' Mark enquires from behind the wheel.

Phinus tries to concentrate on the landscape he must have driven through last night. But nothing looks familiar, in the daylight. 'I really have no idea.'

'Everything looks different at night,' says Katja.

When Aduard's bridge finally comes into view, he can't help bracing himself. They'll be leaning over the railing in their usual spot, Astrid, the brawn, and Melanie, the brain. An ear-splitting ringing starts, and the barriers come down. What just now appeared to be a solid road surface is slowly rising into the air.

'I feel I'm on holiday!' cheers Katja. 'Boats, open bridges! Marvellous!'

He doesn't see the girls. Nor does he see them once the barge has gone past, and the bridge is closed again. They aren't there.

At the inn the landlady comes bearing cold drinks. She enquires sympathetically after the nature of the Vermeer family's injuries, cancels the rest of their reservation saying she quite understands, and charges them only for last night's supper. She personally fetches their coats from the coat rack and brings them, neatly folded with the linings on the outside, out to the BMW in which Mark will take Franka home and the Mercedes which Katja will now be driving. She wishes them a pleasant journey, and a safe ride home.

Stretched out on the back seat, he tries to lead his thoughts in a safe direction. He thinks about the missed breakfast he had been so looking forward to, with the six kinds of bread and the butter under the white earthenware dome. Tea for Franka, black coffee for him. Their contented looks of intimate understanding. Why don't you take a little more of that marmalade, you like it so much. It could have been that way, if . . . If what? Is there really such a thing, in fact, as cause and effect, as action and reaction? Or is everything just pure chance, sheer chaos?

Suddenly he misses his aunts terribly; to them, creating order and harmony was as natural as taking breath. They made the world grow light in the morning by pulling open the curtains in his room, and at night it wasn't until they had carefully closed them again, bumping into each other in the narrow space next to his fold-up bed, that the whole village could go dark. In the springtime they would open his window, having asked the birds to come and whistle a merry little morning tune for him. In the autumn they left the curtains open a crack, so that from beneath his blankets he might see the shooting stars that, at their command, skimmed across the sky with flashing tails. And in the winter they loved to tell him, 'Oh, tomorrow you'd better watch out, watch out!' and then when he woke up the whole windowpane would turn out to be etched with flowery frost. Whatever the aunts said always came true, because they were behind the scenes, quietly but steadfastly manipulating the strings of peace and order. Chaos never stood a chance with them: 'An orphan needs stability.'

Irmgard and Leonoor must now be turning over in their graves. If the dead have any tears, then they have been shedding them incessantly for the past six months, out of shame and disappointment. Their Phinus – a murderer. They would have seen through

204

him immediately, just as Franka had. But would they, too, have kept silent, would they, too, have found pleasure in watching him wrestle with his secret? 'Serves you right.'

The car is slowing down. He lifts his head to see the canopy of a petrol station. Katja gets out. He hears the rattling, the hum and the clatter of the tank being filled. He hastily offers her his wallet through the window.

A little later she returns, an ice cream in each hand.

'Don't get up, you poor thing.' She crouches next to the door, strips the paper off the cornet and tucks it in his hand.

'Oh, Katja . . .'

'That's right, don't think I don't know you two have had a fight. Anyway, at home I always try to make it up with an ice cream. Having kids, Phinus, makes you so damn pragmatic.'

For a moment he'd actually expected her to bend down and say, with a fervent look in her eye, 'I'll always be here for you.' But she wasn't born yesterday, not even this one. Her intuition warns her something's up. In the future, will they all smell trouble as soon as they lay eyes on him? Will women, who have been his sole allies all his life, avoid him like the plague from here on in?

'Oh, and keep in mind, your wallet's almost empty now.' She has half risen when she suddenly spots his feet. Her eyes grow round. 'You've lost a shoe!' Oh, it's always the same things with you kids! At the pool, after gym, at the riding stable — I'm always having to trot after you to keep your things together!

He couldn't care less about his shoe, stuck in the

windowsill of the cottage. 'Doesn't matter,' he says, drained.

She gets in, shaking her head: it's none of her business after all, but if it was her own children, she'd send them back for it. Do you want them to turn into spoilt brats? We're going to have to depend on this generation some day, you know. They're the ones who will inherit our earth!

Crushed by her disapproval, he lies back. He sees the canopy of the petrol station glide away. Then power lines, sharply silhouetted against the bright blue sky. The spindly tops of pine trees stunted by acid rain. A viaduct, with JESUS LIVES on the concrete span. The S is reversed. What do you expect, if you're writing it while hanging upside down from the railing . . . *That's called reversing the situation, Jem, or, rather, looking at it from the other side. Turn 'live' around and what do you get? Evil.* His eyes droop shut and he takes flight in sleep, without even once having to call on his faithful friend the Sandman, bringer of oblivion. The Sandman can just stay where he is, in his little house on the moon, the house made of gold with a chimney of diamonds, with the red cloth on the table, and on the windowsill a . . .

'Hey, look at this, Mel!'

'Looks like a little souvenir left us by Mr Phinus, Ast.'

'Oh yeah, that one. The pathetic loser, right?'

'Yeah. And look over there. There, on the floor!'

'Hey! His watch! After all that, the bloke left his wristwatch behind!'

'I told you, didn't I? He fell for you big time.'

'Can I help it? But with a new strap, that watch could be all right.'

206

'Mrs Phinus should look after her hubby better. What a sleazebag.'

'Velcro, don't you think? A Velcro strap.'

'Are you really going to wear it? It's a symbol, is what he said, innit, a symbol of all the time they spent together. That's what you'll be wearing on your wrist. You'd better look out. Before you know it, it's in your blood.'

What Sanne wants

The front door is still double-locked, and inside, they are greeted by the stale atmosphere of a house that's been closed up for a while: as if the house would just as soon never have seen its inhabitants again, and now, to its distaste, has to suffer windows being opened left and right, and inconsiderate feet disturbing the dust that had just begun to settle so comfortably.

He parks Katja unceremoniously in the living room to await Mark and Franka's arrival. Then he drags himself up the stairs. In the bedroom he kicks off his one shoe and slips into a comfortable pair of loafers. The alarm clock says it's half past five. On to the attic, where his stretching bar hangs from the rafters. He trips over suitcases and stacked boxes. Cobwebs cling to his face as he clamps his fingers round the smoothly turned wood. He takes a deep breath, pulls himself up with both hands and lets his own weight painfully do the rest.

The aunts used to have a book of pictures of people

who practised self-flagellation. They had books on just about every subject, because humankind was an endlessly fascinating study topic to them. From behind the post office window you saw all kinds, but gleaned few explanations. At home, after five, they sought clarification.

'This looks like something religious to me,' said Irmgard, peering at the photograph of a man crawling along a brick path on hands and knees, with a rough wooden cross digging into his shoulder. Clicking her tongue, she wriggled a little deeper into her chair with the ribbed upholstery the colour of pea soup.

'You'll give the child nightmares,' said Leonoor, quickly putting her hand over the page.

The best photo was the one of the man with the turban. For fifty years he had been holding his right arm stiffly up in the air, and as a consequence his nails had grown so long that they twisted in all directions, like snakes. He was doing voluntary penance, Irmgard conjectured out loud, for a theft that had never been discovered. Here on earth he may have escaped his well-deserved punishment, but he knew that the Almighty was keeping a wrathful eye on him, and so he was doing what he could to get a head start on atoning. 'Or it'll be the fires of hell for him, when his time comes.'

Phinus feels the muscles in his arms quivering. The palms of his hands are burning. He endures the pain with eyes open wide. And then it's as if someone's pumping laughing gas up his spine: gravity releasing his crunched discs, one by one. Huffing and puffing, he pulls himself up one more time, but it's pretty much over. When Franka comes home in a little while, he'll be as straight as a young beech again. When she comes home in a little while . . . What does a wife say to a spouse who has gone for her jugular?

Downstairs the doorbell rings.

He stands perfectly still, his senses on high alert. She must have forgotten her key. She is standing on the front step, her eyes cold and hard. But by God, how did she expect him to react? *She knew. She knew all this time.* His heart is pounding. He doesn't know what's going to happen now, he doesn't even know what he would like to happen.

'Phinus!' Katja calls. 'You have a visitor!'

She is waiting for him in the hallway, with Sanne. The girl is wearing a fuchsia sweater with a collar so wide that it's slipped off one shoulder, revealing a childishly narrow bra strap.

'I was just telling her,' chuckles Katja, 'if she'd arrived ten minutes earlier, she would have found the door locked. We just got home, didn't we, Phinus? Are you all straightened out again, by the way? Did it work?'

He is incapable of uttering a word, and Sanne is silent too.

'You know what?' says Katja. 'I'm going to make a pot of tea.' She gives them a push towards the living room and heads for the kitchen.

Standing on the cheerful Third World rug, they both look down at their feet. It feels so strange to be near her again that it makes him stammer. 'Wouldn't you like to sit down?'

'No. Who's that woman?'

'An acquaintance. Sort of a colleague.'

'I came by this morning as well.' She looks at him with bitter mistrust.

'We were away.'

'You and her?'

'No, Franka and I. We were going to—'

Not giving him the chance to finish, she blurts out, 'I need money.'

He stares at the gleaming, unblemished shoulder peeking out of her sweater. The memory of the way her skin feels makes him burn with shame.

'Money for an abortion, I mean.'

Outside, someone is hooting a horn.

'It's Mark and Franka!' Katja yells from the kitchen.

'It can't be true,' he says, in shock.

'Yes it is, I've done one of those tests.'

'Yoo-hoo, Phinus? They're here . . . Oh, OK, I'll get it.'

'But how . . . how do you know that it's . . .' He fails to finish the question. Because of course it's his. There can't be any doubt about it. Every goblin in any old fairy tale you care to think of can tell you what the consequences are going to be if you deflower a girl on top of a brand-new gravestone. And so now Baba-Jaga's services are required, the scary witch in her hut that stands on chicken feet.

Wait. Just wait.

'My parents would murder me if they found out. I have to get rid of it.' She shrugs her shoulders up so high that her ears disappear out of sight. 'You have to help me, you hear? You really have to help me!'

At that moment the figure of Mark fills the doorway. '*Ave!*' he says, raising a hand. His face is drawn into a leer.

Katja, too, comes in, with the teapot. 'We need a little time to ourselves, dear,' she tells Sanne busily. 'Perhaps this wasn't the best time for you to come. Shall I see you to the door? Phinus will give you a ring later.'

211

'Phinus will email you later,' Mark corrects her. He gazes at the limescale-crusted Woolworth's saucers with the withered plants.

We're pregnant. Bewildered, he says, 'Sanne stays. She's a good friend of the family.'

'In that case let me come straight to the point,' says Mark. 'Your wife asked to be dropped off at a friend's house. And she asked if I would fetch the bag with her clothes, which is still in your car. That should keep her going for a few days.'

Katja is bustling around, rattling teacups. 'Here,' she says, 'and just sit down now for a sec, Phinus. Let's all remain calm . . .'

'Where is she?'

'At her friend's house.'

'At whose house? I'm entitled to know whose house, aren't I?'

'I believe that was precisely not the intention.'

'Did she say anything else?' He is trying not to lose it.

'No. Well, let's fetch that bag, shall we?' Mark brushes back his thick hair. He isn't making any attempt to hide his glee.

'Oh dear, oh dear,' Katja sighs. 'Do you want me to talk to Franka, Phinus, when we take her her things?'

'Don't always interfere,' snarls her husband. 'She's with a girlfriend. She doesn't need you for anything.'

'But Phinus may want . . . what *do* you want, Phinus?'

He can't take it in. Couldn't she just have told him to his face, 'I want to be alone for a while'? She needs to recover from what just happened, from all the emotion. There's nothing unreasonable in that, it's forgivable, he can quite understand. But to quietly give

212

him the slip, assisted by Mark, of all people, that creepy-drawers, as she herself called him . . .

'OK, what now?' asks Sanne, who is standing by the bookcase, anxious to go on with her story.

He takes the car keys out of his pocket. A breather, that's exactly what Franka and he need. He sweeps Katja off her chair and onto her feet, so anxious is he, suddenly, to get Mark and her out of his house.

'But we can't just leave you here all alone,' she begins.

'Alone?' says Mark. One corner of his mouth curls up in a sneer.

When he comes back into the room, Sanne is sitting at the table, her head in her hands.

He shuts the door behind him. For a full minute he feasts his eyes on her. He'd like to pick her up by the corners, fold her up carefully and stow her away somewhere safe. She is carrying his child.

'How are you feeling?'

She shrugs. 'I feel sick in the mornings, but not so bad that my mum notices.'

His head spinning, he counts back in time. 'Six weeks?'

'It was the twentieth of February.'

Amazing, that she knows the exact date. But perhaps girls write that sort of thing down in their diary.

'The day of Jem's gravestone.' She traces the grain of the wooden tabletop with the nail of her index finger. 'You could have called me some time, by the way!'

As if he hadn't been on the point of doing that very thing many times. So many times in fact that he knows her number by heart. 'But what would I have said to you?'

'You know. Hello, how are you? Jesus Christ!'

'Oh Sanne.' He wants to hunker down beside her, but his back gives him a warning and he remains standing beside her, like a wooden puppet. 'The thing that took place between us, that time, was a beautiful thing of course, but it really should never have happened.'

'It was only because I missed Jem so much.'

His bewilderment when she'd pushed her pelvis against his. Her arms round his neck. Her tongue inside his mouth, sweet and warm. 'I . . . I was afraid that afterwards, you . . .'

'I'm not a little kid, you know. Jem and I were going to . . . only then he was suddenly dead.' Beads of sweat appear on her forehead. She tosses her hair to the side. 'And that afternoon at the cemetery, I don't know, it seemed so logical, to do it with you, instead.' She looks at him unabashed. *So logical.*

She had murmured into his ear, 'You're the one closest to Jem, after all. You're his father.' Which was more obscene, the fact that she wanted to have sex with *Jem's father*, or that he had said nothing? *I am not really Jem's father.*

He wonders, did I want to get even with Franka, to punish her for her lack of interest in the legal fight? *I'm your husband, I'm doing it for you as well.* Or was this about Jem? Was it with *him* I wanted to get even? Well, damn it all! Always so pig-headedly stubborn, and then just this one time he *had* to go and listen to me, didn't he! How could the kid have been so stupid, stupid, *stupid*! And now *I'm* the one left tearing my hair out for the rest of my life. I can't stand the look of myself in the mirror any more, I can't stand to hear my voice, I'm cursed. Cursed! And you have that on your

214

conscience, you brat. Why couldn't you just have gone ahead and done what *you* wanted to do! Then you could have slept with Sanne yourself.

At that moment the phone rings.

'We're busy now, we're having a conversation, you and me,' says Sanne urgently. She puts her hands on her stomach. 'What are we going to do about this? Do you know how you go about it? Can you look them up in the Yellow Pages?'

'I don't think . . .' he begins. The telephone abruptly stops ringing. The silence briefly throws him. Was it Franka calling, ready with a whole tirade? The thought flashes through his mind that she's probably worried now: why didn't anyone pick up? Should she send someone over, to check on him?

'I want to make an appointment right away,' says Sanne. 'Maybe they can do it on Wednesday morning, that's when I have two free periods.'

'Come on, get real. It's Saturday night. And tomorrow is Easter Sunday. We won't be able to reach anyone before Tuesday morning.'

She frowns.

'Why don't the two of us go and have a bite to eat somewhere? Then we can talk this over calmly.' Impatiently he gestures towards the door.

She thinks it over, then nods. 'OK. Just let me call my mother.' She fishes a cobalt-blue mobile out of her bag. She dials the number and in a routine gesture slides the instrument under her hair. 'Hey, Mum!'

In the warm hollows of her body his genes have made contact with hers. Whether he is to be the father of a son or a daughter has already been decided. It has already been decided whether his child is one that laughs easily, or if it's one that can't sit still, if it will

215

learn to talk early, if it likes music or skating, if it has a talent for happiness. A person has thirty thousand genes, which, if you wrote them all down, would require a billion notations: the genetic information on this new little person would fill a ribbon from here to Tokyo, *oh, at least, and back again!* and half of it belongs to Phinus, fifteen thousand flashing little mirrors. He is no longer alone in the universe. Someone is walking beside him, its little shrimp fingers in his.

Sanne puts the phone back in her bag and takes out a little compact. 'Just got to do my eyes. I've been walking around all day without any make-up on. When I saw that test result this morning, I was so freaked I ran out of the house looking like this.' A mirror, a mascara wand, a cotton bud. 'Can't you sit down for a sec? Else I feel so rushed.'

'To tell you the truth, I'm pretty hungry.'

Unperturbed, she paints her eyelashes. 'What's the shit between you and Franka?'

'It's of no consequence.'

'Well, then I'll ask her herself.' She laughs. Then she peers into the little mirror again. 'Jem used to say that I had the longest lashes in Amsterdam.' She looks at him proudly.

He feels himself getting warm.

'He used to say, "If you cheat on me, I'll cut them off!" Before me, he'd never kissed anyone.' A tender smile hovers around her mouth.

Now he's sweating. 'Are you nearly ready?'

She inspects herself in the mirror. With a critical glance she pulls a lock of hair down over her forehead. 'I think I might as well fix it up properly now, because I'm going out later tonight as well.' She gets up. 'May

216

I borrow Franka's hair spray? My hair is a disaster.'

'Franka doesn't have any hair spray.'

'Yes she does, in the bathroom cabinet. Next to her peroxide, and all the other stuff for her hair. She has a hair mask that costs a fortune' – she kisses her fingertips with a look of longing on her face – 'far out, it's so restorative.'

It isn't until she has galloped up the stairs, until she is heard opening the right cabinet overhead, that he gives himself permission to shudder. Christ, how often have those two sat here together, woman to woman, under his roof? What have they discussed, what confidences have they exchanged? How much does Franka *know*, Franka who apparently keeps a cupboard full of stuff to *restore her hair*? No wonder she didn't trust him with those girls from Aduard, no wonder she blew her top. No wonder she's furious with him.

So here is another thing she has known all this time and never said a word about.

'Oh!' she'd said, stamping her feet with rage. 'He hasn't any idea at all how to quarrel!'

'Well, but it *is* quite an art, all things considered.' That was Irmgard.

But Leonoor shook her head in concern. 'So is quarrelling something you like to do then, lass? What things are really worth fighting over, in the end?'

In years past, when the aunts were cross with each other, they would communicate exclusively in writing. With clenched lips they'd berate each other using a pencil stub on the back of used Giro envelopes. In grim silence, they'd slide these messages across to each other, over the kitchen table with its wobbly leg.

Because even in their angriest moments, they always agreed on one point: that you must never expose a child to screaming or scolding. Quarrels would turn a child – 'and an orphan doubly so, surely!' – into a bed-wetter, a bundle of nerves. That, they said, was clearly spelt out, in black on white, in the handbook for aunts.

He would watch as the envelopes covered in hiero-glyphics shot back and forth over the kitchen table. Irmgard would bang her fist down on it before sending it on its way, as if stamping her message according to postal service directives. Leonoor, who was left-handed ('You can tell she was born to be a post office clerk'), would rattle her bracelets, holding her arm high up in the air like the man with the long finger-nails, before deigning to soil her hands on this kind of missive. Most of the time she'd answer with just a single word.

Quarrelling was a complicated business. You weren't allowed to use the words 'never' or 'always'. Not even in writing. 'You *never* this or that' – wrong! 'You *always* such and such' – wrong again! You had to stick to the immediate present.

It could be sort of cosy, though, when they quarrelled. You'd be sitting in your pyjamas in the warm kitchen, and they'd take turns stroking your head as they licked their pencils, deep in thought. 'Ha!' Irmgard cried out, as new inspiration hit her, and fell to work. And then Leonoor would get up to put the saucepan on the stove, to heat up another cup of milk and honey for you. After a while they got tired of writing. But even then they stuck to the self-imposed rule of the game: they wouldn't exchange a single word, not with each other, at any rate.

'Please tell your aunt that it's a load of nonsense, the things she's got into her head.'

'Please tell her back that I'll make up my own mind about that.'

They rammed the sentences into his mouth as if it was a letterbox, and only when he had carefully delivered them, word for word, down to the very intonation, did they become public, and only then was the other party allowed to react. He found himself right in the epicentre, as it were, of the quarrel: without him, it would go splat like a soap bubble, he kept the whole business going, they couldn't do without him.

After a fight, the big bed would creak and moan twice as loudly as usual in the night, and there would be coffee for breakfast, even if it wasn't Sunday. He could ask for anything, and he'd get it too.

'Did you say some bread for the ducks, poppet?'

'Oh well, you might as well let the child take what's left of the loaf, to make it up to him. I'm not hungry any more anyhow.'

The ducks lived in the ditch at the end of the lane. There were six of them: four brown ones and two black and green ones. They swam around quacking hungrily all day long in the duckweed, if they weren't climbing on top of each other, that is, splashing about like mad. That was called sex, and sex resulted in ducklings. Actually, if you thought about it, this explained why the aunts were the only ones in their street who didn't have children of their own: at home, the bathtub had a heavy wooden plank laid across it, with towering stacks of all kinds of books on top of that. He wondered if they themselves had worked out that that was the problem. Maybe it was even written somewhere in the handbook for aunts, but, oh well, Leonoor always said with a sigh, that was a book that just didn't have an end to it, somehow there was always another chapter to read.

He could always tell them himself, of course.

You don't say, they would exclaim admiringly, why didn't we think of it ourselves! He pictured their delight as they rushed to remove the musty-smelling books and turn on the bath's rusty tap. Within a few seconds they'd be splashing around in the bath together. It was awfully funny, all that thrashing and splashing. But then they began pushing each other's heads under the water, just like the ducks. He dropped the paper bag with the bread on the grass and pressed his fists into his eyes. *Stop it!* Last year, there'd been one duck that hadn't come up again. The one on top had kept going for quite a while before he'd even noticed.

That was called death.

He made up his mind at once: he wouldn't tell them. Because when you were dead, you couldn't do anything any more, not even have a good, cosy quarrel. Man, when you were dead! That's when they stuck you in a box under the ground. Stoutly, he spat on the grass. Then he picked up the bread and began to feed the ducks.

The Spanish-Portuguese restaurant is Sanne's choice. She orders tapas and red wine from the surly waiter. There's languid fandango music playing.

Phinus is sitting up stiffly, his back fearsomely straight.

'Why don't you relax?' she mutters as she begins rolling a thin cigarette.

The wine arrives in something that looks like one of those bottles they give you in the hospital to pee in, plus a little dish of green olives.

She smokes, she drinks.

To stop himself from telling her that alcohol and tobacco are twice as harmful to her now, he carefully straightens the pepper and salt shakers. He has no idea how to broach this, and he's stumped for another subject. Sitting together like this isn't easy.

With downcast eyes she eats a few olives. She pours herself some more wine.

He hastens to order a carafe of water. Which exhausts his conversational repertoire for now.

She starts talking about her history paper. It's a long story. Her teacher is a mixed-up dude, you don't even want to know.

They wait for the meal.

She scratches her bare shoulder.

He straightens the pepper and salt set again, feeling he has somehow landed in a silent film.

Sanne takes a toothpick from the glass and starts paring her fingernails with it.

A man carrying red roses comes up to their table. She whispers, perking up, that those guys are really drug runners. The ones who play the flutes outside the train station too, by the way. She underlines her words with lively gestures. A colourful bracelet is knotted round her right wrist. *The same kind Jem always wore.* He wipes his palms on the paper napkin. Suddenly all he wants to do is go home.

She sinks back in her chair, pulls a wisp of hair down over her nose and starts braiding it, cross-eyed.

Behind her, at the next table, two young girls of around eighteen are cracking up about something. Are

221

they laughing at him? He takes a fresh paper napkin.

Over the sound system comes an Andalusian song about a broken heart, or about the way it used to be, before, in our village, on a summer night, under a full moon, do you remember, darling girl of my dreams?

'You want some more?' Sanne is holding up the urine bottle.

'No. And shouldn't you really be watching what you . . .' There, it almost slipped out after all. But she hasn't heard him, she has long stopped expecting any words from him, she's singing along, softly, to the music.

The waiter comes shambling along with the tapas, on brightly coloured plates. '*Sí, finalmente, finalmente!*'

'God! There's so much!' She surveys the tidbits greedily.

Phinus thinks, she's eating for two. He begins to feel a little better.

She starts on the calamares.

A moment later he says, 'Franka mentioned adoption today.'

The subject doesn't seem to interest her very much. With her pearly white teeth she is testing how much give there is in a piece of squid.

'Because she herself is . . .' The word 'infertile' is so far removed from the way he sees Franka that he changes course. 'She's had cancer, she can't have any more children.' Her barren future stretches out before her pitilessly. For him, on the other hand, a door has always remained open somewhere. His breath catches in his throat.

Sanne sits up. 'Oh, so that's why Jem was an only

child. Just like me. You know, that was what was so special about the thing between the two of us. He understood me completely. He used to say—'

'But now, of course, we are faced, how shall I put it, with a new situation.'

'Don't you want to know what Jem said?'

'I was just in the middle of telling you . . . and no, no, I most certainly do not want to know!' He bangs his fist on the table.

Startled, she flinches away from him.

Behind her back the two young girls crane their necks inquisitively.

The waiter smacks down two water glasses on the table. '*Es su papá vicioso?*' he enquires, suddenly talkative.

'Would you do us a favour and mind your own business? And I mean right now? Thank you! Thank you very much! *Muchas gracias!*' Phinus snatches up the jug of water, pours himself a glass and tries to down his agitation in a few big gulps.

'Jem used to say that you were just like John Cleese. Now I understand what he was getting at! John Cleese in *Fawlty Towers*, remember? One time he was with Manuel, the Spanish waiter, when they . . .' She explodes with laughter. Her hair swishes over her face.

'Here, have a drink of water.'

'That guy can really blow his top.' She's still laughing. She has pegged him as one of the harmless madmen, the comedians you see on TV. Casually she bites into a tortilla. She asks with her mouth full, 'Aren't you going to have some? It's pretty good.'

He puts two sardines on his plate, for appearance's sake. 'So, well now, adoption . . .'

She looks up with an irked expression. 'We were

223

supposed to be talking about me, remember? We've got to work it out. We'll call them on Tuesday. And Wednesday you have to come with me, to pay the bill. And maybe they won't let me walk, so we'll have to go by car.' Her face clouds over. She pushes her plate away. 'And I guess it'll hurt as well.'

'It's not that simple, Sanne! You first have to have a talk with a social worker, and then I think there's a compulsory waiting period to think it over – after all, people do often change their minds. First you look at it this way, and then you look at it that way, experience will teach you this, you can't just act on your initial impulses, otherwise a clinic like that would be a madhouse, impulsive emotions are never our best guide. If you base your decisions on your emotions, you'll almost always end up making the wrong choice!'

Instead of listening to his argument, she has been following an independent train of thought. 'And what if I have to stay in bed? What shall I tell my mother?'

'You see? Don't you see it yourself now? We have to plan this very carefully.'

'I could pretend, of course, that I'm having a very bad period. That I can't walk because of the cramps.' Nervously she rolls a cigarette and lights it, inhaling deeply.

Do they know you smoke, at home? He blurts out, 'And what if you need your parents' consent? You're a minor!' His own words only serve to make him even more frantic. She's only fifteen. How can he expect common sense from a fifteen-year-old?

'But doesn't that mean they help you even sooner? Surely they want you to finish school and stuff, don't they?'

Sanne in the school yard, surrounded by other girls, girls with ponytails and snub noses, laden with bulging backpacks scribbled all over in felt tip with the names of their favourite pop stars. She is still a child herself, she probably sleeps in a bed heaped with stuffed animals. At night her father comes into the girlish bedroom, with its pink and blue wallpaper, to kiss her goodnight.

She looks at her wristwatch. 'I only have another half an hour, OK? I've got to meet a girlfriend in town.'

'But you can't!' he cries and glances at his own watch. The sight of his naked wrist brings back a memory that's already fading somewhat. The piranhas. Hadn't he thought the same thing of them: they're only children? Oh, it's so easy to make that mistake where this generation is concerned. They are adults from birth, in a sense. They are game for anything. He leans forward over the table and grabs Sanne's hand. 'Now listen to me carefully. I'm going to make you a proposition. It may come as a shock at first, but do me a favour and think it over. Keep the baby. Please.' He squeezes her fingers.

Her eyes darken. 'Oh, right. Hel-*lo-o*?'

'No, I don't mean you have to raise it yourself, of course not, that wouldn't be possible, no way, I can see that for myself.'

'Oh. I was wondering.' She laughs uncomfortably.

He increases the pressure of his hand round hers. 'All you've got to do is have it. Franka and I will adopt it. We'll raise it. You won't have to look after it.'

'Oh sure, that's just what Franka needs. Someone else's baby.'

'My baby, I think you mean. The child is mine. And Franka is eager to adopt.' A sudden insight: perhaps

225

that's the reason why she hasn't said anything about his little indiscretion. Sleepless night after sleepless night she's had both the time and the opportunity to rationalize: Phinus took care of her Jem for fourteen long years. So suppose Sanne became pregnant, heaven forbid, by Phinus . . . then wouldn't it be her turn to be just as generous – no, in fact, wouldn't it be an equally precious gift to her?

'What did you say? Your baby?' Sanne's voice is shrill. She yanks her hand free. The ashtray clatters to the floor.

'Yes, mine! It's mine!' He tries to remain calm. 'That's the reason we're discussing it, you and I.'

'It's yours all right, but that doesn't mean you have anything to say about it! It's my life, you know. I'll make my own decision!'

The girls at the next table have their heads cocked sideways so as not to miss anything. Behind the bar the waiter runs a cloth over the counter.

Phinus says quietly, 'Can't we just discuss this reasonably? An abortion isn't a trivial thing. You may regret it all your life. Christ, child, you're still so very young!'

She slaps her hands over her ears. 'I'm not listening to you any more!'

'Sanne, come on. I'll talk to your parents. I'll explain it to them. And if they can't accept it, then you can come live with us for the duration. Believe me, every hurdle can be overcome.'

Seething, she hisses, 'Give me the money. Right now. I'll take care of it myself on Tuesday.'

'The money.' His breath starts coming faster. 'But of course. Naturally I'll pay you well for it. Just tell me how much you want.'

She stares at him, as if she has suddenly discovered that under his Phrygian hat there are asses' ears. *We don't accept credit cards. But we'll accept a debit card, with a pin number.*

He can hardly get the words out fast enough. 'I only mean that we can have a proper contract drawn up, at the solicitor's. That's what's done in the case of surrogate motherhood. So you don't have to worry that anyone is getting one over on you. And if you want' – he's desperately groping around for an extra bonus to throw in – 'whether you decide now or later, we can leave it open for the time being, you can always still claim your rights as the biological mother, we don't want to take anything away from you, we just want to take a burden off your shoulders. We won't keep the child in the dark about it, if that's your decision.' Spent, he concludes, 'The way we were always completely open about it with Jem.'

'With Jem?' Intense concentration, suddenly.

He nods, heartened by her seriousness.

'How do you mean?'

'He was Franka's first husband's, I'm just the—'

'Jem never told me!'

Suddenly everything turns still and calm inside him. He thinks to himself in amazement, it wasn't worth mentioning apparently. It wasn't an issue for Jem.

She's shaking her head, dazed. Then it hits her. 'So you aren't his father at all!' She nearly gags. She jumps up, collects her tobacco pouch and lighter and stuffs them into her purse. 'What *are* you in that case, creep?' Her chair topples over. She's at the door before he's able to haul himself to his feet.

'Stop her!' he shouts in consternation at the waiter.

With a face of steel, the man continues polishing the zinc of his counter.

The door slams shut behind her.

'Stop her!' he repeats mechanically, pushing his way through the tables.

'*Qué? La cuenta?*' the waiter asks stupidly. He bars Phinus's way.

'*Rápido*,' he begs, fumbling for his credit card. '*Rápido!*' He stamps his feet, incapable of coming up with a more urgent phrase. His Spanish dates back to a course he took ten years ago. It was one of those old-fashioned Linguaphone courses, in a hefty boxed set. He had bought it the year Franka, Jem and he were going to spend the summer travelling through southern Europe. Bought it for the holiday that never happened because Franka lost her womb the day before they were supposed to leave, just like that, like money flying out of your wallet.

What Phinus achieves

The entire city is pulsating like a blood vessel about to burst. Neon signs flash. Trams and taxis wedge their way through the streets. Gusts of music come blaring out of the cafés. Tourists clog the pavements. Crowds come streaming out of cinemas at the end of the first show, and with each step you take, you bump into someone. The city is suddenly like some complicated board game, in which each square presents a new obstacle which requires you to throw a double six. One wrong move and it's strictly Go Back to Go for you.

When this critical phase was reached, Aunt Leonoor used to declare firmly, 'I refuse to throw again.' She'd lean back in her chair, the dice clenched in her fist. 'I can't take any more.'

Aunt Irmgard would make a face. 'It isn't a matter of life or death!'

He'd look from one to the other. Were you supposed to take a game seriously, or not? He couldn't figure it out. The aunts staked everything they had on winning, but when they lost, it was suddenly just a game. What was he supposed to believe?

'How quiet the child is,' said Irmgard.

'He is thinking about how he's going to demolish us,' Leonoor replied glumly.

Come to think of it, why wasn't there a game that awarded points for bad luck, for dumb moves, for the spilling of milk on the board? A game that put you in the lead the moment one of your opponents snatched your favourite pawn right from under your nose? A game that would dispense with all the usual rewards and also the penalties! Everybody would be a winner. There would be dozens of ways to win.

If he invented a game like that, he'd become a millionaire, for sure. Then he'd rent a limousine for the aunts on their birthday, with drinks with ice cubes in the back and a liveried chauffeur in the front. They would sink into the leather seats like two queens, with their felt slippers and their gnarled fingers with which (with the help of a little spit) they slicked his hair back behind his ears every morning. He laughed out loud.

'The child is making fun of me,' said Leonoor.

'Go on, throw the dice, or you'll miss your turn,' said Irmgard, rolling her eyes. Of the three, it was she who won most often. Her pawn (always the black one) circumnavigated the Quicksand and Death so imperturbably that it was as if these perils didn't exist for her. She pushed her piece across the board like a tank, leaving everybody else in the dust. And all because she didn't give a fig – not even a *figment*, she'd say, poker-faced. She maintained that Luck would get stroppy with you if you tried to force it to go your way. Luck was a real piece of work: the harder you ran after it, the sooner it would run out on you. Besides, it was only by the grace of Bad Luck – talk about a piece of work! – that Good Luck even existed, and if you tried to catch one, the other was automatically delivered to your door, free of charge.

Leonoor put her hands over Phinus's ears. Only when Irmgard had stopped her ranting did she take her hands away. No, listen, Luck was a fairy in a white dress, in the winter she lived inside a snowdrop, and in summer she lived in the heart of a daisy, where she always kept her ears pricked in case someone was calling. If someone needed her, she would fly to their side, you could count on it. You could, whispered Leonoor, call on Luck yourself. As long as you truly deserved it. There was the rub. You had to be extremely sure of your case. For a heart that was pure, Luck would always have all the time in the world, and all the attention, too.

He comes to a standstill in the middle of the crowded street. Could it be that his motives are not pure? Or does he want the impossible, is he asking too much? His hands are itching to tie a child's hood under its chin, that's all, and to wrap a warm scarf round that. He longs to explain to a little mind that is as yet a blank slate all that stuff about high tide and low tide, the laws of ancient Rome, and Lady Luck. How is that asking for too much?

In a shop selling touristy junk, which is still open in spite of the hour, he buys a tiny T-shirt with tulips on it. Stuffing it into his pocket, he goes outside again. Across the street looms a public telephone. He blinks. He appears to have accidentally landed on a new square on the game board. The square that is known as Nothing Ventured, Nothing Gained.

He squeezes himself into the booth and takes a phone card out of his all but empty wallet. He picks up the receiver and punches in the number. The telephone starts to ring. Twice, three times, four times. Then a click in his ear: there's a connection. He has just a split second to hope that it's the mother, and not the father to whom he was so rude that night at the police station.

It is the mother.

'Vermeer speaking,' he says.

There's a moment's silence. 'Oh, Jem's father.'

He is briefly thrown for a loop.

'Hello? Mr Vermeer?'

Jem has sat in this woman's kitchen, or on her living-room sofa. They've talked. 'My father sits around playing Snakes and Ladders and dominoes all day, and he gets paid for it, too.' Phinus leans his forehead against the glass of the phone booth. He can't get a word out.

'Is Sanne still with you?' Her voice goes up a notch. 'Is there something the matter with Sanne?'

'No. No, she had a date with someone else after dinner, and that's where she's gone off to.'

She waits. Perhaps she's thinking, why is this man calling me? And what does he want from my daughter? Sanne visits the man's wife at the drop of a hat as well. They are completely appropriating her, it isn't healthy. Sanne has to get on with her own life, they shouldn't treat her as a surrogate child, she belongs here, with us.

He quickly brings out, 'That's why I'm calling you.'

'Why? What do you mean?'

'I'm sorry, I'm a little out of breath, because I ran after her when I realized she'd left the restaurant without her bag, it was suddenly much later than we realized, she had to leave while I was waiting for the bill, so if you happen to know where she was supposed to meet her friend, I'll take her her bag, or else she'll be without ... money all evening and without ...'

'Dear heaven,' she says, 'surely you don't imagine that a girl of nearly sixteen tells her mother where she's going?' Why, was that Jem of yours such a mummy's boy, then? We always did find him a bit of a drip. Much too young, in every way, for our Sanne. She's such an independent girl. She'll manage perfectly well tonight without any money, thank you. Her girlfriends will lend her some. She must have arranged to meet Irene at the Heineken Hole, and then on to Gigi's to meet up with the others, or to Dances-at-Jansen's.

'I'm sorry, Mr Vermeer. I have no idea. I can't help you. A good evening to you.' A click and then the dial tone.

He can't get over it. Here's a woman who doesn't give a damn if her own daughter has a tram ticket on her, or the means to buy one, so she can get home safely tonight! Or was his voice a dead giveaway, could she tell he was lying and that he didn't have Sanne's bag at all? They can see right through him, every last one of them, these women. It makes him feel insecure, hounded.

When he steps out of the phone booth, the street seems even more packed than before. It is ten o'clock. The hour when the night really gets going. Boys with spiked hair and girls in high-heeled boots walk by in droves. Everything about them is pointing up, as if they are resolved to go on growing and growing until they're tall enough to crush the whole world beneath their indifferent feet. The city is theirs, they have the whole metropolis in their pocket. They have branded all the walls and shutters with their signature trademark: clashing graffiti in swirling arabesques dripping from every imaginable surface. In every street, on every square, they deliver their unambiguous message: we call the shots around here. We, with our lithe muscles, our quick reflexes, our impeccable straight teeth, we who are not stooped, or leathery or creased, let alone blotched or discoloured, we of the eagle eye, the keen ear and the sharp tongue, we the tireless, the unafraid, the immortal: the rightful inheritors of this planet. We shall still be here when the rest of you are dead and forgotten, keep that in mind, we only barely put up with you and your calcified bones, wrinkled necks, hot flushes and receding gums, we tolerate you, but without much patience or mercy, seeing that you are already, to all intents and purposes, history. You're going to clear out of here soon enough anyway.

Under a lamppost Phinus stands and waits. Three girls pass by, hair bristling with combs, clips, pins and glitter, jeans breathtakingly tight. All three are gabbing into their mobiles. Only the fact that they keep falling over each other with laughter indicates that they're out together.

He starts following the threesome at a safe distance.

Shrieking with laughter into their phones, they enter a café.

Inside, it's so smoky that as soon as he's stepped over the threshold his eyes begin to water. He gropes his way through the overcrowded space, bumping into table corners, disoriented by the noise of monotonously droning music and shrill voices. There's a sweltering smell of ganja, or perhaps it's a blend of perfume, hair gel and warm young bodies. 'Sanne?' he calls out.

Faces turn in his direction. Blonde and dark-haired maidens size him up briefly. Heavy-set and slender. Vivacious and calm ones. And just for a moment, something alarmingly familiar flits across their smooth faces: the women of tomorrow are staring at him, women of the future, women with freckles and women with brains, cheerful women, dull women, sensible, desperate and determined women, women who'll give you lip and women who don't give a damn, smart, sporty, absent-minded and finicky women, women with spunk and women who lisp, immoral women, depressed women, career women, quiet women, greedy, messy, lazy, handy or effusive women, women with a sense of humour and women with none, power-hungry women, wanton women, insatiable women, immoderate women, earnest, brave, gentle, stubborn and unconventional women, women who aren't much trouble and women who have no heart, submissive women, lissome, winsome, loathsome women, women who smell of cinnamon or women who smell of hay, cosy, motherly, adventurous, shy and outspoken women, devastating women, castrating women, women with a sense of mission and women with common sense, strict women, stupid women, haughty, frumpy, egotistic and altruistic women, women hi, women ho, women hi-dee-eye-doh, pious women, poor women, vindictive, serious, impressionable, tough, silly and jolly women . . . and they all see right through him.

For just an instant something like silence settles over the café. Intuitively, using all their senses, the girls plumb the depths of his despair, and something much older than themselves threatens to break through. Then the angry racket starts up again. The glimmer of compassion that was on the verge of showing itself is immediately smothered: what's the fun of inheriting the earth if you keep having to feel sympathy for others?

They turn their backs on him, they pick up their mobiles and punch the numbers in.

He stands at the bar, given the cold shoulder. To cover up his discomfort, he plunges his hand into the bowl of peanuts invitingly set out on the counter. His mouth is so dry that it feels as if he's chewing on sand. He swallows in vain. The nuts stay glued to the roof of his mouth in a thick wad.

'Oh, but now I really have to get going! What if my date . . .'

'. . . so what d'you think I said? I just let it all out, I simply told her . . .'

'Two rum Cokes!'

'Really, it was *so* gross.'

'Well, no, more like Leonardo. Same eyebrows. Real intense.'

They push up against him, scram, out of our way, we're here to regroup, to analyse the situation, we're here to practise how it's done, being human. Taking the nearest girl by the arm, a tubby little thing, he demands, 'Do you know Sanne Hendrikse?'

'No,' she replies, nonplussed.

She isn't an attractive girl. From what he can see, everything conspires against her. The wreath of blackheads around the pale nose. The limp hair, badly cut. The load of chains round her neck and wrists, giving her skin a grubby look, all that unappetizing metal . . . *Jem and his brand-new braces, his mouth open wide, trusting that Dad would know how to replace the rubber bands.*

'Why? Are you her dad?' she asks nervously.

He squares his stiff back. 'Can I buy you a drink?'

Her face lighting up with surprise, she climbs up onto the bar stool beside him. 'A white wine, please.'

He orders two glasses of white wine.

Hesitantly, she says, 'Oh, but of course you must be the father of . . .' She snaps her fingers. At his age, you're automatically someone's father. It stands to reason.

The wine, which comes with ice cubes, is cloyingly sweet. Nevertheless he drains his glass in three or four big gulps. Only then does his tongue feel loose enough to tackle the interrogation. Where else would a cute girl such as herself normally hang out on a Saturday night? Are there other bars that are as cool as this one?

A little colour comes into her cheeks. Eagerly she begins to evaluate the various hotspots. This one costs five guilders to get in, that one ten. Drink chits yadda-this, bouncers yadda-that. This one's more house music, the other mostly heavy metal. 'Only, their loo's a disaster, totally gross,' she tells him. She sounds just as well-informed as Jem, who knew that after four in the morning was the safest time to be out on the street. Phinus immediately tries to bury the memory again, but Jem promptly rises up before him, so real that he can almost touch him. The slouched bearing, the thick lenses, the big feet, the uneasy coordination of a body beset by changes and hormones. How had his peers viewed him? Had he just been a hanger-on, really, one of those boys at the edge of the circle who just miss being hip and cool enough, with the wrong kind of gel in his hair? 'The kid actually *ties* the shoelaces of his Diesels? Oh, man!' Had Jem suffered? Had he lain awake at night dreaming up schemes to become popular, and then hating himself for it?

Phinus thinks to himself, Jem never said anything about it. But that proved nothing. You didn't discuss those kinds of problems at home. At home they had no idea what a fine line there was, at home you had a dad with so little understanding of the right designer logos and the right way of doing things that he'd once even coolly let you walk around with a plastic tiara on your head.

He digs his nails into his palms. *Don't let them get to you, pumpkin. Just tell them to take a flying leap, and remember all the things you're good at! Who can bake an apple pie as sublime as yours? Say, know what? We'll give a Mr Bean party! Yes, that's it. We'll rent every tape in the video shop, we'll have a twenty-four-hour Mr Bean marathon, they're all crazy about Mr Bean, those cool dudes and their girlfriends, and we'll give them your pie to eat, ha-ha! And Franka will make popcorn, and I'll . . . OK, OK, I'll stay behind the scenes. Nobody will notice I'm there. I'll just be in the kitchen, making sure there are clean glasses and plates. But come on, boy, buck up, this too shall pass. Count on it. Before you know it, within a year, two at most, you'll suddenly be . . .*

'. . . at the Escape,' says the chubby girl in a voice tremulous with longing. 'The Escape is the totally coolest.'

He chokes. 'Two more white wines,' he shouts at the girl behind the bar. 'Oh, and I can use my debit card here, can't I?'

'No,' says the blonde. Her piercings look even more threatening than the ones Astrid had. Indifferently she fills up the glasses.

'Do you accept credit cards?'

She shakes her head.

'I just realized, you see, that I don't have any cash on me.' He has to raise his voice to make himself understood over the pounding music.

'You should have thought of that before. Four glasses of white, that'll be eighteen guilders,' she says unhelpfully.

He appeals to the fat girl next to him. Her face sags sullenly. She says, 'Eighteen guilders, that's a whole two hours behind the till at Aldi's for me.' She gets up, takes her glass and disappears with it into the crowd.

The blonde puts her hands on her hips. 'Well?'

He is flustered. 'Surely there's a cash machine nearby?'

'Yeah, round the corner. But how do I know you'll come back?'

'I'll give you some security.' He feels around in his pockets. He has nothing on him of value. 'Here, my credit cards.' He offers her his wallet, after taking out his cash card.

She waves his hand away. 'I'm not going to fall for *that* one.'

'Then come outside with me.'

'And abandon the whole show in here?'

He feels his tic starting to play up again. 'You're not very helpful, are you?'

'No, why should I be? You should have made sure you had cash on you. It's not my problem.'

'If your till doesn't add up at the end of the night, it *will* be your problem. You'll—'

Without taking her eyes off him, she sticks two fingers into her mouth and whistles sharply. Immediately a black youth in a leather jacket pushes his way forward. 'This gentleman here has just announced he wants to leave without paying,' she proclaims loudly, emerging from behind the bar.

Phinus holds up his cash card demonstratively. There's just a tad more than eighteen guilders in his account, it's almost laughable.

Out of the blue, the youth prods him hard in the chest. 'We don't want any trouble here.'

'Ho, ho,' says Phinus, alarmed. What's the best tactic now? *Go back two squares.* He yells to make himself heard over the droning basses, 'I don't want any either. I just have to get some cash.' He waves his card.

'Yeah, that's a good one.' Quick as a flash, the boy takes a step closer and pats down Phinus's jacket.

'Really, I have nothing on me.'

The boy pulls the baby T-shirt with tulips out of his pocket. The girl snatches it out of his hands and holds it up mockingly. 'Oh, look at that, how cute.'

The music switches to a new track, and the decibels increase.

The girl screams, 'He's probably just become a father!'

'Oh well! It shouldn't be allowed, to make babies at his age!'

'And yet he still comes here to pick up girls!'

'What?'

She yells, 'To pick up girls!'

Miss a turn. He takes a step back, but she's grabbed him by the lapels. Veins pop out in her neck as she screams at the top of her lungs in order to be heard over the music, 'Hey, are you a child molester?'

Miss a turn!

'A pervert who doesn't have two cents to rub together!' The boy grins scornfully.

The patrons crowd around, to see what's going on. Oh, it's just that intruder. Go ahead, beat him to a pulp, this is our territory, we can do what we like in here.

The girl waves the tulip T-shirt above her head like a trophy. 'Poor little bugger, with a dad like him! Maybe we should tell the police. They can take away your parental rights, did you know that, you filthy, disgusting . . .'

'But you gotta pay up first, father!'

'Phew, am I glad he isn't *my* father!'

And losing control in the same way Marius H. did on that fateful night, he suddenly pounces on both of them. He grabs them by the scruff of the neck. And as loud screams start up on all sides, he bangs their two heads together, he bangs and he smashes, he bashes them straight to hell.

The devil is waiting for them. Invitingly he holds the door to one of his largest furnaces open wide. A bit befuddled, kiddos? It certainly is quite something, one moment you're a bigshot, not a twinge of pain, and the next you're as dead as a doornail.

But that's life; the earth was created from chaos and blind luck, and chaos and blind luck will be your legacy for as long as you all keep crawling around up there. Your own conception reflects this; it's nothing but dumb luck, after all, whenever some weedy slowpoke of a sperm manages to find that hoity-toity Miss Egg. There are great segments of the population that long for such a hook-up, but in vain; while others, to their dismay, keep hitting the bull's eye, time after time. Let's go, place your bets, ladies and gentlemen, *rien ne va plus!* The whole thing depends on where the ball comes to rest. Generation after generation, mankind has had to rely on this game of roulette. Face it, every one of you exists today only by the grace of blind luck.

So let's have no whining, please, if death reveals itself to be just as arbitrary. It is your lot, after all, to be part of a universe whose very hallmark is that it is flawed and uncontrollable. Nature is simply one enormous buffet; the motto is eat or be eaten. And don't expect any justice, coherence, meaning or mercy either.

But come, let's go inside before we catch cold here outside the cauldron.

A police officer escorts Phinus to a small, windowless room. 'Please sit here. We'll be along in just a few minutes for the interrogation.'

There's an old steel desk with a computer on it and three chairs round it. There's the pungent smell of some cleaning product. In the corridor someone is calling, 'And I'd just given that hairless nithead another warning, too!' Then the door slams shut and it's quiet.

He pulls out a chair and sits down. He places his hands on the table and looks at them. His knuckles are torn to shreds. So. So what was invisible for all those months is now, finally, plain for each and everyone to see: he has blood on his hands.

After a little while he shuts his eyes. His mind is blank. A heating pipe clangs softly. It's hot, but he can't be bothered to take off his jacket. To his surprise he slowly becomes aware of a feeling of peace, such as he hasn't had in half a year. He has landed on exactly the right square – the one square around which the whole game has revolved from the very start; here, within these four bare walls, his interrogation is

242

finally set to begin. Balance will be restored. Justice will have its say.

The officer returns, with a mug of tea and an ashtray. 'My colleague is still in the middle of something.'

Phinus nods, amazed at the politeness of the man's tone. It's as if the world has put aside her recent frightening guise. As if everything has calmed down at once, now that justice will be done at last, now that guilt can be acknowledged, and redeemed by paying the penalty.

'Should we call anyone to warn them you won't be home tonight?'

'No. Thank you.'

The man turns round and leaves the room.

Franka is probably telling her friend right now, 'When I married Phinus, what I got was another child. I'd finally like to be done with nappies for a while.'

His peaceful mood begins to splinter. He gets up, paces up and down, sits down again. He should have jumped in his car as soon as his back was straightened out and gone looking for her! He knows every one of her girlfriends, he'd have found her in no time.

But then Sanne had arrived. *'Jem used to say I had the longest eyelashes in Amsterdam. He said if I ever cheated on him, he'd cut them off!'*

The door swings open. The officer who brought him here enters with his partner. The partner sits down behind the desk. He laces his fingers together and cracks the joints before turning on the computer. 'It doesn't look too good for you. Consider yourself lucky that there were enough people around to overpower you. Otherwise there would have been nothing left of those two youngsters, you were going so utterly berserk.'

The other one says, in a strangely sympathetic tone, 'You were really going off the deep end, you know.'

'Mr Vermeer? Are we getting through to you? Do you understand what the consequences might have been if you'd had the death of a minor on your conscience?'

Phinus looks up. 'Yes,' he says hoarsely. 'That I do know.'

Sighing, the man opens a programme on his computer. He types something in. Then he folds his hands over his stomach. 'Now, where shall we begin?'

At the back of the garden there was a gnarled chestnut tree with branches so thick and so sturdy that they could even have borne the weight of the aunts. It was a very old tree; Leonoor's father had planted it when he was a young boy, yes he did, when he was the exact same age you are now, darling.

On muggy Sunday afternoons, the aunts would seek the shade of this tree. Irmgard with the collar of her blouse open, Leonoor barefoot, her toes wriggling in the grass. They sat in striped deck chairs, head back, prostrate. If you sat on a branch right overhead, the urge to throw something down at them, a little twig or something, was sometimes almost irresistible, but you weren't supposed to snap anything off that belonged to nature, because nature was our teacher.

Lolling in the crotch of his favourite branch, he listened to the chirping of the sparrows. He watched the bugs and the spiders swarming in the grooves of the bark. Whenever someone walked down the little lane behind the garden, he'd raise his hand and call out, 'Hi, neighbour.' It was just wonderful that everyone could see him sitting here like a prince, with his aunts, up in the tree that Leonoor's father had planted.

He must have been a wonderful dad. He felt a little jealous.

'Oh, don't think he was anything special, now,' Leonoor said quickly. 'A grouchy old thing, he was. Always complaining, tarnation this, tarnation that, and kicking up a fuss.'

'Any time Leonoor laughed out loud at something, she'd be sent to bed without her supper,' Irmgard added. 'I mean, really!'

'Or, just as often, to the coal shed.'

'Did you ever tell the child about the time at the well?'

The time at the well. That time on the ice. And oh, *that* time, the report card with the three A-minuses! That had been the worst time of all. That is, if you didn't count the time of the tartan hair bow. No, really, we're not having you on. Why would we? Oh, child, and we haven't even begun to tell you about Irmgard's mother.

'She was the witch from hell,' said Irmgard. 'She'd *bite* me if something failed to please her. On my hand. Or my cheek. And then afterwards she'd rub it with vinegar. So that it would sting like mad.'

Leonoor got up out of her chair. Shielding her eyes from the sun, she looked up at Phinus in the tree. 'Aren't you the lucky one, eh, sweetheart?' Then she walked to the kitchen to prepare sandwiches.

Hopefully there'd be sliced bananas on them.

After a while, Irmgard continued, in a gruff voice, 'Personally, I've never seen the use of parents, really. They consider their children their property. They feel no compunction about bossing them around. They don't have the slightest respect for them. They're always busy *moulding* them. It's true! Trying to mould

245

them in their own image. Naturally. They want their children to be carbon copies of themselves, like peas in a pod.'

An unpleasant sensation filled his stomach, the kind you get when you tell a lie. Nervously he fiddled around with a twig.

'As if you belong to anyone but yourself! As if you aren't just who you are!'

But to belong to yourself wasn't such a good thing at all. With nothing but a couple of fat old aunts.

'So don't you go imagining it's so wonderful. Parents, pooh! As an orphan, you're tempted, of course, to idealize them, but believe you me . . .'

Stop it! The twig snapped in his fingers. For just a split second it felt as if his hand was being held back. Then he threw the twig, with all his strength. With a cool aim nobody had ever taught him, powerful and unerring, he hurled his weapon at Aunt Irmgard.

She screamed. She clapped her hands to her face.

Leonoor, who was just coming out of the house, dropped the plate of sandwiches. She ran up, alarmed.

Hastily he pulled himself up onto a higher branch. His heart was pounding as he nestled deeper inside the tree.

'Don't touch it!' cried Leonoor. 'You'll only make it worse!' She grabbed Irmgard's hands and held them firmly in hers. 'Phinus, go fetch the doctor! Where are you? Phinus!'

He kept quiet as a mouse. He didn't move a muscle.

'Phinus? Oh dear, then I'll just have to go myself. Promise me, Irmgard, that you won't try to pull it out yourself!'

He couldn't see much through the thick leaves. He tried to picture his fat old aunt with the twig stuck right in the centre of her eye. She'd had it coming to her. She really had.

The doctor arrived and drove his aunts to the hospital in his car.

He waited a long time. Then he lowered himself down from the tree. He looked to see if there was any blood around the chairs. Not a speck. He thrust his hands deep into his pockets and went inside.

In his room he couldn't think of anything to do. Moodily he took out his Lego. A castle! But he couldn't manage it. Crestfallen, he dragged himself downstairs, to the deathly quiet living room where Leonoor's collection of porcelain shepherdesses was set out on the sideboard. Girls, he pondered. A girl would never have caused this much trouble. Then, holding his breath, he went and sat down in Irmgard's corduroy chair, and put his hand over one eye. The room suddenly looked as if it had been cut in half.

'Oh darling!' cried Leonoor. She came running in, with Irmgard in her wake. 'Oh, *how* could we have gone out and left you at home all alone! You deserve a glass of squash, to make up for the fright.'

'I had a twig in my eye,' said Irmgard drily. 'That's why.'

In the kitchen they all had a glass of squash. The aunts gibber-jabbered about the trip to the hospital, about how kind the doctor had been, what the nurses had said. It would all turn out all right, it was only a superficial wound, there was just the risk of infection, but they'd been given drops for that, what had they done with that bottle, oh yes, in Leonoor's pocket, and in the meantime they should just let the eye breathe, just let it breathe.

It sounded as if they were talking under water. He didn't dare look at Irmgard.

'Your aunt could use a kiss right now,' said Leonoor.

He nearly burst into tears.

Irmgard's hand stroked his bowed head. 'You don't need to, don't worry. Just go and make me a lovely drawing.'

That night they didn't cook. They went to the Chinese restaurant with the dragons and the lanterns to celebrate the happy outcome. But he couldn't swallow his chop suey. He observed how the waiter looked at Irmgard, as if he'd seen something revolting.

Leonoor saw it too. 'You'd better stay away from the mirror for a couple of weeks. It really isn't a very pleasant sight.'

'Do you think so too?' Irmgard cupped his chin in her hand. He was so startled that he forgot to struggle. Before he knew it, he was looking right into her damaged eye. It bulged out of its socket like a funny red glob. Still, it wasn't as bad as he'd thought.

She let him go. 'It's often worse in your imagination than in real life,' she said amiably. 'You should always look things straight in the eye.'

She could read his thoughts! That must be another trick out of the handbook for aunts. But if she was so good at reading his mind, why hadn't she known what he'd been thinking up in the tree this afternoon – that she should stop saying things that weren't true! Or had she known all along? But then she also knew . . . He yanked his head up.

She was looking at him calmly.

He thought: I did it, and I did it on purpose.

She raised one eyebrow and nodded, almost imperceptibly.

'Does the light hurt your eyes?' asked Leonoor. 'Perhaps we should buy you some sunglasses. It's really too bad, such a stupid accident.'

'Well, it was partly my own fault, I think.' She winked at him with her good eye.

It made him turn red. Quickly he began folding the corner of his placemat into concertina pleats.

'Your own fault? How's that?'

'Oh, things never happen just like that, for no reason. There's always cause and effect. Even' – Irmgard smiled benignly – 'if *you* don't happen to see the connection.'

Leonoor put down her fork. 'But to feel guilty whenever things don't go your way, that's just ridiculous! Are you listening, boy? Never let me catch you doing that.'

'But what if he's got something on his conscience? *Then* is he allowed to feel guilty?'

Leonoor said heatedly, 'If someone's got something on his conscience, Phinus, he just has to confess to his part in it at once, and do his best to put things right again. And if the situation is beyond repair, which is a possibility too, of course, then you just have to try to come to terms with it. Guilt by itself does nobody any good. Pooh! It cuts no ice. It doesn't lead anywhere. Do you understand? It's dead in the water. You have to embrace life, instead of hiding from it.' With a dramatic flourish she stretched her arms and spread them wide over the plates of chop suey and egg foo yong.

'Oh God,' said Irmgard. 'There she goes again, your aunt.'

Leonoor turned her palms up and made a sweeping gesture as if she wanted to gather all the plates and

249

glasses to her bosom at once. 'Wonderful!' she said with a contented sigh.

'Are we going to have a dessert?' demanded Irmgard. 'I wouldn't mind a hot fudge sundae myself.'

They take him to a cell on the floor below. It's quiet down there, because the night is yet young. Or is it simply that ever since his confession, it has grown considerably less dangerous in the city and its environs, as far afield as Aduard? Has everything fallen into place again now that Phinus Vermeer has finally been measured and weighed? Perhaps all the barmaids and bouncers are exchanging banter with their customers again, perhaps all the boys and girls in the clubs and cafés suddenly know how to behave again, and aren't so heartless after all, perhaps Astrid and Melanie are perched innocently on the bridge railing, drawing little hearts on the backs of their hands with a new lipstick. Because doesn't every crocodile under every child's bed turn out in the end to be a camel, *the friendly lemac padding through the desert on its gleaming little hooves, in search of someone to rescue?*

The chaos is lifted; mercy has returned. The everyday, simple mercy of knowing that there is such a thing as justice. Even if sometimes you have to spend a long time looking for it. Even if sometimes you have to make it happen all by yourself.

His mind is calm and clear as he surveys his cell. The fogged-up pane of reinforced glass, the crack in the cement floor that looks like the footprint of a giant chicken, the buzzing fluorescent tube, white in the middle and bluish at the ends. He will be kept in custody here for three days, before being brought before his old friend the Prosecutor. In a few strides he paces off the dimensions of his temporary habitat. For some reason the crowding walls make him aware of the space he himself occupies. It's as if he finally has a sense again of where he begins and where he ends, as if someone has traced his outline with one of those Day-Glo highlighters.

He sits down on the steel bunk and thoughtfully begins to examine, bit by bit, his shoulders, his hips, his knees, his feet. Within these boundaries he exists. *This is me*. And he is hardly done when he notices, with a shock of awe, that a space has opened up *inside* him as well. By admitting his guilt, it has simply evaporated, leaving a weightless, open cavity, which he is free to fill up with whatever he likes. With whatever he knows.

He looks down at his bruised hands. His Aunt Leonoor taught him when he was only five years old that you must not only take responsibility for your actions, but also make your peace with that which can never be made right again. Isn't it high time that he did? What has kept him from doing it all these months, and sent him scurrying time and again to the safe haven of guilt? 'Come on,' Aunt Irmgard would have said, 'just face up to it, and then it won't feel so bad.'

He stands up, his joints creak, and he suddenly feels old. Everything in life, he used to tell Jem, always has another side to it, just like the Rubik's Cube. Twist the blocks round, and new possibilities will promptly open up before you. But that isn't true.

Because 'dad' will always spell 'd-a-d'. And 'dead', reversed, becomes 'd-a-e-d', which isn't much of an improvement either. There's no point turning those words round. No matter what contortions you twist yourself in, no matter which way you look at it, death is not suddenly going to reverse itself and assume a new, different, more hopeful form. Death can be nothing but itself, it can mean nothing but what it is, ruthlessly cutting down everything without mercy. Did it dawn on Jem when he was staring down the barrel of that gun that Phinus had been pulling the wool over his eyes? *Oh, Dad, you and your games. You have deceived me.*

Despair wells up in him. He sinks down on the bunk again.

But when you're fifteen, you are more than just a single stroke of the pen on an otherwise blank piece of paper. You don't just take whatever they tell you at home at face value. Get real, Dad! Jem had long ago set his own course. Phinus is the only one who has kept believing in his own fairy tales, and who is consequently still running from the irreversible, the awe-inspiring irreversibility of what has happened. Running from the open-eyed realization that thousands of casual daily kisses are now irretrievably lost. Running from the certain knowledge that friendly pokes in the ribs will no longer be forthcoming, nor the rowdy wrestling matches. Gone, definitely gone, is the awesome intimacy of the ordinary, of the familiar, the wordless exchanged glances, the shared laughter over nothing much, the astonishing certainty that his love had a destination, a love that from now on will be stamped *return to sender, address unknown.*

How infinitely more bearable it is to get swept up in other feelings, no matter how painful, than to have to endure grief – unappeasable, unstaunchable grief, which is the only possible answer to death! All the diplomas that will never be awarded. All the ideals that can no longer be realized. The motorcycles never purchased, the digs never rented. Nor will there ever be a night in which he keeps himself awake with gallons of coffee in feverish expectation of the re-demptive phone call: 'It's a boy, Dad, and we're naming him Phinus.'

The door lock squeaks. A young officer peers in. 'We have located your wife and apprised her of the situation.'

'Where—'

'She is staying at the second address on the list you gave us.' The man takes his time locking the door again. His face shows a touch of contempt: you don't deserve a woman like that.

Perhaps that's true. But perhaps Franka and he will now be able to find their way back, back to each other again, now that he is finally ready and able to share her grief. It's his grief too, after all. It has been waiting patiently for him, beneath the wreckage of guilt and shame. All he has to do is let it in.

He shuts his eyes.

He folds his hands.

Jem is dead. Jem of the generous heart is dead. Jem of the twinkling eyes is dead. Jem Jem Jem is dead, Jem who was the sum total of himself and his bio-logical parents, but who over the course of fourteen years had also soaked up innumerable bits of Phinus, and hoarded these carefully. Jem, a stranger down to the last of his genes, and yet more Phinus's own than anything that is his. Jem who could never be replaced by any other child. Our Jem.

He thinks about the girl with the longest eyelashes in Amsterdam, the girl who had chosen their son from the sea of eligible boys. He all but smiles. Jem, with that babe.

Jem with his whole life ahead of him.

Without warning, there is a sudden compression of atoms at the base of his windpipe. They pile up, they push their way up his throat into his mouth, they worm open his lips, and emerge as a scream. *Jem.* It's a scream with no end. His arms stretch out of their own accord and that's the way he remains seated, his arms spread wide, as the scream continues to push its way out, continues to come and go, in waves, like labour pains. The membranes that have been keeping his eyes dry all this time, now rupture. He is perched on the edge of the bunk and he is weeping and his arms find his dead child and he embraces him, he hugs him to his chest, overwhelmed with the fathomless loss, the never-ending yearning.

It can finally begin.

THE END

A HEART OF STONE
Renate Dorrestein

'A LITERARY NOVEL WITH A DARK SECRET IN ITS
HEART THAT MAKES READING COMPULSIVE'
Kate Atkinson

Precocious Ellen is the only one of the four close Van
Bemmel children who dreads the arrival of the new baby.
She has told her parents to call the baby Ida, the ugliest
name she could think of, and is secretly afraid that the
curse she has put upon the unborn child will come true.
Her parents, eccentric and devoted to each other, seem to
the outside world to be loving and caring, but after one of
the children has a shocking accident a horror descends
upon this happy household which leads to a disaster even
Ellen is powerless to prevent.

Twenty-five years later a pregnant Ellen returns to the
family home, where she is haunted by the voices of her
dead family. She imagines the questions her own child will
one day ask: 'Mummy, why don't I have a granny? Why no
grandad? No uncles or aunts? Why not?'

A Heart of Stone is an elegant, passionate but chilling
novel from Holland's bestselling writer

'A WONDERFUL FRESH VOICE WITH A STARTLING
AND ULTIMATELY REDEMPTIVE TALE TO TELL. HER
WRITING IS SUPREMELY CONFIDENT AND INTIMATE.
A HEART OF STONE IS A LITERARY NOVEL WITH
A DARK SECRET IN ITS HEART THAT MAKES
READING COMPULSIVE'
Kate Atkinson

'NOT ONLY HIGHLY EMOTIVE AND COMPELLING,
BUT HUMOROUS TOO. I COULD NOT PUT THIS
NOVEL DOWN'
Marika Cobbold

0 552 99836 2

BLACK SWAN

A SELECTED LIST OF FINE WRITING AVAILABLE FROM BLACK SWAN

99313 1	OF LOVE AND SHADOWS	Isabel Allende	£7.99
99915 6	THE NEW CITY	Stephen Amidon	£6.99
99921 0	THE MERCIFUL WOMEN	Federico Andahazi	£6.99
99820 6	FLANDERS	Patricia Anthony	£6.99
99734 X	EMOTIONALLY WEIRD	Kate Atkinson	£6.99
99860 5	IDIOGLOSSIA	Eleanor Bailey	£6.99
99922 9	A GOOD HOUSE	Bonnie Burnard	£6.99
99824 9	THE DANDELION CLOCK	Guy Burt	£6.99
99979 2	GATES OF EDEN	Ethan Coen	£7.99
99686 6	BEACH MUSIC	Pat Conroy	£7.99
99767 6	SISTER OF MY HEART	Chitra Banerjee Divakaruni	£6.99
99836 2	A HEART OF STONE	Renate Dorrestein	£6.99
99925 3	THE BOOK OF THE HEATHEN	Robert Edric	£6.99
99587 8	LIKE WATER FOR CHOCOLATE	Laura Esquivel	£6.99
99898 2	ALL BONES AND LIES	Anne Fine	£6.99
99851 6	REMEMBERING BLUE	Connie May Fowler	£6.99
99978 4	KISSING THE VIRGIN'S MOUTH	Donna Gershten	£6.99
99890 7	DISOBEDIENCE	Jane Hamilton	£6.99
99883 4	FIVE QUARTERS OF THE ORANGE	Joanne Harris	£6.99
99867 2	LIKE WATER IN WILD PLACES	Pamela Jooste	£6.99
99959 8	BACK ROADS	Tawni O'Dell	£6.99
99862 1	A REVOLUTION OF THE SUN	Tim Pears	£6.99
99909 1	LA CUCINA	Lily Prior	£6.99
99777 3	THE SPARROW	Mary Doria Russell	£7.99
99645 9	THE WRONG BOY	Willy Russell	£6.99
99819 2	WHISTLING FOR THE ELEPHANTS	Sandi Toksvig	£6.99